Out of Time

Also by Helen Schulman

Not a Free Show (1988)

Out of Time

Helen Schulman

Atheneum

New York   1991

Maxwell Macmillan Canada
Toronto
Maxwell Macmillan International
New York   Oxford   Singapore   Sydney

This is a work of fiction. Names, characters, places, and incidents either are the product of the author's imagination or are used fictitiously. Any resemblance to events or persons, living or dead, is entirely coincidental.

Atheneum
Macmillan Publishing Company
866 Third Avenue, New York, NY 10022

Maxwell Macmillan Canada, Inc.
1200 Eglinton Avenue East
Suite 200
Don Mills, Ontario M3C 3N1

Macmillan Publishing Company is part of the Maxwell Communication Group of Companies.

Library of Congress Cataloging-in-Publication Data
Schulman, Helen.
    Out of time / Helen Schulman.
        p.   cm.
    ISBN 0-689-12122-9
    I. Title.
    PS3569.C5385O9   1991   90-24110   CIP
813'.54—dc20

10 9 8 7 6 5 4 3 2 1

Printed in the United States of America

FOR VIV

Contents

Acknowledgments

The author would like to thank the guardian angels of this book for their generosity and support: The Corporation of Yaddo where both the first and the last sentence were written, The MacDowell Colony, Joan Aguado, Mrinalini Mazumdar, Rick Moody, Céline Keating, Neil Olson, Eric Ashworth, Lee Goerner, my family, and especially Bruce Handy and dearest Miriam Kuznets.

Out of Time

The Accident

THESE things take time.

I divorced last spring. Will and I, we were a couple for twelve years, married for seven. Our anniversary would have been this month.

He sent me a card: "Thanks for four wonderful years."

Everyone's a comedian.

Still, I like him. We are friends. I don't think I would know how to be a person without being friends with Will. We grew up together, started going out when I was still in my teens. Our friendship bothers our families. People like it better when you split up for a reason, when one spouse does something dreadful to the other. No one can stand the fact that we get along as well as always, it's just that we fell out of love. It's that simple.

Nothing is that simple.

It's beautiful here. The lake is embedded into the valley like a sapphire post. The summers are so green the skin on a girl's arms and shoulders turns opalescent.

Opalescent. I like the word because it implies smell. And shimmering. The fragrance of wavy color.

I teach school, sixth grade, so all summer long I hunt out words to drop during discussion sessions. Last spring when I divorced my kids were going around saying "melancholy," and "nonnegotiable."

For example, Johnny O'Hara said to Little Peg: "If you don't let me cut in line you are going to be very melancholy."

The one who got the most use out of "nonnegotiable" was me: "Homework is nonnegotiable," and "The lake house is nonnegotiable" (where I live now) and "Staying with me is nonnegotiable"—that last slipped out in a moment of panic.

Thank God Will had the good sense to keep on not-listening. The separation has been better for the both of us, or so I tell myself.

Out here on the lake, a serenity enters through the outline of my body, as if the wind that ruffles the water and stirs the trees up into leaf and bird talk passes right through me leaving a cleansing wake.

The house itself was my settlement. Everything inside it smells like cedar. Even me, in the sun I smell like I have been stored in a cedar closet. I have a little A-frame, pointed like a witch's hat. There is not much to it, just a living room with a woodburning stove, a galley kitchen, a screened-in porch with a picnic table, a bath that is sort of primitive and a teeny little bedroom, upstairs, loftlike and slanted—like living among the rafters of a play-cathedral. It is so narrow up there you have to skirt the walls to get in and out of the bed.

When we first moved here, poor Will, six two, was constantly bent, with a skull covered with bumps and welts. I worried that it was tumors, but then we realized it was just from clunking his head.

The bed is a king-size, Will was a flipper, I needed the extra feet for protection. Now, sleeping in its wide expanse is like drowning in something endless. The nights have no boundaries. I spread out as much as I can, but I am little, just five three, so I have taken to piling a whole mess of comforters on Will's side of the bed to balance things. That, plus the cat, so another heart is ticking, so that the empty space above the bed fills with mingled breath.

Our house in town was a different story. A garden apartment, really. Will headed up the grounds work for the University, so coupled with a teacher's salary, well we didn't make out like bandits but we did OK enough. Because Will and I are townies our landlord gave us a break. Everyone hates the students.

Now I rent out a room from one of the other teachers. Will's got the apartment, and most of our other stuff. After seven years you don't even know what you have. In this case what you don't know can't hurt you—it was the stuff and nonsense that tied us down. So I let him have the lot of it.

And like I said we are still friendly. Twice this summer he drove out to the lake, once with these green glass beads that go perfectly with my seafoam dress-up dress, because I was invited out to supper, once with a cooking pot I needed desperately.

"There are no closed chapters to this book," Will is fond of saying—he who has not as much as touched a book since *Ball Four*.

Still, I know he is well-meaning. What he means is we can always count on each other, push-comes-to-shove neither of us is all alone. Especially Will, because he has got a new girl now. A secretary, "an administrator," from up at the college. A little slip of a thing, young, in a good way. A nice girl.

What bugs me about her is this: she is always reaching for him. Will, halfway across the room and she leaping from her chair to brush his leg as he ambles by. Even he says it: "She touches me too much" is what he says, during drunken times. When he is sober he calls it "schoolgirl affection."

She's cute, I think, I mean she has real cute hair and a body that won't quit if you like them skinny. And she wears these outfits, the kind that only she can wear.

I mean I'd rather know the date of my death than see what I would look like in one of her outfits.

But she's not much of a talker, that's it, not much of a talker or for that matter she's not much of a doer. Just work and Will, work and Will, and those fashion magazines while she's waiting around for him. I guess there is something alluring about a person whose life is just the amount of time that passes before they get to be with you.

Alluring. Johnny O'Hara said: "Ms. Parker you look real alluring since your divorce."

Johnny O'Hara was failing sixth grade.

In the beginning when Will went out on a date with this girl, he would call me up for advice.

"Celia," he said, "it's been so long I don't know what to do."

I told him how to date, what were the right and wrong moves, as if I knew.

I told him: "Tell her she is too thin, the breeze could whisk her away"—which is the God's honest truth.

Will asked for my interpretation on every word she spoke, every shake of her head, every flip of the hand she uses to fan the air like a wing. He even asked me about

6

sex, but I drew the line. When she broke up with him for two weeks last month he said: "How long did it take you to get over me dumping you?" not in a nasty way, but as a question. Only then did I realize who left who, that I was the clever one.

Last summer I had Joshua and Will both up here on alternating weekends. This summer is the summer of good, lonely times. I wake soft. Stretch and pull, talk myself into leaving the bed and the feather comforter, light for summer. It takes me a solid half hour to convince myself to step out into the day. I negotiate the stairs, a ladder really, wooden slats shallow as ledges when you are climbing a cliff. I proceed drunken on the last clung-to shreds of sleep. It feels like I'm grabbing at the bed-clothes a lover rolls themselves away in, uses to build up a cocoon. Either I can't let go of dreaming, or it's just my low blood pressure.

Then coffee, always, for the smell warming up the house like a family lives there, for the mug that I take to the porch still in my pajamas, so that with the trees weeping green that way, with the birds chattering the breeze awake, with the sunlight sliding over the lake, the trees, the hills, spreading out like golden stain, I feel like a coffee commercial. It's rare that I drink more than a sip—coffee breath is a bad breath—but I warm my hands, and I press them against the grain of the cup's handmade ceramic—a present from Little Peg.

I begin this way every day except for rain. When it rains sometimes I wouldn't even root myself from bed, except the cat always needs feeding, another reason why I have her.

When Joshua was here it was different, we were too busy clutching, worried about how to lengthen a day. Dreaming was unnecessary. I loved him. Joshua. I loved

7

the name in my mouth. I loved the sound in my throat rising to call him.

Nobody ever liked anybody for being nice. You like them for other things. Affairs are symptomatic. A dumb person would blame Joshua for the disintegration of my marriage. A very dumb person.

I, for example, would blame Joshua.

But that is neither here nor there. Today I will swim. I spread the water with my hands the way a man spreads a woman's legs, lovingly but with purpose. I will pass back and forth over the skin of the lake patting it smooth as a sheet on a bed.

I will lie out on the rocks that tip so much they could force a dive into the water and when I flatten out onto its surface, my surface will flatten out into me and I will wonder where the curves go, and because of the angle, worry a little that I will slide in.

I will suck up the sun, eat it with my body, store up the warmth for winter and what is to come. Then I will go back to the house and I will garden. Or read. Or not.

What I like best about being at the lake house is the not-gardening, the not-reading.

But for now I will sit with my coffee and look out.

1. Lugubrious.
2. Lackadaisical.
3. Serene.

Words for next year.

The last night Joshua and I were in this house was the night I told him about Will. That he was leaving me. That he left, Will. The rest is history. The last thing Joshua wanted was a woman that was free.

We fought so hard and for so long and with so much tears and sweat and congestion that when we finally got down to sex and finishing we both conked out, fell asleep.

At first I thought my heart was crashing—corny, but true. I thought, those old songs were based on something. But when I woke I knew. I knew from experience.

It was a college boy, wasted. That tree always gets boys and specific ones. It happens every year like a season. And be damned if this town would change the road, cut down that tree. I knew it was not a local, the tree didn't have it in for locals, and a girl, a girl has sense.

I knew it as Joshua rushed out in a pair of boxers.

I knew it as I slipped down the staircase, practically breaking my neck and bruising the right side of my body, long as an ink spill from hip to ribs. And as I called the sheriff and the campus police, I knew. I knew it the way sometimes you know the fabric of your life even before you've woven it.

The boy was dead.

If the boy were dying we could have done everything in our power to heal him. We would have no guilt if the boy were dying.

Joshua was from out of town. He had a special fellowship up at the University. Physics. He could explain so many things, how a boy traveling forward would still travel even after the vehicle the boy was traveling in was forced to stop.

How even though the science teacher tried so hard to convince my kids in school that if you travel fast enough time will go backwards, Joshua said that straight as an arrow time marches on.

Remember all that stuff that didn't make sense about if a mother was sent up in a spaceship and a baby stayed put, the mother could end up younger than her child?

That if the mother died in childbirth, the kid could go back and be by her while she was still alive?

Misconceptions, according to Joshua.

He explained how in limit cycles all it took was a tiny change to set the whole thing out of kilter, how with people the world went the very same way.

Remember how everyone always told you that there was only so much one person could do? Myself for example, my big line to Joshua was: "I am only one person."

"Not true," said Joshua. "Hitler, Elvis, Rosa Parks. An individual and his actions can change everything." He said: "You do nothing to realize your potential."

Joshua spent a year with me, then went back to the city after that accident. I stayed right out here as I like it. And Will, he went on to the girl who touches him too much, for my taste, in each and every way.

The night the boy drove into the tree we waited for the highway patrol, for the ambulance, me in the doorway, Joshua out there with a blanket. We helped fill out the forms when they came and took the kid away.

Taking the boy away was not easy, as he had encrusted and hardened around the steering wheel in the same manner as coral. Or roots and rocks. Or mortar and stone. Or the heart, my soft tissue, wending its way around the soul of Joshua, covering him like a skin, holding him in, holding on to him.

Then, when we went back to the house, Joshua banged on things, the table, a chair, broke glassware and dishes like someone out of the movies. He cried, Joshua, and his eyes rolled back and mucus poured over his cheeks and mouth and chin like a glaze.

He pounded his fists against the door until they were raw. He left bloody fist prints against the white wall the way the younger kids in my school make potato prints on long sheets of white paper. He was bent on making patterns until I told him I was afraid. That I would call those police right back here. But I wasn't afraid, I was calm. Energy and shock waves, fields of light and sound, swirled around me; pure, untouched, I felt dead, not dying. When the thing you fear most occurs there is no room left for being afraid.

I had authority. Joshua slept then, he slept perfectly. And he was gone for good the next day.

It was a week before the mother came; seven days that car carcass pushed up against the tree. She brought the boy's brother, her living son, along with her. After a week the boy's blood was long dried and it lifted into flakes that floated like dust motes when his brother crawled along the cracked leather.

What the kid rescued was this: a pipe, a comb, a marijuana pouch, a sunglasses case.

I saw all this while I poured them lemonade. Then I called up Will who, trouper that he is, came and spent the night, without bothering me with any sexy stuff, probably for lack of wanting any.

The next morning Will and I had coffee. We packed a lunch and biked around the lake. He was kind, Will. He listened. Which now, listener-elect that I am, I am able to see was big of him. Now, I realize how little he was invested. It is easy to listen when you don't really care.

After supper we went for a night swim. The water was black in the shadows, silver where the moon walked. Across the stage that was the lake I watched Will's arms swing his body forward and away from me. I followed in his wake. When he reached the footholds he hesitated, performed one last surface dive, his back arched and strong as a dancer's foot.

Will was in the spotlight, the moonlight, and I could see him clearly from the shadows where I waited. He climbed out first and reached his hand back, he swung me up and out, easily. Then we rubbed each other hard with big beach towels. It was cold out there in the night where we were.

After Will left, I sat out on the porch, wrapped in a quilt like I was taking a cure, and drank hot chocolate. And I counted my blessings: that I was alive, that Will was my friend, that I had this house to live in.

I try to remember this.

Mostly what I do now is read, hunt out words for next year, and thank God that I have no children.

Getting Over

IT WASN'T like he was my best friend or anything. I mean we liked each other okay, me and Ken. We were in a Bio lab together, before he dropped it. We both slept with this one loser girl Orientation Week which sort of linked us. Plus, we knew a lot of the same people, so when I got the deal down by the lake and I heard Ken needed a place to crash for Six-Week Session, well it made things easy. We were housemates, which doesn't have a whole lot to do with like or dislike, it just instantly elevates you to family status. Just-add-water loyalty. Members of the same team.

I mean he got on my nerves. So what? And I bugged him. All right, I know I bugged him. I was used to living alone. It was amazing to me to find out I was so annoying. When you're on your own long enough you have no clue to how weird you really are, and I'd been on my own a long time, my whole life, really; except for six months of me and Sue but that's history and I don't want to talk about it. So the truth was: I bugged Ken and he bugged me. Which made it even, neutralized us like a positive and minus charge. What I mean to say is it really freaked me out when he bit it, I mean it hurt me a lot when Ken died.

The name's Scott, Scott Levine, but my buddies call me Charlie. Who knows why? They also call me J.D. (because it's my drink), Smoke (because I do—the wacky stuff) and Barney (because I have this weird thing about "Barney Miller." I mean I *love* that show, don't ask. I mean I plan my class schedule around the reruns). Ken called me Scotty Wrong because I have a hard time doing things right. "Scotty Wrong" was one of those things about Ken that really bugged me. I called him Kenth, rhymes with tenth, for no particular reason except it kept me from what I really wanted to call him.

If you would like a taste of hell before you die you should try spending October through May in the frozen tundra of this poor excuse for a town our school lives in. Purgatory would be July and August. September, the season of torrential rains and flash floodings. But June is pure joy. Just terrific. A sexy, sexy month. It seduced me.

There I was a victim of post-exam delirium, where the thought of shlepping my shit back to Larchmont and spending another summer commuting with my dad and wearing a tie seemed worse than a bad tab of acid, when I saw this rather nifty sublet sign. The day was a great day. The breeze felt like what it looks like a cat feels when she's petted. The breeze gave you fur, and stroked it. The air was soft. The green greener than green, the sky's blue the bluest. Everything was at its most intense color. And that sublet sign. The sun hit it just right, hit it like a Hopper. The details, they were lacquered by white light; the price was shaded. There was a drawing of a ying-yang. Above the symbol it read: "Balance your Karma."

Below, it said: "Two bedrooms, two couches, two blocks from the water. Hear the lake's heartbeat—great for meditation."

That was it, I craved two couches, I craved balanced Karma. Since I'd spent the last four semesters renting a room at Zeta Psi, living in an actual apartment, hotplate and toaster oven, sounded real inviting. I took it sight unseen which was stupid. I admit it. But in a way I lucked out all the same. The place was a dump. Ken put it succinctly. But it was "Our Dump," he said, and we were two blocks from the lake which sits like a cool blue pearl at the bottom of several rock gorges, and we had this great porch to piss and spit off.

It was unclear who could piss farthest, mine a long, low graceful curve, Ken's a hard, full-throttle stream, but when it came to arcing seeds, Ken was hands down the winner. He'd take a biteful, suck and blow, soft pink bits of melon meat extending his gumline to his teeth. Our porch overhung a weedy yard, an alley really, and night after night we'd throw some chicken on the hibachi, maybe order in a pizza, crack a few beers and then piss and spit our way through the evening. Ken swore that below, among some of those nasty greens and vines, the bicycle wheel, an old sink, his watermelon seeds were growing. Ken said it was his piss that got them going, Fucking Fantastic Fertilizer.

It was summer. Ken, the quintessential Liberal Artsie, was taking Six-Week Session, science requirement. So far he had walked in and out of Bio I, Chem, Astrology and Physics for Poets. Now he was enrolled in Rocks for Jocks, which was okay by him because the town where we lived has some of the coolest rock gorges in the world and twice a week for lab he got to horse around in them. I was painting houses. College Pro Painters. By the end of the summer when I figured out all of my expenses, my co-workers' wages, having to replace the wrecked truck, my final earnings would amount to five maybe six dollars. A completely loser-effort. But then, during the first few weeks of August I felt flush, and even sprung for beers a couple of nights in a row. It was a special time in my life. I felt very free. A little bored, maybe, but very loose and easy, like everything was up to me. It was that incredible space between kid and grown-up. I made all the decisions but I had very little responsibility. It was perfect, sort of.

"Check it out," said Ken.

He spit five in a row like buckshot.

"She wants me," he said.

He tilted his chair back, put his feet up on the railing, hung precariously enough so that if there had been a mother, anyone's mother, anywhere within a five-mile radius she'd have screamed: "Watch out, you're going to break your neck!"

I lay back on the hammock.

"Who you trying to kid," I said.

Ken said: "I tell you I know women, she wants me buddy. She wants me to do her long and slow."

Ken bucked suggestively in his chair, practically tumbling to the porch floor. I caught a wooden leg and steadied him.

"What about Sylvie?" I said.

"What about her?" said Ken.

"What about her?" said me.

"We decided to take the summer off," he said. "If that's okay with you?" he added. Snidely.

It was okay with me. It was fine. Like any typical heterosexual human with at least one stray male hormone, I was crushed out on her. Sylvie had something special, something mysterious, and forgive me God, Ken wasn't

it. I don't even think he knew what was so great about
her. How she wasn't pretty, she was really pale, but she
was great looking; how she was inarticulate and unhappy,
but she could identify and talk about things you felt your
whole life, you just could never identify or talk about them
before. When she spoke, you felt a sense of recognition.
She had "aha" value. The amazing thing about Sylvie
was that when you were with her it was impossible to feel
lonely. She was the only cure I ever knew of (except for
those last few seconds of whacking off) for the human
condition, my human condition. She made you forget, for
a while at least, that someday you too were going to end
up as dust.

So I liked her, Sylvie. So I didn't mind that they were
taking the summer off. So I didn't care that Ken had
made his way through a ton of freshmen and A.P. students
already that summer. I just liked to remind him of what
he was doing, sleazing around with a couple of sixteen-
year-old APE's when he had the chance to be with a real
live goddess. That was the thing about Ken, babes loved
him. I guess he was pretty cute, but cuteness fades, you
know? Sylvie's words: "Cuteness fades," she said to me
one night when she called on the phone and Ken was
obviously not in the shower the way I said he was, when
Ken was obviously not home.

Ken scratched his bare belly. His shirt was unbuttoned, open, it opened him up like a book. He was white
and exposed and readable. I remember looking at him
hard. I remember thinking there is flesh, there is blood,
there is a heart pumping.

I remember remembering this, but I don't know if it
is the actual moment that I remember, or just my memory
of it, shaped by the fact that within nine stupid hours,
Ken would be a dead man.

He was weird to look at. The planes of his face were flat and at opposing angles. His eyes were the color of afternoon. They were long open tunnels that stretched back to the sky behind him, as if the afternoon sky shone through. Blue. That two-toned hair of his drove the girls wild, or so they tell me. Overall he was dark as metal, but the right eye sported grayish-whitish lashes with a matching eyebrow and in the front his cowlick was silver. The silver dusted back so that from behind, on one side, you thought he was a well-preserved old guy, gray-templed.

Why this drove the girls wild, don't ask me. Girls can be strange that way. I thought it made him look a little demonic myself. Although I have to admit I envied him his Pepsodent-bit, teeth as white and even as a mouth full of Chiclets. At that exact moment, however, he had a black seed lodged against his left front tooth and his smile was kind of crooked. His lips spread in different directions. Which made me wonder what girls saw in him at all. Really.

Sue said, "He has geeky good looks."

"*Geeky* good looks," Sue said.

Something about too skinny, fine-boned, hot eyes. But I have no desire whatsoever to discuss anything that Sue said.

"I've been thinking a lot, Wrong-Man," Ken said to me, "I've been thinking a lot about this man-woman thing."

I'd been thinking about it too.

"Love, physical love, emotional love, even, is not about possession," Ken said.

"What's it about then?" said me.

As far as I could tell the whole point was in *having*

someone. That was the trouble with Sue. She wouldn't let me have her.

"What it's about," said Ken, "is the experience."

For him, this was per usual. Ken liked to get deep. Some nights we'd stay out on the porch and shoot the shit for hours. He didn't always make sense, but you had to give him credit for spending a hell of a lot of time on thinking about stuff.

"It's the work," Ken said, first slowly, as if a great big cartoon of a light bulb was brightening over his head. As if an earth-shattering theory was *dawning* on him. And then more lecturey: "Whether the work is scholar stuff, the art of love, or the really noble business of physical labor, you've got to be in it for the work," Ken said.

He who had never worked a day in his life.

"I assume," I said, "the art of love is synonymous with shtupping?"

"The whole wham-banger. The big boff," said Ken, this somewhere around eight and a half hours before he nodded out—we think—and drove his car into a tree. You see, they could never pinpoint the exact time of death precisely. Between 2:00 and 2:30.

Whoever *they* were.

Which is something I wonder about, now, from time to time. Who was that poor guy whose job was to determine the moment when some shmucky kid went out and totaled the car his parents bought for him? Was that any way for that guy to spend his life? And what about the rest of us, the majority of the Eastern Seaboard: when Ken became history we were counting Z's, sawing wood, safely in our beds. Why? I don't get it. I'll never get it. I'll never understand the distance, maybe ten, maybe fifteen feet, between the people in the burning building and the people outside the burning building, watching. I mean, during those rare (and I mean rare) moments when I consider myself truly happy, somebody's dad somewhere is saying his goodbyes.

How did I get so lucky?

It was dusky out. Those with apartments on the other side of the house had the privilege of reacting to a devastating sunset, a mind-expanding sunset, an electric hot-fucking sunset, one of the rare positive attractions for which this ridiculously inclement region was famous. (The others being those three glorious weeks in June, terrific ice cream, and the best burritos in New York State—which isn't saying much.)

What we were seeing was what was left when the colors go. The absence of sunset. The anti-sunset. Us, stuck on the side facing away from it all.

"Who's she this time?" I said.

"Katiya?" said Ken. "She's an artist."

All his girls were named names like Katiya. They were all artistas or modern dancers. Unless they were bizarre Philosophy Department geniuses.

A little secret. I was jealous of him. I bet you could have guessed that one on your own. I'll let you in on another. For one brief second after I heard Ken kicked it, I thought to myself: I won.

I won.

"She's working with organic matter. For months now she's been saving her menstrual blood on natural sponges."

"Gross." I said: "Gross me out." I said: "You're shitting me. Right, boy?"

"You have to embrace the body," Ken said. "You have to see it as beautiful. All of it. Its secretions and lubrications."

Lubrications?

Ugh.

I cracked open another beer.

"You really should come with me to the sweat lodge. I told Running Bear all about you."

Ken was into this Native American stuff. And meditation, and astrology, and Zen Buddhism, and a religious following of the Dow Jones Industrial. He'd recently inherited a mess of blue chips; I figured he was set for life.

"Maybe," I said, although I meant never. I said "Maybe" because in spite of myself it sounded kind of cool. Chanting and fasting and sweating your white American suburban ass down the fast track to enlightenment.

"It would do you good, man," said Ken.

And he got that look, that look where his eyes went so wild they made that two-toned hair of his look normal. Wild eyes and a face so blank, without those eyes blazing and burning, his face looked like nothing alive could live there.

This was the danger point. I knew Ken. I fucking *lived* with him. Maybe Sylvie had X-ray vision into his soul, maybe that wacky sister of his was the only one who *understood* him. But I lived with him. I knew what magazines he read in the bathroom, for Christssake. I knew all about his weird foods—apricots in ginger ale, cottage cheese and ketchup. When he got all pedantic and godlike like that, when he started in like he was Moses with those tablets, I tell you it could get ugly. He could want to steal a car or something. Trip out on six drops of acid. Do pull-ups off the suspension bridge. Ken could go crazy.

"The thing about life is you got to embrace it."

Ken said this. And even then, knowing how he could go off, get possessed, let fly, before we had any hint he was near the end, he had authority. He had gone to the edge and back. He fell through the ice while ice-skating as a kid, he'd been one of those ice-cube miracle boys. He said he was without vital signs for actual minutes. And he came back exactly as he was before. That's what Ken said. Except that he had seen the hereafter. Said it was pink. Pink as a dog's dick. Bright and inescapable. Said the whole time he was out of it he heard Charlie Parker. That God was obviously cool, very cool. So when Ken went on and on and on again about what Life was about, I listened to him. I may have been a skeptic, but I listened. I think now that somewhere in my bones I knew.

This is what I told Sue, when I got her to hold my hand, after. When I was trying to impress her. I told her I had seen the future.

"It's about action," said Ken.

So that's how he motivated me into going out and buying the rope, even though it was late and I was semi-wasted. That's how he convinced me to ride out with him to the res, even though they were cracking down on the swimming and nude sunbathing that summer in our town was all about. Ken coerced me. I was innocent.

I tied the rope around his waist. I secured the other end to the tree. I think I checked the tree's roots for tree rot.

And I lowered him, slowly, over the edge, flashlight in one hand, sketch pad and pencil in his teeth (which was a mouthful), the other hand holding on to the rope like a true mountaineer. And I stood there, legs braced, hands clenched, suffering rope burns for God's sake as Ken had his transcendental experience. He sketched the rock's face in the fading light of day. He shined his high-beam on them. He drew abstractly, geometrically, deconstructivistly. He was in his post-neo-geo-supra-modernist phase. He was lousy at it.

And after twenty sweaty minutes of waiting for him to

apply his finishing touches I hauled him up. Me. I pulled Kenneth Gordon Gold to safety.

Him with his seven hours to go.

Now that I know, it all seems so obvious. As if everything in his life was leading him up to that moment. Predestination. I mean you never think about it, at camp, in kindergarten, at high school graduation. At least one of the bunch isn't going to get to grow up. Ken was set up from the start. He was the kid who was going to die.

I still have that drawing. I meant to frame it, to hang it, but it's leaning against the wall on the dresser in my room. I don't know. When I look at it I feel something. It reminds me not to be too lazy, it reminds me that I am alway near the end. It reminds me to wear it today, that today is the first day of the rest of my life, that my life is what I make it.

After it does all that reminding, that drawing, I stay the very same way that I am. Which I suppose is, in and of itself, a lesson in denial. In survival. But at least now I wake up and think: go for it, grab it, take it.

Reality: the difference in my life since Ken died is that now I think in slogans.

It was amazing. While he was hanging from that rope, I cursed him. I wanted to kill him. I hated him. Me with the rope burning through my palm-skin, me yelling: Hurry up there Dog-Breath, Kenth you asshole, you Jerk, me with the calf cramps from bracing against the tree. But when he emerged, slightly red-faced, but triumphant, we got high off of it, I swear it. We jumped around and whooped in the air. We had gotten over—Ken's never-failed trick for feeling great. Then we hiked down to the falls. Went in with our clothes on. The water was a liquid glass curtain between Ken and me. And our clothes plastered clear to our bodies. It was the destruction of obstruction, even the night-dark was light, and daring, sculpting new bones into Ken's bony face, working him over like a surgeon. The sky was bright. I have no idea why. It was early, yet, for moonlight.

The rest is fact and well documented. His mother made me go over it a hundred times. We drove back to the apartment, The Doors blaring, Ken singing hard, off-key.

When we got home, I let Ken shower first because he had a date, and me, I had nothing. Just a ménage à trois between the hammock and the porch and yours truly. When Ken emerged, he looked pretty spiffy. One of those guayabera shirts unbuttoned so that his lack of chest hair was obvious, but okay-looking. Sort of clean. Young. And my favorite pair of jeans. Without asking. My favorite jeans that he died in. It took me a long time to get those jeans in that condition, soft, bleached white at the seams, fraying at one knee, but the crotch still solid. It took me a year and half of everyday wear to get them where I wanted them to be. On Ken they looked terrific.

"Fuck you," I said. "Take them off."

He said: "Wrong-Man, old pal, old buddy."

He grinned his crazy-grin.

"What could happen to them?" said Ken.

Then he headed out for Katiya's. I wished him luck.

I said: "I hope you get to bone her."

Ken gave me the high sign.

He said: "Later."

So I hung out awhile not-calling Sue, pounded back a few, smoked a doobie, got a little buzz going, and fell asleep in the hammock. I never did take that shower.

At about five in the morning I was woken up by a phone call. It must have rung about eighteen rings. I stumbled into the kitchen and answered it. At first they asked if he was home. I said, give the guy a break, it's five o'clock in the morning. That's when they told me.

Isn't it funny, but I expected more.

I sat still, I was at my stillest. I remember thinking: Do I even *like* Ken—because at the time I wasn't really hurting. And then I thought: I wonder if I can use this to get Sue back. My first thought: how can I get this to help me?

And that was the best of it really, sitting in our pit of an apartment, quietly scheming, surrounded by Ken's dirt. It wasn't until later, much later that it got hard, then bad, then worse. But at the time it was a breeze actually, I even made a pot of tea, and I sat there, sort of round and whole, just being. Nothing had changed yet.

That afternoon Sue came over. That's the kind of girl Sue is, she came because she felt sorry for me. And we did it, I don't mind telling you, I think it's probably good for me. Confession. Makes me wish I was a Catholic. Sue and I did it on our kitchen table. It was out of the movies. Ken was dead and I was living. And with Sue, well this is the weirdest, but I didn't want her after that, which is sort of hard to explain, since up until that point my whole reason for being seemed to revolve around wanting Sue. I mean I can't be with her anymore, I can't talk to her on the phone, I can't look at her picture, I wish that she'd just disappear.

The Indispensable Man

HANNAH'S house smelled like Hannah's house: the oven
was going. A clean green scent came from all her potting
and pruning, the work of spring and summer divided up,
taken in, so that falling leaves were everywhere, in and
outside Hannah's house. And that boy smell was locked
inside too: athletic, something to do with sneakers and
socks—only not repulsive—that and leather and the
almost plastic odor of new sporting goods.

The scent of sage wafted through Hannah's house, the
perfume of it burning as Cara lit yet another smudge stick
and pirouetted through the rooms; a dance full of purpose,
Cara's purpose being to transform the southeastern part
of Connecticut into the southwestern part of the country,
she herself outfitted in Navajo this and that, luminous
tears of turquoise dribbling from silver chains encircling
her wrists, her waist, her neck, turquoise dewdrops crying
from her ears.

Doug and Madeleine were arguing, about poetry it
seemed, or art. Madeleine's black sheet of hair swung

side to side or bobbed and lengthened depending upon whether she agreed at all with Doug or not. They shared a clove cigarette, an Oriental smell, mingling mystical and foreign, permeating the atmosphere so that it seemed a lot like Christmas in a house that had never had a Christmas as far as anyone could be sure—still, that smell seemed to be universal, it conjured memories of times that had not occurred before. Doug and Madeleine sat at the kitchen table and passed the slow-burning stick, back and forth, mouth to mouth, as if it were a respirator that connected them, heart and breath, flesh and bones and body.

Only Jeremy had no scent, but a white scent; he smelled clean. If he smelled like anything, he smelled like a baby. It was a chalky non-scent: powder, things that crumble, Jeremy smelled of the charcoals he used for sketching, his scent *felt* that way in your nose, it felt without really smelling. Surrounded the way that he was surrounded, the delicacy of Jeremy's non-scent traced away, it melted around him.

At last amidst this cacophony of desirable and undesirable odor was Hannah herself, the hair released finally into gray waves, the body loose in the folds of something reminiscent of what used to be called a caftan. Hannah. Smelling badly really, from the cologne the kids had bought her last birthday. Something expensive that had turned, Hannah thought. Something on the sale shelf.

Jack used to say, "Make the house smell good, you know, Hannah, honey, the way you do" when things were not good, and so two and a half years after he left finally, left them all, she was determined to make the house reek with happiness, with soothing homey smells, redolent of completion. She wanted the holiday to be more than a holiday, she wanted it to be proof positive of the smashing job she did as a mother. She was dying for a success.

Many pots were cooking, more than necessary—asparagus, tender green furled feathers steamed to their brightest bright; beets boiled and buttered and peppered, laced over by onions ringed and sliced. She had pies baking—Hannah who had never baked a pie in her life. Cherry and mince, from a can no less; who knew what went into mince really, thought Hannah. Who would want to? She had stuffing stuffed in the turkey, and also browning in a separate Pyrex dish for Cara, the vegetarian. Oranges hollowed out and filled with sweet-potato mush topped by little marshmallow caps sat on the counter ready for a last-minute broil. These were for Jeremy. He was crazy for them ever since he was a kid. Hannah tried to please her children, each and every one and their lovers too, for that matter. She'd bought a carton of Lactaid instead of milk because Madeleine was intolerant. Even the cat, this year, got special claim to the turkey's hindquarters, a delicacy that Jack had coveted—in some ways, Jack's departure was really better for everyone. The last couple of Thanksgivings had been pretty miserable with Jack gone. Hannah couldn't seem to quite pull it together, and ended up hating the kids for bearing witness to her weakness.

This year, Hannah was giddy with newfound freedom. The house was her house. For the first time in her life she could have things the way she wanted them: skylights in her bathroom, for example, in her bedroom a large Clark Gable poster. She was "expressing" herself, finally—according to Cara, the resident pre–Psychology major, the feminist, wise woman, intuitive interpreter, the teenage witch.

"God, Mom," said Cara, "I spent my entire adolescence wondering if you were going to implode." Cara was sixteen.

Implode, explode, not sure if bursting out was really

any different from caving in, Hannah knew her kid had a point. Clearly, it wasn't any fun being left by Jack, but then toward the end, the last eight years, it wasn't exactly fun being married to him either. A secret Hannah kept to herself—aside from the rage, the fear, when Jack told her about that young girl, that girl turning forty—Hannah felt something close to release. Finally, she thought. After a whole lifetime of wondering: when will I die, what will become of my children, will I ever divorce, Hannah possessed an answer. Endings held a simple comfort for her; no more worrying about the outcome.

Hannah bit into a seal of plastic, broke the vacuum, and poured, nuts, assorted nuts, into a large wooden bowl. She slid it down the kitchen table to Doug and Madeleine.

"Earn your keep," said Hannah. "I need walnuts for the frosting."

Madeleine made a half-hearted effort, Doug was too caught up in their argument. Madeleine, silver nutcracker in hand, picked through the pile, her fingers light and random as waves over water until she found an almond smooth as a stone. She squeezed it open, the shell disintegrating rather than cracking, the shell threadbare, the nut-meat available in the tiny nest in her hand. She wore a silver band on her ring finger although she was not married. Hannah noticed this, and it annoyed her. Why were those two so bent on living a married-life if they were so insistent upon not-marrying?

"That's an almond," said Hannah.

"That's bullshit," said Doug.

"Oh," said Madeleine. "Oh."

"Not you, Ma," said Doug, "Madeleine."

"What?" said Hannah.

"It's bullshit to think you can raise the collective consciousness through artistic measures," Doug said.

" 'There was no poet and so the city died'—
Cervantes," Madeleine said.

" 'Fuck you,' " Doug said. "—David Mamet."

"Who?" said Cara, as she came twirling in. "Who?"

"You sound like an owl," Doug said. "Who? Who?"

"Fuck you," Madeleine said, "Madeleine Rappaport."

"Cara, darling," Hannah said, "could you rid the
house of evil spirits in another room? It smells like a barn
in here."

"Fuck you," Cara said, "Cara Running Doe Gold,"
and she twirled out.

"Running Doe?" said Doug.

"It's her *real* name," said Hannah. "Kenny named her."

"Be good, Douglas," said Madeleine.

"Speaking of which, where is that no-good son of
mine?" said Hannah, broadly, as if she were imitating
herself.

"Probably still upstate studying, Ma," Doug said,
winking like Popeye, "probably passed out in the library
from intellectual exhaustion."

"I'm counting on him," said Hannah.

The kitchen really did smell like a barn, in a nice
way, the burnt sage smelled like harvest: blond, musky,
sweet. The water set to boil, boiled over, and Hannah
went to the stove to turn it down.

"Has anyone seen Jeremy?" she said over her shoulder.

She said it to no one in particular. No one in particular
bothered to answer her.

Jeremy was outside, in the back, at the picnic table which
rested unevenly on the brick patio that Kenny, his older
brother, in a fit of charitableness and with a firm if passing
"religious" conviction in the work ethic, had laid two

summers before. Everything was off-balance. The table rocked. The benches teetered, and even the cat, snoozing in a pocket of cool sunshine, seemed to waver in his perch on the edge of the raised flower beds. Overhead clouds crowded out the blue. Where it burst through, that blue looked icy. The cat was rocked by fleeting shadows, but anchored by the light.

Jeremy stared into the house. Through the sliding glass doors that he himself once walked through—even now he remembered the embarrassment, all of it, painfully enough to make him shudder, want to hide. The crashing clarity of impact, his forehead, the splintered light. Kenny and his buddies drinking beer, their open mouths like donuts, frozen laughter. Mom being away. What felt like sweat but was really blood. All that glass . . . It made him sick just to think about it. Through those enemy doors (*now* affixed with stickers of flowers for godssakes so that it looked like one of those bathmats) he could see the d-table set, that plus the card table (company was coming) and that corny cornucopia thing that Cara begged for at the farm stand. Still-life in suburbia, Jeremy thought, Still-life.

A pebble flew.

"I was aiming at the cat," said Cara, barefoot in the cold, with bells on her ankles, Cara with the little removable butterfly tattoo buried in the hair near her sock line.

She was beautiful. Silly, but beautiful.

"You are pretty today," said Jeremy.

"What do you mean 'today,' " said Cara, "aren't I always pretty?"

"Yes and no," said Jeremy, which was the truth.

Cara frowned. She shook her hair, dark curls that grew out rather than down, her earrings—three on one ear, God knew how many more on the other—jingled.

"Was there someone else out here?" Cara said. "Was there someone else out here, but they went inside to the bathroom? It feels like there was someone else out here, but now they're missing," Cara said to him.

"Just me," said Jeremy.

"It's Kenny, isn't it? He's here, he's hiding," Cara said.

"Nope," said Jeremy, "not home yet."

A breeze swaddled her dress around her. It blew Jeremy's fine, light hair up like a skirt. It took the cat's fur in the wrong direction.

"He looks like he has feathers," said Cara.

"The cat?" said Jeremy.

"Yes, the cat," said Cara. "Yessiree Bob, the cat," she said. She waited a second, expectantly, as if to see if the breeze would come back. "You know the feeling you get sometimes when the wind blows against your face a certain way and you think to yourself: this is the eighteenth century and I am a Russian peasant? You know that feeling? I had that feeling, just now," said Cara.

"I don't know that feeling," said Jeremy.

Cara balance-beamed the brick wall of the raised flower bed. When she got to the cat she nudged him with her toe.

"Move, Lardo," said Cara.

That cat ignored her so Cara did a little leap over him. Jeremy watched her. It was hard for him to believe she was three years older than he was.

"You look like a little kid," Jeremy told her.

With the tips of two fingers Cara showed him the inside of her nose.

"You act like one," said Jeremy.

"You," said Cara, "you."

The earth rotated under a cloud, moved away from the sun. The cat yawned, lifted his tail toward God, then started to stalk off. Cara swooped in on her target, slipped an arm under the fur-balled belly, and carried the cat high. The cat wriggled uncomfortably against the graying expanse of sky.

"Quit torturing him," said Jeremy.

"He likes it," said Cara, when clearly the cat did anything but.

"Jeremy, where are you?" Hannah's voice rang out.

"Nowhere, Ma," said Jeremy.

The kids, if anyone could still call them that, were sitting in the living room. Doug was blowing smoke rings. Cara was climbing the furniture. Her dirty feet sunk down deep into the velveteen sofa. Jeremy sat on the floor, leaning against the ottoman. Out in the kitchen Madeleine was playing the good girlfriend and helping Hannah out. She was chopping and peeling and spooning. She was instrumental in a pie's resurrection, the crust on top having already reduced itself to tar paper. It had been Madeleine's idea to schlag cream all over it, and considering her own relationship with dairy products, Hannah was suspicious, although Madeleine assured her it looked wonderful.

"The pie looks wonderful, Hannah, really," said Madeleine a little too loudly. The kids in the living room could have heard her, if anyone was listening, which they weren't, not an ear to out back, not an ear for one another.

Hannah looked at her hard. She liked her, Madeleine, she just wished she wouldn't call her Hannah. Mrs. Gold. That would be better, or better still, nothing at all.

In the living room, Jeremy, the resident ventriloquist, was throwing voices. He'd learned how to do this, on his own, as a kid. The sofa talked to Cara, for example. The sofa said: "Hey, Running Doe, don't tread on me." Cara ignored him.

"What's with this Running Doe stuff anyway?" said Doug.

"Another nonbeliever," said the chair that Doug sat on.

"Cut it out," said Cara to the chair, and then to Jeremy: "Cut it out. I can't stand it when you do that." She leapt from the sofa to the recliner.

"Dad hated it too," said Jeremy.

"I couldn't care less what Dad hated," said Cara, crossing her legs and then sitting quickly, her calves folding, her dress falling into a puff.

"Let's make the predictions now," said Doug, "before Abigail and Fred," he said. "Jeremy, go get a piece of paper."

Jeremy obeyed him. He went up into his room and came down with a page of the fancy stuff. He took out his fountain pen and ink and in an elegant hand scripted "Predictions" across the top.

"Doug," said the sofa, "you start."

Doug glared at Jeremy. Cara interrupted. "I predict," said Cara, "that Jeremy will be all zits by next year."

"*Douglas,*" the sofa was insistent.

"All right, all right," said Doug. "Next year. Next year will be a good year. We'll elect a Democratic House, the Talking Heads will put out another album, Madeleine will get some of her stuff published. Me I'll be a little clearer on what I want to be."

"Be?" said Cara. "Be? You are already hopelessly what you are."

Doug ignored her, sort of. He went on. "Things will get easier for Mom, she'll adjust more; Cara might or might not be less of a JAP, and at this time next year you all will spend Thanksgiving with Madeleine and me on the farm. We'll eat only the stuff we've grown."

"How groovy," said Cara. "Make me barf." She did an around-the-world in her chair.

Jeremy scribbled furiously. He accompanied the disharmony of his siblings.

"Next year I'm going to be with Kenny," said Cara. "Next year that dork better definitely show up. Show up on time," she added for good measure. "Write that part down in big letters," she said to Jeremy. "Make it look foreboding."

Jeremy inked in a couple of lightning bolts.

"Next year," said Cara, "in New Mexico." She said it like "next year in Jerusalem." "Next year I want to spend Thanksgiving far from home."

"I'm going to be with Dad next year," said Jeremy.

"You do that, creep," said Cara.

"Shut up," said Jeremy.

"Children," said Doug in a mocking tone.

"You know," said Cara straight at Doug, "I've always hated your guts."

In the kitchen Madeleine was proving the existence of God. She did this by distinguishing between what she referred to as "biology" and "emotion." Emotion was her proof. Biology made sense; the nature of human feeling, that was another story. It was the product of an inquisitive and scheming mind.

"It's illogical," said Madeleine to Hannah over the crudités. "Emotions are illogical. Reproductive organs, fur, incisors—those make sense. They insure the propagation of the species. What do feelings do? All they insure is chaos. It's nonsensical for an orderly science, for biology

35

to create emotional attachments—love, for a lack of a better word . . ."

"Love," said Hannah.

"Love," said Madeleine, "it's excess baggage. Nature makes it inevitable that a love object or loved one will be removed . . ." said Madeleine, who at that point in her marvelous young life had yet to lose, or be rejected by, anyone.

"Will die," said Hannah.

"Will die," said Madeleine, "before its partner, or before its offspring can take care of themselves, or worse yet . . ." she paused for emphasis . . . "even if they are *biologically* independent, they're bound to be a catastrophe emotions-wise." She paused again. "If they're human," said Madeleine.

"I don't understand your differentiation," said Hannah. "How can you separate biology and emotion? Can you whip up some extra cream? This batch is beginning to melt."

Madeleine placed the pie in the refrigerator. She took out a little paper carton.

"And anyway," continued Hannah. "I'm not sure how this all proves the existence of God. I mean it seems to me that you are *dis*proving Him by illustrating one of the inherent injustices of life."

"Hannah," said Madeleine. "You are assuming that if there is a God that God is kind."

"*Madeleine*," said Hannah. "I'm not assuming anything. Why don't you add in a little vanilla this time."

Madeleine was beating the cream into peaks. "The truth is," said Madeleine, "only a mind would bother to think up something as cruel and unnecessary, as infinitely *interesting* as quote-unquote love."

"Define 'mind,' " said Doug, lounging in the doorway.

"Mind," said Hannah. "I am beginning to mind this conversation."

"You're threatened by it," said Doug. "It threatens your atheistic, knee-jerk liberal philosophies."

Hannah drizzled melted apricot preserves over some mixed-fruit tartlets.

"The amount of food here, Ma, it's ridiculous," Doug said.

"Why don't you two set the table. Please," said Hannah.

Madeleine set the table, Doug supervised, the two of them fought, as usual. Madeleine's hair swept across the cloth, the plates, the silver, the tips of her hair swinging across the table like a brush. Doug reached out and twisted it, all that hair, his hand full of that amazing stuff, and he used it to bend her back at the neck and kiss her. The quiet, the absence of argument, startled them both, even with the muffled chewing sounds that come along with lips going, tongues going, an occasional tooth grind, a quiet surrounded them for the first time that morning. Doug came up for air, he laughed down at Madeleine, he twirled a side lock with his forefinger, until her face was punctuated on one side by a straggling curl, a question mark.

"God, I love your hair," said Doug, and then they continued arguing.

Cara entered. She always entered, Cara, she never just came into a room.

"Bicker, bicker," said Cara. "Why don't you two get married?" Cara was nibbling at a piece of cauliflower.

"We don't believe in marriage," said Doug. And then, "Yo, Chow-Hound, what was that . . . Running Dough-Ball, Running Dough-Ball's your real name?"

"Douglas, it's a piece of cauliflower for godsake," said Madeleine.

The truth was that Cara was sort of plump, but in a nice way. "Zaftig," Hannah called it. Still, tears stood in Cara's eyes. She turned to Madeleine. "Do you think I'm fat?" said Cara. "Am I lardette, am I? Am I a real load?"

"More of you to love," said a voice out of nowhere, Kenny's voice, Kenny who just appeared in the middle of the room. His hair, his strange, personal hair—the result of some weird pigmentation thing, the right side distinctively lighter than the left, the right brow white, ditto the lashes—that hair was longer and stranger than ever. He was bearded, sort of, as bearded as a boy his age with his hormones and his heredity could be. He was wearing a dashiki. It hung down almost to his knees. He was wearing a Guatemalan sweater, which was shorter.

Kenny was home.

"Ka-knee!" Cara shrieked, and she was all over him like a puppy.

"Hey, man," said Doug, and he offered his hand, which Kenny took when he could navigate his way around his sister. "We weren't sure you were going to make it. Mom know you're here?"

"I did it in two rides," said Kenny. "Met up with some hippie in Binghamton who was going to the City, but after I got him stoned he said he'd drive me home to Connecticut. That weed was so awesome I could have gotten his firstborn off of him." Kenny grinned his crazy-grin.

"Hey, Mad," he said to Madeleine, even though Doug had told him a million times Madeleine hated it when he called her that.

"Hey yourself," said Madeleine, but she leaned past Cara to kiss him.

"Kenny, you're an absolute wreck," said Cara happily. "Mom will have an absolute fit."

"You are a bit scuzzy, son," said Doug. Madeleine shook that lovely head of hair of hers and giggled.

"Scuzzy's too kind," said Hannah, for she had arrived at once, sensing the presence of her offspring.

"My yiddishe mama," said Kenny, and Frankensteinlike, with his arms outstretched and his tongue lolling, he lurched toward her.

Hannah hugged him hard. "Thank God," she said. She stepped back, gave him a good once-over, and held him at arm's length. "Shower and shave," Hannah commanded, "there's company coming." And then, "Young man, what is that smell?" Hannah sniffed him.

"You sound exactly like some sit-com mother," said Cara.

"Where do you think they get it from," said Doug, under his breath.

"Kenny," said Hannah.

"It's pot, Mom, it's wacky weed, marijuana, it's ganja," said Kenny.

"You left out *reefers*," said Hannah.

"It's reefer, Mom," said Kenny.

"I know what it is," said Hannah. "Go clean up." As he started toward the stairs, she continued, "You are in trouble and you don't even know it."

"*Reefers*," said Cara, "Oh Mo*ther*."

"Yo, Jerm," shouted Kenny. The bathroom door was open, steam ghosting his mother's room. "Yo, Jerm, a towel." The shower was running.

Jeremy sat on the king-sized bed.

"Don't call me that," said Jeremy.

"What," said Kenny, loudly, because the shower was running.

"I said, don't call me that," said Jeremy.

"I can't hear you, Jerm," said Kenny.

"I said, don't fucking call me that name," screamed Jeremy.

The water turned off. Kenny walked out of the steam, emerged like a sea monster from a lake, like a rock star and that stage smoke, hot-ice. He stood totally naked.

"You're right, man," said Kenny. "You're absolutely right. I'll never fucking call you that name anymore, man," said Kenny, and he smiled right at his brother.

Jeremy threw Kenny a guest towel, a towel laid out for company. Jeremy had taken it from the guest bathroom.

"Thanks, man," said Kenny. "Check it out," he said wrapping the towel around his waist, high, near his chest, like an old man would. He looked funny. He stood next to the Clark Gable poster. "Separated at birth," said Kenny.

"Yeah, right," said Jeremy.

In came Cara, singing: "You better hurry, you better scurry, you better get the lead out, Lead-Head, Mom said, before they get here—Abigail and Fred, or you'll be dead, Mom said," sang Cara.

"Abigail and Fred?" said Kenny. "What other nightmares await?"

"Every insane relative Mom could dig up," said Jeremy.

"Kenny," said Cara, on tiptoe, her nose to his armpit. "You are the only person alive who smells terrible coming out of the shower." She was beaming.

Kenny bent his neck, lifted his arm into a frame for his face and snorted. "Ahhh, nectar," said Kenny.

Cara went silly with laughing. "Wh-what are you, what are you ..." Her giggles hiccupped her words. "What are you going to wear?" said Cara.

"Wear," said Kenny. "Wear?"

"A white shirt, a jacket, a tie," said Hannah, who was in the doorway, carrying said articles of clothing.

"My white shirt, my jacket, my tie," said Doug, who came in after her, carrying nothing at all.

"I didn't know you owned a tie," said Madeleine, bringing up the rear, a leather belt in one hand, two shoes hanging precariously from the finger joints of the other, swinging her hair over her shoulder like an accent, with a swimmer's toss of the head.

"Doug doesn't have to wear a tie," said Kenny.

"Doug doesn't have to wear a tie," said Doug in a baby voice.

"You're not Doug," said Hannah and Cara on top of one another.

Even Hannah had to laugh at that one.

Jeremy handed Kenny a pair of shorts, which Kenny slipped on beneath his towel. Kenny then did a mock bump and grind, the towel hitting Cara squarely in the face, the corner landing in her eyes.

"You knocked my eye out," cried Cara.

"Oh dear," said Hannah. "Honey, let me see."

Cara held one hand fiercely cupped to her eye. "The towel sucked the eye-juice out of it. It burns," cried Cara.

"Zhere ess only von vay to put zee eye-juice back in zee eye-ball," said Kenny.

"Shut up," said Cara.

"And zhat is to tickle it out of zee stomache," said Kenny, and he chased Cara, Cara laughing and sobbing, around the room until he tackled her to the bed and tortured her into fits of screaming giggles.

"I gave birth to this?" said Hannah. "Kenneth Gordon Gold you must get dressed, NOW," she said.

"If you want my body," sang Kenny, "and you think

I'm sexy," he sang to his reflection in Hannah's wall mirror. Hannah went into the bathroom and came out with a comb, which she used as a weapon really, to desnarl and untangle Kenny's long hair. Kenny kept on singing, arms stretched out into a wingspan like he was Kate Smith or somebody. Doug pulled the sleeves of *his* white man-tailored over Kenny's outstretched arms and buttoned him down. Cara held out the trousers for Kenny to step into, which he did without missing a crooked note. Even Madeleine got into the picture—she tied his tie, looped that purple and red fabric around his throat, then tightened it into a knot. Cara threaded his belt, Jack's old one, through his loops. Jeremy sat on the bed and watched his family in action. It was a group effort, a theatrical extravaganza, this getting Kenny presentable. Jeremy was the audience.

"Something's burning," said the mirror. "You can smell it."

Everyone looked at Jeremy.

"God, Jerm," said Kenny, "I've always wondered how you did that."

The kitchen was filled with smoke. Cara rushed around opening windows, she was as much a source of wind as anything else. Hannah stood over the turkey, scorched to blackness, tested a leg that slid down limp rather than reflex-kicked.

"Look what you made me do," said Hannah. She was near tears. "Look what you made me do." She turned her evil eye on her children. They cowered as if they were a collective, guilty six-year-old, reduced by their mother's anger.

"Now, Mother," said Cara, "don't have a breakdown."

Kenny, bridled by his tie, his slacks, his coat, was tossing back a beer, although he still looked uncomfortable. He shushed her. "Shush, Cara," said Kenny. The way he said it, it sounded like a prayer.

"I wanted things to be nice for a change," said Hannah. She was sobbing.

Jeremy left the room. He couldn't take it.

"Goddamnit," said Hannah.

There was silence. For a while, no one interrupted.

Then, "Doug," Madeleine said, in an almost whisper, "Doug, this is like the theory of the indispensable man," said Madeleine.

"The what?" said Cara.

"Madeleine," Doug said.

Madeleine's left hand floated up to her left shoulder. Her arm lay bent, winglike, graceful. Her wrist looked so slight, so snappable, angling in that way, folded in on herself like a letter.

"You know," said Madeleine. "I had that professor at school who said if a company loses its indispensable man that's when you know how strong your company is."

"Indispensable *person*," countered Cara.

"Indispensable person," agreed Madeleine.

"I mean, now, Hannah, you know how good your meal is," said Madeleine.

"You could look at it that way," said Hannah. "I suppose."

"You could," said Doug.

"I mean you only know what you have when something else is missing," said Madeleine. "It's all comparative, I mean relative. Oh, you know what I mean," she said.

"Like with Dad," said Cara, "what are we missing?" She held out her arms as if to signify "nothing at all."

"I don't know if I agree with you on this, Madeleine," said Doug. "Define indispensable," he said. "You are assuming a lot. I mean the only way you could really test this theory of yours would be by removing the potatoes and the pies, by removing man after man, until you found out which dish, which man was the indispensable one."

"Person," said Cara. "Person."

"You said that already," said Doug.

"When someone's indispensable you know it," said Madeleine. She sounded exasperated.

"Here they go," said Cara.

Hannah, meanwhile, had lifted off the turkey's skin and was doctoring the carcass. Thanksgiving. It was less than a year away from the car accident that was already coming to take Kenny's life. It was two and a half years to the day before Cara's first breakdown. The mathematics involved were astounding. Later, in hindsight, when all her memories took on a strange significance, a significance that was useless, it seemed to Hannah that the clues had been everywhere. The worst thing that could happen to her would happen to her: Hannah would outlive her child.

At that moment, however, bent over the turkey ruins, her arm elbow-deep in the bird's wet cavity, her hand reaching to bring outside what had been inside, intent as if it were some sort of offering and largely unaware of her children, Hannah was still innocent. She was back to thinking of that simplistic God of Madeleine's, a God oblivious as a whacked-out scientist, conducting experiments for the sheer pleasure of observing response and behavior. The idea amused her. She carved some decent-enough slices and laid them attractively on the platter.

Jeremy crept back into the kitchen. He hugged the countertop.

"It's cold in here," he said.

"It smells like snow," said Cara, retracing her recent typhoon-past, shutting all the windows with as much energy as she had expended in flinging them open. She closed them with such a healthy gusto the panes rattled. She closed them as she would a finished book.

"It smells like mud," said Kenny, "like spring. It smells like the year is in reverse."

"It smells like snow," said Cara as if she meant business.

"It smells that way to me, too," said Jeremy.

"Which way," said Cara. "My way or Kenny's way?"

"Both ways," said Jeremy. "They're the same. It smells like the way the snow will smell coming and going."

"You're weird," said Cara. She sniffed the air loudly. "I changed my mind. Kenny's right, it smells inside out. Besides, where would snow go anyway? I mean where would you go if you were snow?"

"Anywhere where it was quiet," said Jeremy.

Whatever Happened to Daddy

HE WAS in no mood.

Cara pushed up the sleeves of her sweater, plunked her elbows down as if she meant business. Then she twitched around some. Swiveled her gaze around the bar. Profiled. Balanced precariously between the well-thought-out casual chic of looking arty, and an unconscious aura of deprivation that caught Jack there, in the heart.

She lit another cigarette. Ran her hand through a headbanded mop of unparted, unbrushed curls—curls glossed not unattractively, he thought, though oddly enough, in eggplant, deep purple—then yanked the black sleeves down long to cover her.

They were misshapen and stretched out, the sleeves were. They matched her pants which were also knit, though tight, tucked into spiky black boots: all in the monochrome of her uniform color.

Those sleeves, they swallowed her up like two black hoses, both skinny arms and half of her palm bottoms. The right sleeve was ragged, so if you knew enough to look for it, and he knew that much, you could see the little white half-moon, raised and smooth, the tender crescent that made that wrist her wrist, the scarred wrist that was the signature of his daughter.

"I need to get to the next level," she said, "Father."

He couldn't bear this psycho-culty stuff. It had been a long trek into the city, first Park and Ride, then two hours on Metro North, plus a twenty-minute wait in which he was twice splashed by an insensitive driver, all for a ten-minute cab ride.

This, out in the rain and him without his galoshes.

His socks were wet. He would catch cold, he would bet on it. Emily, of course, had warned him.

She said, "Wear your boots, old man, or you will catch your death."

And then she laughed at herself. "Catch your death, what an expression! As if you could hold it in your hand. I must have heard it in one of your old movies."

It was stubbornness that prevented him. It was the "old man" that sunk him.

Jack shifted his toes within the wet wool, the wet wool that was growing colder. He would catch his death, all right. His wife was on the money. His second wife. She knew him. And as if to prove his point and her point (it had taken some doing but now the spouses were both in full agreement), he sneezed several times, uncontrollably.

Cara did not take notice. She was on her second Sambucca. She was chewing on the coffee beans.

He tried not to let this annoy him.

It was odd, this café where they were. It appeared to have once been an old gas station, now converted in front to look like someone's partially redone garage— halfhearted.

It hit him hard when he first walked in. The bicycles

against the wall, the unfinished projects, a stereo's blar-
ings, the black-light rock posters, the old "Gasoline"
signs, several spare tires, even two longhairs in a hammock smoking pot. It reminded him of the boys when they
were younger.

The back room, however, where Cara sat, nervously
tall and theatrical in the booth side of a wooden table,
looked like a charming Soho-like wine bar—all old wood
and fresh flowers and piped-in, sometimes switched-on,
Bach harpsichord concertos. It was a compromise on her
part, Jack was sure. A little bit of what she thought of
him, a little bit of how he saw her, both a little bit off the
mark. This is what happens to fathers and daughters.

"I want to earn my clear bracelet," said Cara.

Jack wished she didn't live in this neighborhood.
Although he had to admit it was changing, tenement to
tenement, some filled with junkies, artists and young kids,
poor families, others spiffed up and teeming with yuppies.
He saw the draw of it sure, the surprise of art gallery or
bookstore nestled among the rot, the nightlife. Hadn't he
too been young once? But she was so fragile.

Jack said this to her mother, who replied, "Fragile from
too much support."

Em said, "Let the kid alone, she knows what's best
for her."

Em said, "It's time she had some fun."

And on one of their handful of visits Em said to Cara
somewhat wistfully: "This reminds me of Mags' and my
old place before I met your father."

Cara's floors slanted, and were kept bare, so she had
all guests take their shoes off before they entered. Another
way she could wield control, he thought. Like something
out of *Grey Gardens* her ceiling peeled in strips, cavelike,
like stalicites or whatever you call them. They festooned

down like a Halloween party. The walls were okay, though they had their oddities too; she covered them with tapestries and rugs, which made the place feel topsy-turvy.

But the furniture was comforting, for the most part it was familiar. It was Jack's first furniture actually, his "young married" stuff, now graced by Elvis throw pillows and that old moosie cat coughing up fur balls on her mother's once precious velveteen sofa. And there was a nonworking fireplace, with that picture of Ken, shrined, up on the mantel.

Jack himself had taken that shot of his middle son, six months before Kenny drove his car into a tree. Kenny's dark hair was long, whitening prematurely in spots. Some odd pigmentation problem from the boy's mother's side of the family. He was born this way, one blue eye winged by black lashes, the other outlined by a feathering of gray-white. Same for the brow, a splash of light on the right side. As a child it gave him an odd, quizzical look, but as a young man with a good jaw and bones that stretched his skin tight as tarp, his strange coloring had definitely been an asset—all Jack's boys had a way with the girls. When it came to his head hair, Ken sported a tuft of silver in the front which sprayed backwards, dissipating on one side into a pepper-and-salt just like his mother. She, of course, used to dye hers but he always looked like he just came in out of the snow, even though the picture was shot in early spring—Spring Break to pinpoint it precisely. He wasn't smiling, Kenny.

There were no pictures of Cara's two other brothers. Or of him, or of her mother, or of some beau, for that matter. Or Em, though that would be too much to hope for.

A good sign last time were the drawings on the fridge by her nephews, his grandsons. His oldest started out the same way that he did—blinded to a bad first marriage by a fierce pride in his two sons, in manhood. This, Jack felt certain, would change later with the next crop of offspring. What was so clear to him was invisible to his children. Life as a series of repetitions. At times he was so sure of the outcome, he wondered why he had to bother to keep on living. It seemed so predictable, inevitable. And yet, there are always those moments you can't prepare for. The good stuff, for one. And then again, for Cara. For Kenny. His son.

"What's with this clear bracelet stuff?" he said. "Honey."

"You don't even try," said Cara.

She fingered the crystal that hung from her necklace.

His feet went first. A chill startled through the rest of him. His skin smelled moist and damp and oddly enough of the old garage furniture the boys used to use for their "clubhouse." Perhaps this last was a nasal hallucination. Who knows? This business, this rare, awkward father-daughter lunch, this "confrontation" brought it all back to him, his life before Mags, before Em, his life before. Which wasn't the most pleasant of sensations, but wasn't totally without some pleasure.

"Cara, baby, they just want your money. My money. Cara, you don't even have any money," said Jack.

"Father," she said, "please."

"What's with this Father bit?" said Jack. "Whatever happened to 'Daddy'?"

The waiter came over. His electric-blue hair sprouted in patches. It was cut and shaved, ragged, along the curve of his head. He looked like he'd been through massive amounts of chemotherapy. There were five earrings in one ear, countless more in the other. He even had a safety pin drawn through his cheek. It looked like it was meant to hurt him.

He poured them more water. He brought her another

drink. He gabbed with Cara about his new performance piece. He asked her about Ilana. Who was Ilana? He asked how Group was going. What was Group, a rock group, a dance group, group therapy? Who was this man? This man who knew his daughter.

This man was Aquarius. In the 1980s. Aquarius.

He introduced himself. Cara was too busy displaying the left side of her face, half-cocked like a parrot, and puckering, which gave her hollows, cheekbones. Aquarius caught her right indentation with his lips, the kiss hidden from her father. Then, frosty glass pitcher in hand (the flirtation of ice and lemon slices reminding Jack somehow of chimes), Aquarius floated his way over to another table.

There was silence.

With his shoes off Jack's socks were drying.

Where at this moment, he wondered, was Em? In her darkroom? Outside with the kid in the teepee? God no, it was raining too hard out there for it not to be still raining in Connecticut. What did they do on Wednesday afternoons, Em and her daughter? Did the kid come home and watch TV or was today one of the days of her many art, or music or movement classes? What the hell is a movement class anyway? Mags' real father is a flutist, the kid takes violin. Her instrument is so lovely, so tiny, like a toy, the bow not much more than a matchstick.

"Look," Cara said, "if I can't come to terms with the way you acted after the accident then I can't get to the next level. It's that simple," she said, but her voice was trembling. Her face began to break.

"The way *I* acted," Jack said. "At least I didn't add insult to injury." Which he instantly regretted.

Cara pulled down her sleeve again. The half-moon was shadowed out of existence.

In families, tragedy brings tragedy. Jack learned this the night his daughter attempted to take her own life. For himself, he had been determined to break the cycle.

Cara started crying softly. Everything with this kid was a disaster. The other one was so different. Sure he was moody, that was a family trademark, but he had a lighter side to him. He enjoyed things. All that adolescent angst stuff was what he would have lived to grow out of, Jack was sure. Sometimes Jack liked to imagine Ken off in Paris writing poetry with that hero of his, that Jim Morrison, carrying on with a new, secret life. Who could blame him for trying to escape his family? And then there was that sneaking suspicion Jack always had that they had buried someone else's body. He even dreams about it, that he comes upon Kenny in a home for the disabled or worse yet, a loony bin, and Kenny says: "Dad, where have you been all these years? How come you haven't visited me? Why don't you take me home?" That was worst of all. Jack had refused to view him. He left the viewing to the boy's mother. More. He left her all the arranging. This, his therapist believes, all designed to preserve that little bit of doubt. But who knows?

Cara looked at him with anger, with desperation.

"I need to know," she said. "I need to know something."

What, he thought, could he possibly tell her. What did she need to know? What magic fact would cure her?

He'd grab at straws to satisfy her.

"I can tell you that you are very beautiful, very talented, very gifted. I can tell you that you have a whole host of wonderful things to look forward to in your young and promising life."

His words bounced off of her.

"Your mother and I love you very much," he said.

"Em loves you, the boys love you. The grandkids are crazy about you."

It was useless.

Cara was biting at her nails, stripping the cuticles until her fingers were raw, were bloody.

He hated her.

"You hate me," said Cara.

"What do you want from me?" said Jack. "What do you want? Do you want me to say that he drove himself into the tree on purpose? Is that what you want from me?" He hissed this at her.

"I wasn't there, was I?"

"Do you want me to say he was drunk?" Jack said. "The coroner's report said he wasn't drunk. You know that. We've been over it a thousand times."

In this strange bar he was shouting at his daughter. She was crying, her face as tight and wrinkled as a peach pit. It turned his stomach.

Outside in the rain was the gas-up part of the old gas station. It looked like one of the little kid's dioramas. The sky was washed the same ash-gray as the surrounding tenements, as the garbage cans, as the gray alley cats that crawled in and out of them. Someone had turned the area around the pumps into a sculpture garden. Most of the pieces were large and angry-looking, fluted by fencing and barbed wire. Long steel loops caught the rain as it was falling, channeled it into streams that led out into the street. The gutters were rivers. Newspaper, empty cigarette packs, and leaves that had fallen from some far-off and mysterious tree, sailed curb high, then snailed down toward the drain grid that was dammed with trash at the bottom. There were the beginnings of a flood. The pouring had stopped, but the steady steady hum of falling rain was so continuous it seemed unendable. It had the same reassuring rhythm of a fountain or a waterfall—the promise that no matter where or how far away he traveled, in this spot the rain would always fall.

Fountains will run even when we are not watching them. Waterfalls and rivers churn and pump like circles—without end. A person is not necessary to verify their existence. Whether or not he lived or died, around the world water was falling. Jack could do nothing to stop it. The wet that wet the air here, so heavy, so rich, was the same wet that swelled the breeze back home in Connecticut. Throughout time this same rain had been raining. It was recycled through the earth. It rained on the Greeks, the Romans, it rained in Paris and in Tahiti. It rained on Em, on his first wife, on Cara, on each and every one of his children. It rained on his dead son, broke him down into elements, returned him to the soil. This was the very same rain that fell on his own uncovered head when he was just a boy. Now, it was falling heavily.

"You know what Ken's first words were," he said to her.

She shook her head "no."

Jack said, "He was a slow starter, Kenny. He didn't speak until he was about three years old. But when he finally opened that big mouth of his he never shut it up."

Cara smiled at this, she sniffled.

"He spoke in sentences," said Jack, Jack who was warming up. "No goo-goo, no ga-ga for my son."

He had Cara's attention.

"He spoke his first words when you were born," said Jack and he looked at her, looked at her hard. Remembering what it was like when she was a brand new tiny baby.

" 'Throw her out on a dusty road,' " said Jack. "That's what Ken said."

" 'Throw her out on a dusty road'?" said Cara. " 'Throw her out on a dusty road'? No way. He did not," said Cara.

"Did too," said Jack.

"Did not," said Cara.

"Did," said Jack. And then he began to laugh.

"I never heard that one before," said Cara, "it's not true." But she laughed too. She laughed too. He got a rise out of her. And she was kind of pretty there, too skinny, but pretty, pretty laughing in the wet, the gray, the air oddly visible—a nameless essence that replaces light.

"Do you need any money, honey?" said Jack, although he knew this was the wrong thing to say.

"No," said Cara, "I don't need any money."

He looked at his watch. Time had passed. It was amazing.

"I should be getting back," said Jack.

Cara said nothing.

At home was Em, perhaps a fire, soup that Em made not from a can, but from those red and green and yellow beans she kept like sand paintings in a round glass jar. Clean, soft socks would be rolled and waiting in his drawer, there would be those fat depositions to sift through. He was a good two hours away from all that, and no matter how hard he wished it, no matter that he would sell his soul even, Jack could do nothing. He was no time machine. He accepted this, naturally, although he longed for the other. He was stuck, for another fifteen minutes, maybe half an hour, depending on her, on Cara. Depending on how much he and she would let him get away with. And on the trip back he would chastise himself for failing her so. He would forgive himself. Then he would declare her spoiled, disturbed, paranoid, neurotic.

He would grow ever more anxious the closer the train brought him toward town, time ballooning backwards, moving excruciatingly slower and slower the nearer he got to where he wanted to go. Would he ever get there? Would he live to make it home?

This was what troubled him. It had nothing to do with leaving, or arriving. It was the going that was so difficult. Going home to Em and that soup of hers, to that ridiculous teepee in the yard. And home, home to Mags, that fortunate, only child.

Throwing Voices

"JERM-A-FAT? Not really. Jeremy. I mean *that's* funny."
Here Steven snorted, laughed a little. "I mean that's
really, truly cruel. Kids. Kids, hunh. How come kids can
be such little bastards? How could anyone be mean to you?"
Steven's touch was soft. He unended me. I was one
smooth continuum pressed petal-flat against his freshly
ironed sheets. He ironed them, white with teal borders.
He was the only one I knew who would take the time
out to touch up permanent-press—except for Hannah, the
mother of my young adulthood. Her ironing board out
always now—as kids we were all perpetually wrinkled—
like a piece of furniture, part of the decor, going at shirts
and blouses, sheets and towels, underwear if you can
believe it. Hannah irons underwear in her desperate
search for things to do. She's a fisherman, my mother,
casting out worthless errands for the sole purpose of reeling back in time.
I lay flat as paper. Steven leaned over me, translating
his shadows into sentences, his long hair curling across

my chest like fancy script. He passed over me, my belly, down past my hips, my legs, my thick thighs, his hair writing out the story of my life as he heard it, from my lips through Steven's body, my story through the hand-writing of his hair, the sweep of his hair across my endless sheets of skin that he, that Steven, invented. When he got to my toes he disappeared over the edge of the bed and I thought, my God, it's true, the earth is flat. I couldn't see past my own horizon. So, I said his name, me pinned smooth as a poster to the tablet of his bed. I said: "Steven, hey Steven," because the last thing I wanted was to be without him.

And when I heard his voice, it seemed disconnected which was odd, because I had always been the ventrilo-quist. He said, "What did you call him back?" but I couldn't answer because I never had a name for him, a secret name I mean. I never had a name to call my brother, which was part of the problem really. I didn't know Ken, and then he died.

But Steven I knew, I knew him from the bones in his skeleton, from the soft tissue that surrounded them, through his capillaries' delicate webbing, his seven layers of skin. We were in the same English class in junior year. He sat three rows ahead of me, the light from the window warming his golden head. I could feel the heat in my fingertips just sitting back there. From the front, his lion's head surrounded by a halo gave me an icy chill that streaked down my lower back as I took attendance from the front of the class. Hot, cold. He made my thermometer go out of whack.

I remember the moment it hit. I was marking Steven absent, absent for the seventh time. I held that little card in my hand and read the writing that came from Steven's hand through Steven's pen onto the card that I was holding and I memorized the address, over and over again, 166 Linden, 166 Linden, until I wanted to go over there to Linden Avenue with a hacksaw or a machete and kill his whole family because they, not me, had the privilege of living with him, of watching him do the dishes, or seeing him reading a book curled up in an armchair before going to bed. It was the first time in my whole life I remember ever really wanting anything.

My brother died five years ago in a car accident. He just drove his car into a tree. A tree, a car, my brother. Such everyday, normal things. What did one have to do with the other? My sister Cara is at F.I.T. which means she studies design, and once in a while she drops out and studies acting—anything as long as she can justify wearing all-black clothing. My oldest brother Doug is married with kids, Evan and Kenneth, the baby. I get a kick out of my nephews, although I don't see them much, just holidays or when Cara is having a breakdown. My Dad lives with my stepmother and her daughter Mags, about four towns away, but miles away in his heart. So, basically, it is me and Hannah, the two of us in that big house, with those empty rooms, a whole lot of nothing. Just me and her. And her plants. Hannah's got a green thumb.

The first time Steven and I did it in the greenhouse. It was steamy, wet, it was sultry. I let the plants do the speaking for me. An orchid whispered soft words over Steven's head. A daff said a couple of things that were funny. I threw my voice in circles around Steven. All those green things growing, spinning out vines of a foreign language, words I couldn't say, didn't know.

When an iris dipped and swayed, spoke of the silkiness of his inner thigh, hushed through petaled lips, a long full throat, when the iris opened its mouth to say: "Make me come, darling," Steven said: "Cut it out."

He wanted to hear me from me, from my gut to my throat to my lips to Steven's ears. I said: "Steve." I said: "Honey." Then I choked. It was all I could do. I can barely speak or write. It's only in the velvet insides of my head that I have language.

I learned to throw my voice when I was still a little kid, by accident. The first time it happened was when Ken, always Ken, fell through the ice at Beebee Lake when he was about fourteen. If he was fourteen, I was eight or seven. The police called, I answered. They passed on their information. Hannah was in the family room—it was around 2:30—she and I had just gotten home from school.

Back then Hannah was a sort of guidance counselor. Now, actual kid-contact is too much for her. She says the uncertainty of their futures makes her crazy; all she can imagine are tragic endings. Worse still are those landmark occasions: graduation, the Prom; while everyone else is looking hopefully toward the future Hannah can only shiver over the horrors yet to come. Who else but my mother? Worrying about seventeen-year-olds' future diseases and divorces. These days she's an administrator, but in those days when Ken could still pull off a scam like falling through the ice and living to joke about it, when Ken seemed destined to be able to get away with anything, Hannah needed to be available. Tuesdays and Thursdays she followed us to school.

With the police on the line I needed to get her to the phone, but my mouth couldn't shape out her name. The word lived in the back of my throat. So I threw it, I threw the word out of my throat across the room. Ma. Like a sheep's bleating. It bounced off the refrigerator, bounced out in the hall to Hannah. Later, Hannah said, she knew that something had been wrong, there was a different caliber to my voice. She said I sounded like me, only farther away from myself than usual.

When Ken died, they called us at 7:00 in the morning. I got to the phone first. Hannah was right behind me. I didn't even bother to try, but just passed the phone silently to my mother.

"Bless my blond heart," Steven said. This was one of his greatest expressions. I was on the floor now, he was on the bed. He leaned his head over the side, his hair surrounding me, curtaining me off, saving me from what was out there—the living world that wrapped itself around us.

"Bless my blond heart," Steven said.

You see I'd been trying. I'd been trying to tell Steven about Ken. Steven was infinitely interested.

I went at it again. I said: "He was always leaping."

"Leaping," said Steven, upside down, cheeks reddening.

"He would just do things," I said, "crazy things."

"Crazy," said Steven.

"Come here and say that," said Steven's TV.

"Cut that shit out," said Steven. "Jeremy."

I didn't know what to say. How do you reveal a person maybe you didn't like so much, a person you didn't know? The thing that always struck me about Ken was the way he would take action. You know that feeling when you walk over a bridge and for a split second you want to throw yourself off? Or if you drive past your exit on the highway you might be tempted to go into reverse? How about during some staged performance, when the theater's quiet, the audience hushed, and out of nowhere there's the desire to jump on stage, piss everybody off? The imp of the perverse. The guy who would put a cigarette out in his palm just to see what it felt like. Take whatever drug was offered. Fuck anyone. This was my brother, my dead brother that turned Steven on more than I did.

"Are you sure he was straight?" said Steven, too often for my liking.

"Sure I'm sure," I said, although how was I to be sure, how was I to be sure about anything? Like, why couldn't Steven just give it up already, why was he goading me on?

"He was such a looker," said Steven. "I had my eye on him since the third grade. Tell me more," he said, "talk."

I didn't want to talk. I wanted his tongue.

"Help me," I said, so Steven helped me. We had our fun. We did what we did without voices.

I am nineteen, too old to live at home. This is a fact and unarguable. Cara says: "Grow up, jerk, and get your butt out of the house." Cara, who's on the dole from Dad, Cara who weasels Mom into greenlighting all of her black clothing. She looks witchy, my sister. Hundreds of dollars on outfits that make her appear exactly the same as she did the day before.

I go to U. Conn., which is why I still am where I am, close by, where it's convenient, cheaper, at home with my mourning mother. Hannah irons a lot, did I tell you? Sometimes when I walk past the dining room where she's set up shop, she'll say: "Take off your shirt and I'll iron it." I'll stand there bare-chested in the parlor while she touches up a collar, or worse, steams the writing off. On bad days, I've seen her iron slipcovers.

Steven skipped out on school, one month into his first semester. He likes to read, anything—novels, plays, poetry—he even likes philosophy, the kind no one can understand (including Steven), but he was never much of a school person. He wants to read what *he* wants to read, and he wants to talk about it the way *he* wants to talk about it. Plus, he was totally burned out on Connecticut. "NYC is the place for me," said Steven, so he got his great-aunt Sylvia to set him up in an apartment in Manhattan—Barrow Street. He wants to be an actor. His place is a studio, one room with an exposed brick wall. I spent an entire week helping him chip away paint and plaster. Then I drew in moldings for him, on the baseboards and where the beams connect to the ceiling—me backbending on a ladder, brush in hand, always afraid to fall. I did a mural of a fireplace on his other wall. See, I like to draw.

Steven says: "Face it kid, you're an artist. Enough is enough with the dirt."

I am an agronomy major. Who knows why?

Steven knows.

We are in the City. We are eating Chinese takeout. We are naked, sharing chopsticks, digging through container after container. I go down deep into the moo shu vegetable. I hunt out stray pieces of pork. Steven is a vegetarian.

Steven says: "Jeremy, who knows you better than I do?"

That's an easy one, no one does. I nod at him.

Steven says: "I think this dirt-thing has something to do with your mother-thing and your mother's-thing with plants."

He's a sage, that Steven. He's also in therapy (a precondition of great-aunt Sylvia's generosity) and full of it. Aunt Sylvia is sure that he just hasn't found the right girl. With me it's different, no one, except Cara, even knows, although they must know. How could they not know?

"No bullshit," asked Cara, in August. She was still lounging around in that fancy psych ward, some happy-making fluid dripping through her veins. My sister, the only person I ever heard of on IV antidepressants. "You're a fagilah or what?" I didn't say anything. What was there to say? "Big fucking deal," said Cara. Her way with words is why I love her.

"I like dirt," I say to Steven. What I like is its cyclical nature. Dirt makes it clear to me that energy is never destroyed or created. What happens is that it gets translated. Ken's internal life-stuff charging the soil that is food for the plants that are my mother's life-supports. The calcium in Ken's bones came from the very same earth which had been rained on by elements resulting from the death of strange and distant stars. Bizarrely, I find this comforting. The star-business has something to do with the dirt-business which has something to do with the mother-business which has something to do with feeling responsible for her and afraid—which has to do with Ken. Again. At least that's how I figure it. Go figure it.

Steven puts down his sesame noodles. He stretches out face down on the bed. His hands reach over his head as if he were diving. He begins a downward slide, over his previously ironed sheets, toward the floor where I am sitting Indian-style. He dives down in slow motion, sheets and Sylvia's old comforter coming with him as if he were a swelling shift in tide. He lies on the floor like a heap of used linens.

"Jeremy," he says, head buried. "Stay with me."

Steven never lifts his head.

*   *   *

Hannah and I at home: She's repotting, shears out, cutting back an ivy's root system before refreshing the soil,
pebbling some nice new terra-cotta, and shoving the whole
living mess back in again. I keep her company by sitting
by her. We are in the kitchen so that Hannah can get up
from time to time and stir the soup. I am working in pen
and ink. What do I draw? I draw Steven. His hands.

"Ma," I say, "tell me a story about you and Dad."

Hannah looks at me, oddly; streaks of dirt mark her
forehead and her chin. She blows away a stray hair that
has curled out of her hairknot and rested annoyingly
against her lip. I reach up and move the hair away for her.

"Thanks, kid," says Hannah.

She starts in on a rhododendron.

I dip my pen, blot lightly, then stroke out the light
bones, puppet strings that allow Steven to play his fingers.
His hands are long and old, way older than Steven is.
Blond hairs glide across the surface like tiny breezes. His
skin is leathered—too much sun perhaps, perhaps some
symbolic surfacing of the soul. He has Georgia O'Keeffe's
hands, her aching, stretched-out fingers.

Hannah refreshes her soil. Will she speak, won't she
speak? You never can be sure. I try to sneak my questions
by her. The rhododendron gives it another go. From my
lips to its leaf to Hannah's ears: "Talk."

She sighs, loudly. "Jeremy, this is pathological." The
"this" is my ability to throw voices. It annoys her, but
there is nothing Hannah won't do for her kids. She would
do anything, so she obliges me.

"When we lived on St. Marks we were very, very
poor," says Hannah. "Dad was still in law school, I was
working at the Community Center for next to nothing.

We went from his mother's to my mother's to my sister's house for dinner, so we could save on food. One night when I was heating up some leftover brown meat your grandmother had sent over, I started to cry for absolutely no reason. I was happy then, Jeremy," says Hannah.

Hannah and I both stop for a moment, thinking of Hannah happy.

"But I was crying just the same. I remember I was surprised to see my tears bounce when they landed in that hot pan. Jack said: 'Let's go out, take a walk. Brown meat is brown meat, it can wait.' So we bundled up, did I tell you it was winter? And we walked up and down St. Marks Place. When we got to Tompkins Park, Jack bent over and picked up a ten dollar bill. Ten dollars was a lot in those days. We couldn't believe it. Daddy said: 'You only live once,' so we went to this really terrific expensive little Italian place in the West Village—what was it called, I can't remember—and we spent every penny." Hannah is pink now, she's looking rosy. Her fingers are kneading some loam into the peat.

"The funny thing was that next year when we had Douglas we were out walking one night and at the very same spot your father found another ten dollar bill. How's that for luck?" Hannah is dreamy. The earth rises beneath her hands. I don't want to disturb her, but there are things I need to understand.

"Ma," I say, "how did you know Dad was your right person?"

"Right person?" says Hannah. "Your father was my wrong person, Jeremy." And she's back in the land of the living. The soup boils over, so she gets up, lowers the flame. "I'm the last one to be handing out advice," says Hannah, but she gives me the once-over, looking for clues, of what? Some budding heterosexual signs of life?

My ink bubbles then blots. An age spot blooms over Steven's right knuckle.

"Carmela's," says Hannah, "that was the name of the restaurant." She is elbow deep in dirt. She is retrenching.

"Carmela's," I echo her. I like the sound.

"Since Ken died, I can't remember loving your father. I mean I know I loved him, I wouldn't have married him if I didn't love him, I just can't remember what loving him felt like."

That was Hannah's voice, coming out of nowhere. I believe Hannah is the one to say this, as there are no other people in the room. We look away from each other for a while. Then we both return to our representational reconstructions: me and Steven, my mother and my brother.

"Stevie." Steven's magic window whines. "Lift up those golden tresses."

"Jeremy," says Steven. "Get a life."

With his head bent that way, I can see the back of his neck, my favorite part of Steven. I cover it with my hand. His hair is lighter than my skin. I reach my fingers up and bury them—sign language. What's to say?

Steven lifts his head, finally. It is bright, bright red from lying in the wrong direction. His face is full of blood. He flips over onto his back. I keep my hand steady so that now it is a clamshell, protecting the muscle of his throat.

I love him. I love Steven more than I can imagine loving anyone.

If I could I would slide out of my body, enter through his ear, his mouth, his ass, my form's distillation, the liquid light of my essence threading its way inside him. I want to see all there is to see of him. I want to ride the corpuscles in his blood.

I watch his eyes move beneath their lids' shiny membrane.

"Help," I say. It's meant as a whisper, but it comes out like a croak.

Steven laughs in spite of himself. His eyes break open, two light blue yolks.

"You sound like your voice is changing, Jerm," says Steven.

"Hey, don't call him that," says Steven's sofa cushion.

"Jerm," says Steven.

"Jeremy," says the door.

"Jerm-a-fat," says Steven, and he sits up. "Jerm-a-fucking-fat," he says.

"No," says the door. "Shut up."

"Jerm-a-fat," sings Steven. He sings it like a brat would. "Jerm-a-fat-fat-fat, you are a tub of lard."

"Shut up," I say. "Steven, shut up." This last part comes out as shouting.

"Fat-fat-fat," says Steven.

"Shut up," I scream this at him.

How did we get to our feet? Steven is in my face. I slap him. Hard.

"Fat-fat-fat," sings Steven. "Fat-fucking-faggot."

I hit him again, harder.

"Jerm-a-fag, Jerm-a-faggot, is that what your brother called you?" Steven sings this out.

I punch Steven in the gut. His breath whooshes by my cheek. Steven folds. He cramps up like a muscle. This is too much. I run away to the bathroom, slamming the door on Steven.

* * *

I sit in the tub. It's one of those old-time tubs with feet. There is no water in the tub, just me. My legs swing over the side, my body is encased in porcelain, a jewelry box, a white, white coffin. I look at the dark hairs that wink across my skin. I am all lids, no eyes.

I hit Steven.

He comes to the bathroom door. His face is white, his chest still heaving.

Me in the tub, Steven in the door. Waiting.

"You shouldn't have hit me," says Steven.

"I know."

"Don't ever hit me again," says Steven.

"No," I say. "I'll never hit you again. I promise." And it's true, I'd rather die, I will never again hit Steven.

Steven comes closer, he sits on the bathtub ridge. "Why are you sitting in the tub?" says Steven.

"I always sit in the tub," I say. "When I was a kid I'd go sit in a tub whenever my brother beat me up." It was the farthest place in the house I could go to get away from him.

"Doug or Ken," says Steven.

"Doug was too old to care about beating me up. It was Ken," I say. "Kenny."

And then Steven starts to cry. "I hate that bastard," says Steven, Steven, naked at the tub's edge, Steven redeyed, leaky. "I hate that bastard for being mean to you."

I can't believe I hit Steven. I say it: "I can't believe I hit you, Steven." I say it from deep down within my body. And then I'm crying too. "Fucking Ken," I say. "Fucking bastard." I don't know why I say this. It's as if someone else has taken over. "I hate him," I say, "I always hated him. Bastard"—which I'm not even sure is the truth. That last part comes out in shudders because I'm crying hard now, really hard, but I don't feel at all like I'm crying. I feel like I am circling above me, above the whirling grief, lazing above the mourning. But I know I'm crying because I can hear it, and there is stuff in the back of my throat, and because Steven is crooning, softly softly, "Good Jeremy, good boy," petting me with his angel hand. I watch the tears, the sounds. It's as if I am outside myself.

"I'm glad Ken's dead," I say.

"Good boy," says Steven. "*Now*, you're talking."

A Good Time

WHEN Kenneth Gordon Gold was fifteen, he fell through the ice at Beebee Lake and lived to brag about it.

The day Kenny fell through the ice was a Tuesday, bright, blue and cold as metal. Both Kenny and Cara, his baby sister, had the week color-coded since they were little. Thursdays were mustard, Mondays were canary yellow. They discovered this when Cara had to make a calendar for school. Without stopping to think, she used colored squares instead of names. Pink was her color for Saturday afternoons. Kenny objected. "That's wrong," he said, "it's purple." Because she believed in him Cara didn't bother to fight. While an occasional Sunday could be tinged by a watery blue, Tuesday's blues were the bluest, as loud and available as Kenny's eyes. They pressed Cara outside of herself. They met her before she had half a chance to rise from her internal chair. Those blue eyes lifted her, shooting Cara up, up, high as a dancer, far away from herself.

The Tuesday that Kenneth Gordon Gold fell through

the ice his Mom was social-working over at the high school. Tuesdays and Thursdays. His Dad was in The City at The Firm. His Dad took The Train to The Cab Service to The Office. No other cities or firms or trains or cab services existed, but his Dad's, which was something none of the children could stand about him. Kenny's younger brother Jeremy was in school. His older brother Doug was out of school, a problem really, Doug's taking a year off to find himself and all that, but not being able to stay out of Connecticut—having been to Alaska and back, and one horrible week in Paris where all his Alaska money plus his passport and backpack had been ripped off by this Dutch guy he was traveling with. Doug didn't know what to do with himself, so he spent a lot of time torturing his younger siblings. Mom said it was because Doug wanted to punish himself, but it didn't look that way to Kenny who loved Doug, or to Cara who was born hating Doug's guts.

The morning of the day that Kenny fell through the ice, Doug was supposed to drive Cara to school. Their folks had devised little chores for him, chores that Doug was paid for so that he could continue acting out his wanderlust, still have his pre-college adventure, no matter that he had done everything in his power to botch it up so far. Of course these chores had all been freebies before, part of Doug's duty as a member of this family, but whenever Cara brought these things up, Dad told her to "can it," which was hard for Cara. She was dying to really let go and whine. Still, even Cara knew when whining would get her only so far and no farther, so she did her best to shut up, wait it out and pick her best time.

On Tuesdays and Thursdays Mom left the house early. If Kenny bothered to get up, he could catch a ride. Otherwise he was to take his bike. That was the deal. Mom could easily have dropped Cara off at the Middle School on her way, but this would have left Doug with another entire day without any sort of purpose. Doug was to drive Cara and a gaggle of giggling girlfriends to school. If he felt like it, he could also give Kenny a lift, but that was up to Doug. Any and all of them could choose to walk. These were the ground rules, according to Mom. Dad, of course, stayed out of it.

Jeremy took the bus. He was still just a little kid. And a "space-muffin," as Cara called him. He'd wander dreamily to the bus stop, his coat half off, flapping like a sail behind him. It was evens or odds if he remembered to get on the bus at all. More than once, Cara and Doug found him still sitting on the bench, the bus long gone, history, as they turned the corner in the old white station wagon. If they found Jeremy, their duty was to take him to the Elementary School and deposit him; this was Addendum Number 1. Also, it was Cara's job to make sure Jeremy had his lunch. She took the job seriously. Every few minutes, during breakfast, and while he was getting dressed, Cara shouted out to him: "Better not forget," which could have made the poor kid a nervous wreck if he bothered to pay any attention to her. More often than not, Cara had to run out of the house after him, carrying his lunch box with his thermos of soup, his banana, and his peanut-butter-and-jelly. Mom was sure that Jeremy would grow up to be an artist, because he could draw, and because he was so sensitive.

So it was clear, everybody had their own specific little duty to perform. This was the way Mom set it up, so they would learn responsibility, so that all the kids would be safe. Therefore, according to Cara, Kenny's falling through the ice was really Doug's fault. If Doug hadn't been such an asshole, if he had done what he was supposed to do, Kenny wouldn't have been out on the ice at all. Doug didn't see it that way. He never told Kenny to go out there, where it was thin, where it could break.

To catch a ride the girls met at Cara's, which was fine with them, more than one was a little bit in love with Doug, crushed out on him. Ilana's crush was the ultimate betrayal, Ilana being Cara's best friend practically from the moment she was born; their mothers gave birth during the same week at the very same hospital—Jewish Memorial. As far as Cara was concerned, Ilana was beginning to show signs of being a traitor way before the day that Kenny fell through the ice, but that was the day that clinched it.

Cara had forgotten her bandana. Everyone was tying bandanas around their legs or through the loops of their carpenter's pants—you wouldn't want to be in school without one. Cara ran back inside the house to get hers. The wagon was full. Mindy and Melissa were in the way back. Joan and Mimi were in the middle. Ilana, little bitch that she was, sat up front with Doug.

Cara was in and out of the house within two minutes, but two minutes was long enough for Doug to turn all five of her best friends against her. It was all over by the time she got to the curb. Just as she reached for the door handle, Doug hit the gas and drove the car about ten feet up. He stopped there, waited for Cara, so, without think- ing, she ran to him. If she thought about it, she would have realized that running after Doug was exactly what Doug wanted. Her panting after him. If she had time to think, if she wasn't the type to so instantly react to him, she would have just coolly given him the finger, and walked. Or stuck out her thumb and hitchhiked to school with some amazing older jock. Or called a cab, and charged it, making Doug pay out of his adventure fund. There were options, sure. But not for Cara as far as Doug was concerned. His effect on her was immediate, like a lit match, its flaming head pressed against her finger. He burned her. She had no time to brush him off.

Cara pressed after them. Again, as before, just as she got to the door, Doug's foot hit the pedal. Inside the car the girls squealed like pigs. Ilana pressed her face against the glass, her tongue, the veins of its underbelly like worms, fat and purple, was folded over and all smushed up. Cara got close, close enough to see Ilana-spit, like a white streak of lace across the window. Cara's hand touched the metal of the door handle, so cold it was hot, so hot her skin stuck to it. Doug geared up and screeched off. The door handle yanked her fingers loose. He pulled up the block another couple of yards.

Cara ran after them. Getting redder and redder, Cara cried in anger. Her girlfriends were laughing at her. Her very own brother was driving them on, driving them off.

Cara's misery was so intense she felt she couldn't live another second. How far could the minutes stretch? Behind the Schaeffer house was a field of silver-white birches. She veered toward them. She ran and fell, splitting the knee of her carpenter's pants. She tasted dirt. The dirt fueled her. Cara got up from the ground, ran across the Schaeffers' lawn as fast as she could into the trees. She heard Doug, the girls, calling out for her. But it was too late. Cara hated them. She did not have one forgiving bone in her body. She was born that way, but all this reconfirmed it, especially after Doug shouted: "C'mon Cara, can't you take a joke?"

If she'd had a gun, she would have shot him.

*   *   *

Lying at the base of the trees, angling her vision up, the silver birches looked like the legs of a pack of giant dalmatians. Cara liked it there. She wrapped her arm around a thickened paw and bawled her heart out. If she stayed long enough she was sure to die of exposure. Those assholes would all suffer for what they did to her. The idea of this pleased Cara: Doug and Ilana suffering, snubbed by everyone because of their nasty, babyish behavior. She was beginning to feel better when she heard Kenny sing out her name.

"Cara." He trilled it. It sounded like a bird song.

She loved him with every cell in her body. Kenny had probably started off to school in time for the tail end of the Cara-Doug fight to the finish, but he had seen enough to satisfy him, to pick a side. And he picked hers. Cara's heart swelled, it was brimming. The whole horrible incident seemed worth living through now that Kenny was there to the rescue. He came to her out of the trees.

"Cara-Rose, I love your nose." Kenny sang his older-brother song.

He looked good. He was not as good-looking as Doug, but he looked good to her. He had a cold sore on his upper lip, which swelled the right side out of proportion. The sore itself was a raised hot bubble, and sat like a single splatter of melted fat against his mouth. It was the mystery of Kenny that he could make even a cold sore look cool. Good thing, because it seemed like in the winter he spent more time with one than without one.

Cara arranged herself so that she would seem more pitiful. She collapsed around the tree.

"Aloha," said Kenny. He pressed a wet tea bag against his injured lip.

Cara continued with her sobbing.

"Cara, quit it," said Kenny. "You don't want to be a crybaby your whole life."

He was mean. Newborn tears flooded her eyes. Something dropped to her stomach's base, everything fell inside her. He tricked her, Kenny. He cut her to the quick. Cara hated him, she hated all her brothers, even innocent little Jeremy, who existed out of space, out of time. She hated Jeremy too, because he was related to this traitor.

She recoiled from him. "Get the hell out of here," Cara screamed. She slithered around the trunk to the other side. She focused away from Kenny. She refused to look at him, even when he tethered one long monkey arm to the tree, and swung after her.

He brought his nose to her nose, but again she turned away. Cara wouldn't give him the satisfaction of face-to-facing him, but she wailed a little louder.

He knelt down. "Feel this," said Kenny. He held the tea bag out to her.

Cara ventured out a finger. The tea bag was as hot as if it had just been immersed in tea water.

"It sucks out the fire. Isn't that wild?" said Kenny.

Cara nodded. He almost had her.

"Now it needs something cool," Kenny said. He leaned forward and rested the sore against Cara's tear-stained cheek. She felt its heat throbbing through her skin. She let him hold it there.

"Doug's a bastard," Cara whispered.

"It was pretty rotten," Kenny agreed. He agreed with her. When he spoke, she felt his blister move. Cara loved him, she loved him. There wasn't anything in the world she loved more than this brother. He was hot against her face.

"Does it hurt?" she asked him.

77

"You cured me," said Kenny.

He sat back on his heels. She still felt the heat of the tiny circle he imprinted on her cheek. She brushed it with her fingertips. There was a little bit of golden crust. She examined it, but it did not bother her. She rolled it into sand, into dust, between two fingers until it traced away.

"Doug drove the girls to school," Kenny said.

"I couldn't care less," said Cara.

"He asked me to go after you." Kenny closed his eyes when he said this.

The sky lost all its color. Cara never remembered which was which, the sky reflecting the water or the water the sky's glassy mirror. Whatever directions colors go, sky and water were endlessly supplied by the flash of Kenny's iris, the flickering of his eyes. He shut them off when he was lying.

"Yeah, right," said Cara.

They both went quiet for a while, Kenny pressing his lip with his tea bag, Cara using a stick to hack away at the dry dirt. No snow had fallen all winter. It was cold, but they didn't feel cold, there in the trees, the trees breaking the wind. Most of the neighborhood was houses now, but still behind the Schaeffer house, the Carter house, and Billy Gallagher's, there were woods.

The Golds went to the woods in times like these when someone was unhappy. They went to the woods when there was a secret to tell, or in Cara's case, a secret to be kept. She'd hop around among the trees as if she had to go to the bathroom. Not-telling was hard for Cara, but being left out was worse. She wanted desperately to be confided in. There, secrets were safe with her, simply because in the woods, most of the time, there was no one to leak her gossip to, and hopefully, the urge would pass.

To get high, all the kids went there. To chug: beers,

Thunderbird, Boonesfarm Strawberry Hill. At night, Kenny and his buddies went to the woods to smoke cigarettes, their red tips glowing, Morse-coding in the dark. Cara and her girlfriends went to bite wintergreen Life Savers hard, their mouths open, green sparks flying like fireflies. Kenny had begun to go there with girls, Phyllis Newman to be specific, who was two years older than he was, and a hippie-freak, which made her doubly cool, a super fox.

Doug had just grown out of this. He boldly brought his girls home when M & D were out of the house. It seemed like whenever Kenny was just getting ready to be old enough for whatever Doug was into, Doug was on to the next level. He could never catch up to Doug. And Doug would never wait for him, the way Kenny was willing to wait for Cara, Kenny reaching back to her, Cara reaching up.

Jeremy was his own generation. He went to the woods to play, be by himself.

Cara's teeth chattered. The cold snuck up on her. She was at that awkward bony stage anyway. Dad had said, "You are at that awkward stage," which made her run into her room, slam the door hard and loud, and cry—forcing Dad to send Kenny upstairs after her. Her legs were growing, but nothing else was, and she had slimmed down to a stick. Crumpled on the ground that way, still curled against the tree, she looked like an optical illusion, no body just endless thighs and feet. Her curly dark hair was puffed out of place. In her angst, her hands had snagged up a bunch of hairbumps, her head shaped like a magnified berry. She looked pitiful when she finally had forgotten about trying to look pitiful. Perhaps it was this rare, unchoreographed moment that moved her brother most.

"Fuck school," said Kenny.

He was instant happiness.

Kenny jumped to his feet. He extended a hand, lifted Cara up. He had that look, that Kenny-look, when anything could happen.

Cara would gladly have followed him off of a cliff, she would have raised her hand, volunteered to go after him. In fact Mom was always saying to her, "If he jumped off the Empire State Building would you jump too?" and Cara shook her head "No," rolled her eyes even, but inside she said "Yes, yes" because jumping off the Empire State Building with Kenny would be a good time. Anywhere with Kenny was better than anywhere without him. He completed her. He filled up the empty space inside of her that yawned open and then closed again, like a mouth, like a talking wound. Yes, she would follow Kenny, she would have followed him to school even, right then, if she had to.

They made their way out of the trees. Birds swam through the air like fat little flying fish. Their gills were streaked with color. As Kenny and Cara single-filed the trail, the birds skittered in and out of reach. And when they got to one specific silver birch, Kenny first, Cara second, a tree like all the other silver birches in the birch field, each reached out and touched its blistered skin. This is what linked them, the fact that while they never spoke about it, neither brother nor sister could leave the woods without touching the bark of this particular tree. Once, Cara even tried, she got all the way to her own front yard when something came over her, as if she were under a spell, hypnotized, and she ran back to the tree without even breathing. She wasn't brave enough. She had to touch their tree. Cara did not want to be responsible for what could happen if she hadn't.

* * *

The station wagon was in the driveway. Doug was home. Sometimes he left the key in the ignition. Cara figured that the key in the ignition was a lot of what the day was to be about. Joyriding. Kenny whipping them around Connecticut's fastest curves. She loved it when they stole the car. First off, she got to ride up front. She'd take Mom's sunglasses out of the glove compartment and wear them like a headband. She'd flip the sunshade down and put on Mom's lipstick, as carefully as she could with Kenny at the wheel. And like Mom, she'd check her teeth in the mini-mirror for little slash marks. Sometimes she'd even smoke a cigarette, a Camel, one of Kenny's. She'd lean over and extract it with long fingers from the pack in his breast pocket. She'd push in the automatic lighter, wait for it to pop. That was the best part, really, bringing that glowing coil, a little branding iron, up to the cigarette, dragging the heat and smoke through the thin white funnel, pulling it back to her lips. Yes, stealing the car would be A-OK with Cara.

Kenny had other things in mind.

He bypassed the station wagon altogether. He walked his Indian walk, one foot after the other, silent as a trapper. He went in through the back door into the kitchen. Cara went in after him. Her nose was running. It was good to be inside, where it was warm. She ripped off a section of paper toweling from the roll, put it to her nose and blew. She sounded like a trumpet. Kenny swung his head back, threw her a silencing look.

They continued through the downstairs of the house. When they hit the den instead of veering in toward the living room, Kenny headed toward the playroom and climbed up the back staircase. This staircase led to the second floor where Kenny and Cara and Jeremy, and Mom and Dad, all had their bedrooms. After graduation Doug got to live in the attic, which you could only get to by the main stairs. At the top of the back stairs was a big picture window. Kenny pushed it open and stepped out onto the roof. He reached back, lifted Cara, swung her to safety.

Now it was obvious. Cara could see what Kenny had in his head. They were going to spy on Doug. How simple. How boring. What could this possibly have to do with revenge? Unless he had a girl with him, Doug usually wasn't much to spy on. He hung out all day smoking pot, listening to his headphones. Mom called it depressed, Dad, "a wasted life" which made Cara snicker, Dad didn't have a clue to how "wasted" Doug was half the time. Still, Kenny seemed to find Doug more interesting than television. He watched him a lot. Kenny watched him as if he, Kenny, were waiting for something. Cara went with Kenny, sometimes, sometimes not; she didn't care, Doug seemed the same as he always was—horrible. Kenny was on his own in missing his brother.

But she went with Kenny this time, Cara did, out of the window, onto the roof, because there wasn't anything better to do. She went, because she wanted to be with him. Except for one narrow ledge, getting to Doug's window was a cinch, because the roof was broad-based. Some nights they met out there to tell ghost stories, look at the stars. The roof was outlawed, of course, but it was familiar territory. In the summer, if Mom wasn't around, Cara and Ilana went out there to sunbathe. The tar had reflective powers. Ilana read this in a magazine.

Cara's favorite part was the scary part, when Kenny held her hand. They sidestepped the ledge, their backs flat against the house, like they were part of some movie caper. They inched their way around to the other side. Kenny's grasp was firm. Cara wasn't sure what good it would do, if one fell, the other would sail kitelike after them, but she knew in her heart this linkage was worth the risk. It bound her to him. Besides, thought Cara, anything could happen. It was always possible that they would fly.

Doug had taken off his shirt. They could see this from outside the attic window. His stomach was all hairy. The room was a mess. Magazines, beer bottles, ashtrays spilling ashes, butts, wads of gum wrapped in gum paper. Underwear everywhere. There were socks. Jeans pulled inside out lay flopped on the floor as if inhabited by phantom bodies. The mattress was bare except for Doug's sleeping bag, which was balled up and punched down into a corner. It was a good thing Mom wasn't allowed up there, Doug being an adult now, entitled to privacy. If Mom had been up there, seen the rotting banana skins, the half-burnt towel (he must have used it to smother something), Mom would have died.

Cara wondered briefly about all the dried-up snot and toenail clippings, all the human flickings Doug had flicked up there in the attic. But it was too disgusting even for Cara to think about for a prolonged period of time. Kenny had not yet let go of her hand, which was odd. Cara stayed very still, so that no movement would remind him.

Doug stood in front of the mirror. No lights were on, but the sun was so strong, even from the roof they saw his reflection. He was smoking a cigarette. At first Kenny and Cara thought that he was mugging, which was something they both did in private, in secret, posing and posturing like a pair of movie stars. They could relate to this.

But Doug was not mugging, he was staring at his shirtless self. He dragged on his cigarette. The ash trailed long, longer than seemed possible.

It was cold on the roof, but they didn't feel cold. They didn't feel anything.

Doug put his right hand to his head. His fingers got lost in the thick, dark carded wool of his hair—what all the girls went crazy over. He clenched them up, his fingers, and he pulled as hard as he could. He pulled his own hair out of his head.

Doug cried out. His face contorted, but still he continued to pull. He pulled until it seemed like he could no longer stand it, and then he pulled a little longer. When he opened his fist, hair fell out of his hand. He grabbed again. His knees bent. His neck knuckled under from the force of his fingers, but his expression twisted up, his eyes fixed on the mirror. All three siblings were joined together by the draw of watching Doug. His face broke into jagged edges, red and white from straining, and it was slick with fluid. He looked like an internal organ. He did not look the way their brother looked.

"He hates himself," said Kenny.

Doug relaxed his hand. He was breathing heavily, his belly rolling. He lifted the dead cigarette to his mouth, and watched in the mirror as his face made its way back to normal.

Kenny tugged at Cara, an electrical impulse shooting up an invisible wire to her neck. Cara didn't say anything, but she followed. She'd go anywhere as long as she didn't have to relinquish his hand, give Kenny back to Kenny.

They went back across the roof the way they came, silent, in tandem. Cara thought many things, frightened things, nasty things, things like "I told you he belongs in a nut house," but she did not say a word.

When they got downstairs to the kitchen Kenny said, "Let's go to the lake," which was fine with her. He didn't say anything about taking their skates; everybody knew it was cold, but probably not cold enough for skating anyway. Then he traded her hand for a fresh wet tea bag. His lip was beginning to puff all over again, and he looked lopsided. The tea bag steamed when it hit his face. Cara started to say something, but he shushed her.

Beebee Lake wasn't that far from their house, but Kenny walked fast, like he was racing to get there. Walking fast was a good thing, because it kept Cara warm; it was a bad thing, because Kenny got way ahead of her. She'd walk two steps then trot some, at first in order to keep up, and then just to keep her sight of him.

"Wait," called Cara.

He slowed, but he didn't wait up for her. When he got to the mouth of the trail that led to the lake, Cara lost him altogether. He dissolved into the trees, far ahead of her.

The sky was blue and endless. The sun, high. By this time it must have been about 11:30, 12 o'clock. Cara was getting hungry. Her stomach growled so loud it sounded like an animal, an alien, growing deep inside her. She started to get pissed off.

"Kenny, you jerk," she called. "You asshole."

She continued down the path after him. By now she felt so mad she practically skipped. She'd give her brother hell to pay. The path seemed longer than she remembered. She started to panic just as the lake came into sight.

The path had been closed. Now, nothing seemed more open. It felt like going outside from the inside. The lake was a glistening expanse. The ice, a diamond skin over the blue blood of the water. It threw off a whiteness that hurt. Cara's hands lifted involuntarily, to shield her from the light.

That's when she saw Kenny. He stood out there in the middle of all that was blinding, all that was bright. She had no idea how in the world he got there. The ice retracted from the shore. It looked like what had been shielding the water, was healing the water. Puddles of blue shone through in hot spots. It seemed as if Kenny had descended out of the air. He really was dead center.

After Kenny fell through the ice there were a lot of noise and a lot of lights. A crowd gathered. One guy even remembered a helicopter, but he was a lonely kid, the type to remember a lot of things that he really saw the night before on television. A lady was out walking her dog. The dog chased a squirrel. The squirrel leapt in a series of flying stitches, hemming the trail to the lake. The dog, the lady, flew after it, far down the path to the water.

It was a good thing the dog dragged that lady, Mrs. Weiss, or Kenny might have died; although later after the real catastrophe was over, there was some talk about a dislocated shoulder. Whatever—she arrived just in time to see Kenny go under, to see the surface of the lake give, shaped like a platform, as if Kenny were descending in some sideless, roofless elevator, all in one piece. Mrs. Weiss arrived just in time to hear the ice crack like a shot, although bizarrely, she remembered the sound a lot sooner than the sight, as if the looping weren't synchronized quite right.

Cara was at the shoreline, mouth open, frozen in motion, like a movie frame, like a watch that stopped without warning. Her arm was carved still, in midwave, midflight.

Mrs. Weiss dropped the leash, finally, ran back to the road and summoned the assistance that saved Kenny. What she did was run in front of a car that stopped, thank God. In hindsight, to Kenny and Cara it all seemed sort of funny, but not at the time. The car was being driven by a doctor and his wife. And miraculously, a state trooper was cruising by. In the suburbs. A state trooper who stopped to find out why anyone in their right mind would run in front of a moving vehicle.

After, everyone said, Mom and Dad included (and neither of them inclined to say such things) that Kenny was born under a lucky star. He had been without vital signs for actual minutes. He said he heard music. Jazz. He said that it was cooler than the water. When he bragged about it, about his survival, Kenny said he kissed Death's stony face and then he got the hell out of there. Death looked pretty boring. "Later for that," said Kenny.

Although Cara's turning into a statue was widely concluded to be the result of life-threatening fear, a natural and an appropriate reaction (Mom assured her), that was not the whole truth. She wanted to stop time, Cara. She wanted to freeze-frame it. She believed in him. It never occurred to her that Kenny would leave and not come back for her. She was still just a little girl.

Cara had been terrified to see Kenny alone, at the center of the lake. She waved her hand, flagged him down, called out to him. "Kenny," called Cara, but her voice seemed too young to reach him.

A cloud passed overhead, the weakened sun grayed the ice. What was once pure white was the white-blue of the milk that swims around old eyes. A clap rang out. The sound of ice wrenched from ice.

His ground shifted, and for a moment Kenny struggled with his balance. Cracks shot across the surface of the lake like a shattered windshield. On the shore, Cara waved frantically, as if she could create enough wind to buoy her brother.

And then Kenny stabilized, the ice seemed strong enough to hold him. He relaxed into his weight. A second passed and then another. He raised his hand in victory and waved to her. Kenny grinned his crazy-grin.

It was the grin that saved her. And that was enough for Cara. She was reeling with the joy of it. It was clear, Kenny would be pulling these stunts his whole life; and get away with them. She waved back to him. Her own hand froze in midair, miming him, Cara Kenny's mirror. Their palms touched in the way of divided prisoners. Separated, but on parallel lines. There was nothing in the world she loved more than this brother.

He was a boy. He would be fine.

Everything was going to be all right.

Enemies

THE WORLD is your enemy when you're a mother. If they're still little, electrical outlets loom like live wires, medicine cabinets with their M & M–shaped poisons deliberately confuse, entice. Playgrounds—those torture chambers—invite every conceivable neurological injury with their jungle gyms and their concrete floors and those swings that swing too high, all designed to maim, to paralyze your angel, your monkey. Other kids' germs swirl around your kids in endless life-threatening tornados. The alcoholism of their friends' parents, their wanton ways, endanger your offspring's moral fiber. The head-injury factor of bunk beds during sleep-overs is enough to keep you up all night.

As they age—miraculously, every second of every day, microbes and organisms bombarding the tiny cells of your child's precious body—it gets worse. When you think of all the things that could happen to them—meningitis, wandering sexual offenders, childhood leukemia, falling off their bikes—when they actually survive and prosper long enough, grow first strange and sunken and sticklike, then blossom out in all kinds of shapes and directions, *they* turn into the enemy themselves. What you have then is running away and drugs and sexually transmitted diseases, teenage pregnancy, anorexia.

The sun is harmful to your children. Milk now clogs the intricate web of their arteries. The air is too polluted for the delicate tissue of their lungs, their bloodstreams are streamed with all their ingested garbage.

You wake every morning in terror, if you've managed to sleep at all. The nights stretch so long and unwieldy that they are virtually unlivable until you hear the sound of that junk heap of a car pulling into the garage and you flip in bed toward the direction of sleep, and you whisper first to your husband and then to the pillow and then later (if you're lucky and had time between all that worrying to pay a little attention to yourself) to your second husband or more likely your make-believe boyfriend and say: "Thank God." And he says, relax a little. And you can't, you say, until they turn thirty—although everyone knows that you're a liar. After thirty you worry that they don't even remember who you are.

The moment during birth when you first hear that lusty screech of life, that's the moment when you are ruined as a person in your own right.

The more you have, the worse the odds. Four children insured me that some would remain living. Four insured me a gamut of experiences, of personalities, of sexual orientations. I tried to prepare myself. I played "what if." I thought the unthinkable. I figured if I thought the unthinkable nothing would happen. Nothing ever happens the way you imagine it. Things happen other ways. I imagined every gruesome instance I could not bear to think of; I did this to protect my children.

I could not protect my children.

After my middle son Kenny died, after he cracked up the car his father bought for him, for one brief second I thought about poisoning us all—if only to get it over with, keep it short, swift. Mercy. At least then I could control the outcome.

I used to think that anything known was better than anything unknown. Nothing could be worse, I thought, than my own imagination.

My son died weeks before he turned twenty-one. For once, I was prepared for his birthday ahead of time. I had his gift. A gold-plated pocket watch. Inscribed. "For twenty-one years of faithful service."

I have three other children, two boys, the oldest and the youngest, and one sad little daughter, who is not so little any longer. Did you know that in Korean you cannot say "my wife," "my son." Instead you say "the woman that is married to me," "the child I gave birth to." In Korean, you cannot possess another person. My dead child might translate into "the one to whom I gave life, who left life before me."

It rained the morning of Ken's funeral, and it was cold, windswept, blustery. I had the flu. My nose was swollen and white-pink as the inner leaves of an onion.

It was warm the morning of Ken's funeral. It was August. There was no wind. The sun shone blue, a concentration of bright, white light.

I remember rain. I remember the heat of the exhaust like a hand-dryer in a public washroom as I circled around the back of the limo. I remember the splash of mud against my stockings as we walked, his father and I, like strangers to the gravesite. I remember worms on the sidewalk, treachery to all those pumps and high-heeled shoes and me sliding, and Jack, the boy's father, catching my elbow as I slid. I remember hugging my arms around me for warmth because I had nothing black for a coat.

But all of this is untrue. It was a beautiful hot day; the air was perfect. The earth welcomed my boy in his glossy wooden casket into her warm, dry bed. Cara, my daughter, said if Ken had lived until the day of his funeral he would have lived—period. Cara said anyone alive that day could never die; that day promised too much to live for. She was young then, Cara. Me, I remember monsoons. I was blind.

Sunset Memorial Chapel. A parking lot. The promise of his father's face. The smell of bread, a thick, yeasty air, from the shopping center across the parkway. A smell that would do better in winter. Why was the kid in such a hurry?

Abigail pulled up first. She'd had to borrow my car. Fred was away on business, and Jews, well, we bury them fast. Fred had no time. No one had time; we were unprepared. Sometimes I wonder if it had been different, if we were prepared, if he had some terminal but chronic illness, if we wouldn't have fared better. Jeremy, my youngest, his ex-boyfriend, Steven, recently diagnosed with cancer—Kaposi's sarcoma. Do I have to tell you that I steep myself in worry, although Jeremy assures me that he is, indeed, "all right"? And poor Steven. Who can bear it, that bright, blond, handsome boy. Is it better, all that prolonged agony? I don't know. I never met his mother.

By the time Jeremy came out of the closet nothing could faze me. I was numb.

The morning of my son's funeral Abigail parked crooked as usual; by the end of the day there would be two scratches along the Saab's body, a dent in the left rear fender. Abigail. My best friend. We met in Cuba, on our honeymoons. Our husbands, newly hatched, found something to talk about; they were both lawyers. We bought our houses three doors away from each other. Twenty-five years later, Abigail buried my son. She wore a red dress with a black blazer in that heat. I never forgave her. She teetered toward the chapel on black spike heels, heels that would sink into the sod, later. She made the arrangements for me, Abigail. I was eternally grateful. She made the arrangements wrong. I can't get this out of my head.

I curse the day I met her.

The chapel was awful—tacky; and the rabbi was a jerk. The casket should have been a pine box, simple, biodegradable, of the earth, but my Ken's was lined in soft velvet. The service was Jewish, which he would have hated. At the time of his death he considered himself a Zen Buddhist. What would he have considered himself next if he had lived? I buried him Jewish for myself. He was dead. Who cared what he wanted. What about what I wanted? Did he think of me when he plowed that car into a tree?

You'd think I'd remember more about the funeral, but it's the funny things that I remember—Scott, his roommate, wearing Kenny's one tie: it literally looked like a slice of pizza with silk-screened sausage and pepperoni. I remember that tie, the dented car, my fat cousin Nathan wedged into one of those tiny seats. He was the only one from my side of the family who could make the funeral. Every day I thank God my own mother was dead. She would never have been able to survive this.

And the things that never happened, those I remember: Cara, wailing, throwing herself on the casket, plunging into the dirt. Reality check (as Cara would say), she was quiet as a mouse all day, even well-behaved, if anyone could believe it. She wore some pretty peasant-thing and clung onto Jeremy's hand. She looked expectant, as if Kenny would pop out of the casket like a jack-in-the-box, as if this was all part of another one of his scams. He had survived several death-defying feats before, why would he abandon her now? Later, in family therapy, this is how Cara explained it. Doug came alone, my eldest; alone, no girlfriend. He never shed a tear. Jack, their father, was with his new wife; they left their little girl at home. I remember no wife; I remember Jack hanging from my arm. I remember his shirt against my face, the graying chest hairs visible through the wet spot of my tears.

I remember nothing real, except for Abigail's red dress, Scott's slice-of-pizza tie, Cara's pink batik cloud of a skirt—that dazzling display of living color. The rest of the day was supplied to me by my family, what was left of it.

So what do we do? We move on. We left Ken in the cemetery and continued. Was there a choice? I needed something to make the years pass. Work. Kids. Gardening. Gratitude toward God for making life a finite procedure. I managed.

Today, at the shopping center, more than a decade since the day I buried Ken, who do I run into in front of the pet store? Scott, the roommate. Scott of the pizza-tie. He looks taller, heavier, his brown hair, poor thing, has begun to thin. He's wearing pinstripes and wingtips. He had been such a little hippie boy. Now, a gold wedding ring. I stop him. For a second he looks like he wants to run. Then he smiles, shyly. It embarrasses him to see me. After Ken died, I embarrassed everyone.

"Mrs. Gold," says Scott.

"Scott," I say. "How are you? Scott. You look wonderful," I say, which is the truth. He is tall inside his suit.
He looks like a man.

I've seen him twice since the boy's funeral, but how I
interrogated that kid on the phone! He was one of the last
people to see my son before he died. They spent the better
part of the evening together, although Ken had also visited with some not very helpful girl—I could barely get
her to say "boo" to me, and she didn't bother to show
her face at the funeral. I made him break it down, Scott.
We spoke for hours and hours of long-distance about the
music Kenny listened to (The Doors), what he had eaten
(chicken and watermelon), any drugs he might have
ingested (a couple of beers). I was looking for clues, pieces
to the puzzle. It wasn't until months later that I realized
that even if "it" were solvable, even if I could pinpoint
the one thing (a snooze, a sneeze, a flying insect) that
diverted Ken's attention from the road in front of him
long enough so that he couldn't help but crash into that
tree, it wouldn't matter. Like the crushing disappointment
of failed therapy, identifying the problem wouldn't neces-
sarily bring about the solution; understanding will not
bring my son back to me.

Scott and the other guys came around once to return
the pizza-tie (which I told him to hang onto—what was
I going to do with it? Create a shrine?); and they came
once out of duty, to see how I was, then they each
returned to the short and selfish process of growing up.

"Scott," I say. "Scott."

"It's *my wife's* birthday," says Scott. He says "my wife"
in a way that is exaggerated, like it's a joke, like the words
are too large for his mouth. "I'm thinking of getting her
a kitten."

His wife.

I say: "You're married."

"I'm an old married man," Scott says and rolls his eyes. "It's been four months," he says, "and I still can't say 'my wife' with a straight face." He smiles, but he looks down at his feet. "We met in law school."

Law school.

"What are you doing in this neck of the woods?" I ask him. The words are too loud. My voice hurts my ears.

"We bought a house," says Scott, and he begins to color. A creeping blush rises up his neck, above the tie and tie clip.

"A little house," Scott says.

"But you're so young, a baby," I say this low, even to myself it sounds like pleading, so I cough to cover up.

"I'm twenty-nine, Mrs. Gold," Scott says. "Almost thirty. I'm even going bald." He bends forward so that I can see the shiny pink of his scalp. The hair Scott's got is combed over; I notice a little dandruff.

I laugh, because I have nothing to say. This relieves him. It seems like for the first time since we've started talking that Scott is actually breathing.

"My wife thinks this will be a good place to raise kids," he says.

Does this wife of his have a name?

"Yes, it is a good place for kids," I tell him. And it is, the schools are strong, the neighborhood is still woodsy, it's not too far from the City which is a Godsend when they get older; and it's safe.

"It's safe," I tell Scott.

He nods. And for the life of me I don't know why—I never knew Scott all that well, not like some of the other boys, Rip and Jake and Doc, and after all Scott and Kenny only roomed together that one summer—but I reach out my hand and touch his face.

Scott looks like he wants to melt right into the pavement.

"Good luck to you, Scott," I say.

"Thanks, Mrs. Gold," he says, "nice to see you, too."

And that's that. Scott's mother's son goes off, rubbing his cheek, the spot that itches, where I caressed him.

Tonight, Scott will come home from work with a new kitty. He will tie a ribbon around its sweet neck. His young anonymous wife will be enraptured.

"Oh, honey," she says, "I love her." And she watches happily as he plays with the kitty, thinking what a good father Scott will be some day, congratulating herself on making all the right choices.

Sometime in the evening, still at the table, maybe after dinner, but before they will make love, Scott says: "Honey, remember that dead guy I told you about, the one I roomed with up at college?"

And that sweet young girl nods gravely. Her hand flutters up to her throat. For a moment she thinks about what her world would be like if it had been *her* husband instead of *my* boy; an imagined life of loneliness and spinsterhood unfolds before her. At her age she still believes that there is a special someone for everyone on earth, that she and Scott were *made* for each other. And now, when faced with some shadowy ideas about my son's death, she wonders for a few seconds what I have wondered for years: where out there in the world, bewildered and confused, lives Ken's future wife? Does she go through life knowing something's missing? Is she holding out, waiting for him to show? Or has she married reluctantly, wondering what is wrong with her—why *is* it she has never really been in love?

"Well," Scott continues, "I ran into his mother today.

97

It was so weird, I told her all about you." At this, his new wife brightens. "And Mrs. Gold was very happy for us and all that . . ." Here young Scott trails off.

"Sweetie, I can always tell when something is bothering you," says his wife. "What's wrong, my love?"

And then maybe she rubs his shoulders a little, maybe she kisses him on his bald spot.

"Well, it might be me," Scott says. A hand drops to pet his little kitten, and he leans back into the softness of his wife. "But Ken's mom, oh God, I don't know."

"Scott," says the girl. "Come on. The truth."

"Well," says Scott, a little red now, "you want the truth? I'll tell you the truth." Poor Scott begins to sputter. "The old bitch. She made me feel guilty for being alive."

His wife is silent.

"You asked for the truth," Scott says. "You got it."

"Don't think about it," says his wife. "Put it out of your mind. It's still my birthday. The rule is you have to do everything I want."

I suspect that Scott obliges her.

So all right, Scott and Mrs. Scott, enjoy your young love. Forget my boy. I apologize for living. See this for what it is—Scott's the age Ken would be, and, okay, Scott reminds me of him. There's no more to it than that. Ken's death was just a tragic episode when Scott was a kid, a death that seasoned Scott (that taught him to always wear his seat belt); Ken's death helped usher Scott into manhood. Look at the benefits—why don't you both?

But once in a while, Scott, tomorrow, Scott, when you're in your office, at a boring meeting, playing hoops at the health club, for my sake, for your sake, flashback to his funeral, revel a little in being haunted; as a pallbearer you could feel his light, light body sliding within the casket. Think about how boring the service was, how much Kenny would have hated it, how you had to go to the bathroom the whole time. Remember the pizza-tie and laugh, and wonder where it is, maybe in a box of mementos at your mother's. Then, abandon my boy to youth, continue on without him. Go on, gain maturity, knowledge. Be married, Scott, pay taxes. Leave my child in the dust.

Scott and Mrs. Scott, get bald, get fatter. Give in; have a family of your own. Learn the hell, the joy, the rapture of being a parent. Go into debt, buy furniture on time. Get too busy to read a book. Travel to Europe, go skiing, have affairs, fights, varicose veins, hernias. Be on school boards, help with homework, pay tuition bills, and camp bills, bail them out of jail. Never get a good night's sleep.

Garden, iron, listen to music, get bifocals, do aerobics. Vote and party and dance and nap. Lie to one another. Go into therapy: alone, as a couple, as a family. Struggle and laugh and wish you were dead. Eat all the kinds of food you can think of: knishes and burritos, fugu and fungi, calamari and scungilli. Be of age, drink legally, knowing full well that my Ken never had a legal drink in his life.

Listen to the rap music my boy never heard of, watch the tearing down of the Berlin Wall on your wide-screen TV—a sight he never lived to see. Discuss the ending of the Cold War, know about compact discs and cordless phones, AIDS, crack, artificial fat, Dan Quayle, Madonna, Iran-Contra, Savings & Loans, turn on the tube and see a freed Nelson Mandela. If the miracle happened and Ken came back for a day, the history of the world's most precious hour, my poor child would be hopelessly lost, out of touch, out of time. How could he talk to you? He's still a kid, for eternity a kid, his decades are the sixties, the seventies, "def" is deaf, "dis" is this, "cool" is "hot." How could he know from Retin-A, post-postmodernism, cyber punk? Go ahead, Scott and Mrs. Scott, speak another language than my son. Live, well into the next century.

And all the time, everywhere, see danger, in the schools, on the buses, in the playground, in the company your children keep, the people they will grow up to sleep with. There is salmonella in their eggs, nitrates in the meat they eat, herpes in the hot tub, poisons in the water. The air, the air! The earth is turning into a hothouse, your children will be seared and steamed.

Worry for your kids; worry that they are too privileged, too talented, too handsome, too lucky.

Know your enemy, Scott.

Embrace life.

Welcome to the Club

JEFF was supposed to bring his soon-to-be-ex-girlfriend to supper, but when Madeleine buzzed him in through two sets of locked entryways, before swinging wide her own front door, he arrived empty-handed. He even forgot the requested jug wine (wine that Madeleine had nudged him about that morning on the telephone); forgot, which was both par for the course and a bad sign.

"Where's your soon-to-be-ex-girlfriend, Jeff?" said Madeleine, as she leaned over to kiss him. It was a wet kiss. It was a damp night. Jeff's cheek was so moist it felt like lips, like anyplace where inner skin was stretched all the way to the outside.

Jeff smelled, but Madeleine was used to this, he was her husband's best friend. Consequently, he was around a lot. He'd biked all the way up Riverside to their apartment, and he was both the type to sweat and the type to not believe in deodorant. Begonia, his real ex-girlfriend, had raised him on organic yings and yangs, and from her he had received a religious training on the healing powers of garlic. Jeff wasn't dirty, exactly, but the complicated layering of his various odors produced a sum that was greater than its parts. He was lucky he was so gorgeous, Madeleine often thought. He had those natural good looks that one finds in a leaf or a tree. All browns and greens.

Stan, Madeleine's husband, leaned past her in the entryway to shake Jeff's hand.

"Where's your soon-to-be-ex-girlfriend, buddy?" said Stan, leaning. And then in a justifiable-but-mock recoil (he was used to this too, after all Jeff was *his* best pal, the guy he had moved to New York with after school, his old roommate even, before Jeff and Begonia fell madly in love and set up their personal house of horrors) he said: "Buddy. Take a shower."

Jeff took a shower.

While Jeff went at it, messing up the bathroom they had fought over cleaning just that morning (it *had* been three weeks), Madeleine slipped out to buy some wine. Stan was cooking dinner. Stan loved to cook dinner; he was good at it. He was, in fact, a much better cook than Madeleine. This disturbed her. There were things she liked to make, too—escarole and white bean soup with pasta wheels, wheels that swelled to monstrous proportions when left over and parked in the fridge. "Scary soup," Stan called it. She liked to make cauliflower–potato-crust pie. Hippie food. That's what Madeleine was good at. Salad that might have a tiny trace of dirt clinging to its leaves. Still, during the course of their marriage, Madeleine handed the kitchen over to Stan. For the most part they were on the run anyway, eating with friends, ordering in. They cooked for company, or on exhaustion Saturdays when they would take turns: getting things done, passing out. One would shop, one would nap, they would share in the preparation. The careful choreography of their lives had come through good-humored trial and error. They knew what worked for them. And while Madeleine wasn't always crazy about it, she'd sit on the other side of the counter that divided the living space from the kitchen space (they had no "rooms" in their apartment) and watch Stan make his magic. These were charged evenings: Madeleine sipping wine, staring Stan down.

Clearly, wine had become a necessity. It was a red-wine dinner that they were having: mussels, pasta, veggie pâté, and more than once Madeleine's mind had blinked over the thought that perhaps living through dinner would be more uncomfortable without that jug there. The idea of dependency, any dependency, annoyed her, so she shrugged it off, patted Stan—who was already on automatic and didn't really seem to notice her slipping into his denim jacket, her short black boy's hair hidden by his silly cap—and headed out into the night.

On the street the air was wet, bright. It had misted all day and the tiny bubbles of moisture had entrapped hard little dots of light which glowed against the darkness. It couldn't exactly be called rain, this mist, but by the time Madeleine walked the two blocks to Broadway and the liquor store, she was coated. Everything was slick. The oily asphalt, the lights from the cars sliding on and off of one another, even the garbage that spilled from the cans and out of black plastic bags (food, newspapers, cracked glass) seemed to have decomposed into some shiny slime that slithered on the sidewalks. Madeleine felt slippery where she was exposed: the tips of her fingers (her arms were long, Stan's arms were longer, his sleeves swallowed her up practically whole, just the second and third joints of her fingers, like fishtails, peeking out of their mouths), her face, the uncovered skin between her dirty little white sneakers and her pants' legs. The mist turned her soft, but left her solid. Open. Exchanging intrinsic fluids with the air. She felt like an eye.

It happened to her just before she got to the recessed glass door of the store, in a short hallway that was lined with some of those gold-veined mirrors, one or two steps up. It always hit the same way, like a seizure. Out of nowhere. No aura, no nothing. She'd say his name. "Doug." She'd say it when she wasn't even thinking about him, when she literally hadn't given him a thought in months. In fact, in recent years she wondered more about saying his name than about the guy himself. It would fall, his name, out of the sky, out of her mouth. This was nothing new to her. Other things fell out of the sky, out of her mouth. She screamed, for example. In college, she'd scream sometimes out of the blue—dormmates rushing from their rooms to see if she was all right. Later, when they knew her, they'd say reassuringly to each other, "It's only Mad, screaming again" (as if they didn't know she hated to have her name shortened that way), as if her little cry were just another piece of punctuation in their day, like the ringing of the clock tower. Her family was, naturally, used to her.

Other things came rushing out of Madeleine's mouth, little bits of songs, maybe a sentence that she wished she said in real life. But these things made sense to her. An acting teacher had called it "releasing your vocal urges" and approved of it, especially the sounds of Madeleine's own language, coming, honestly, from her gut.

It wasn't like it happened all the time, anyway. And when it did, often she was alone or capable of hiding it. She had even had to explain it to Stan, one of those after-sex whispers, when she felt she owed it to him to give something up. When she confided, he was holding her in his wondrous arms, long enough to wrap and wrap like ribbons, turn her into a gift, wide enough to feel male and close enough to what she dreamed about as a young girl to make the whole of it—marriage, aging—seem worthwhile. Hadn't he heard her small outcries? Wasn't this something he did too, maybe at the gym or on his walks at night? Couldn't they pretend they shared some horrible little quirk, some potentially shameful but tiny oddity?

Stan was, of course, curious and accepting. He was a kind and generous man. But he wasn't quite sure what she meant, exactly. She promised to point it out next time; Madeleine's voice leaving her body as if it were giving up a ghost.

That night, frozen in the doorway of the Buy-Rite, it just slipped out, like an extra little particle of breath.

"Doug," she said.

Doug, who was this guy she had lived with for a while in and out of college. Who she had done the whole Vermont farm trip with. Doug, who she hadn't even seen in years, and when she did last see him he was someone she didn't even like. Doug, who couldn't stand it when her mouth would open and words would fly.

Madeleine said his name and then forgot about him. She went into the store and bought her wine.

The guys were already eating when Madeleine got back. Stan had put out two big bowls: chips and salsa, not because they made sense with the meal, but because they would keep Jeff happy. They were drinking beers out of the bottle.

"I bought wine," said Madeleine, plucking off her wet things like shedded skin, lifting them up and away from her body. She hung the jacket and the cap on the pegs she'd forced Stan to nail to the hallway. Neither of them liked to hammer.

"Maybe later," said Stan.

Madeleine went into the bathroom to dry her face. The little rug was bunched and kicked into a corner. A bottle of shampoo was oozing on its side. She picked it up from the tub rim, tightened the cap, and rinsed the plastic in the sink. There were whiskers at the bottom, Stan must have made him shave, she thought. They looked like little lead filings. She ran the water until they were gone, the sink as white and empty as an empty, white bowl. There were moments, moments like this, where Madeleine felt some kinship with inanimate objects. It happened once when she opened a can of coffee, some essence of herself lifting up to meet her. She looked at the sink, then, for a second, with recognition. She looked at herself hard in the mirror. Her hair was flattened against her skull. She wiped her face with a paper towel, then leaned from the waist and shook her hair out. When she stood up, too quickly, she got a rush. She gave herself another tousled look—It's only Jeff, she thought. Then she went out into the living area of the subdivided room that was their home. Jeff was on the hammock, Stan in a slung-back leather chair from her parents' basement. The whole apartment really looked a lot like someone's rec room. Piles climbed everywhere: Union notes, copies of the rag she wrote for, their books, their bicycles, their tapes and their records. Somewhere along the line Madeleine had lost her possessions. How would they ever divide this stuff if they were to break up?

"Sit, Madela," said Stan. He had picked this Madela-shtick up from her mother.

Like a flash, it hit her that he was losing his hair.

Obviously this was something she was aware of, she looked at Stan, happily, every day; but there beneath the harsh light of the old lamp the two parallel roads of his temples encroached farther back along his scalp. One day they would converge, leaving a patch of hair, an island. I will be married to a bald man, thought Madeleine. So many things in life you think will never happen.

"Wine," said Madeleine. She went behind the counter to search for the corkscrew.

Stan was talking about the Union. He'd met Madeleine while he was organizing the weekly where she worked. When he walked into the office, so long ago now it had already become another memory of a memory, Madeleine had thought to herself: Why don't I ever meet men like that? He was so wonderfully big, Stan, so full of purpose. That's what Madeleine needed then, a lover with a reason to live. Stan *believed* in unions. At that time in her life, Madeleine had stopped believing in anything. Stan was an infusion.

Jeff had been an organizer once himself. Stan and he met at a college of Industrial and Labor Relations, upstate. Doug had a brother who went to school up there, who died up there in a car accident, which was something Madeleine didn't like to think about. He'd been a nice enough kid, not that she knew him all that well, just from family get-togethers, holidays, times when Madeleine had to be on best behavior. The whole thing was so tragic. Privately, what really felt tragic to Madeleine was the fact that the death of someone she knew tangentially, clearly as an appendage to someone she loved, would go on to inform her whole life. His death had wrecked everything, although everything had been pretty much wrecked before. He was her excuse out. She ran so far she couldn't find her way back. Stan was way too old to have known this kid at school—good thing. She would not have been able to date him if he had.

Since Begonia, Jeff was a struggling actor.

Madeleine sat down at Stan's feet. She passed him the bottle and the corkscrew, which he inserted and turned with an even hand. He poured the wine into a glass they had stolen from their own wedding. Stan didn't miss a beat . . . The Union was suing the Union. The Union was threatening to go on strike. This was always the trouble with the Left, it factionalized itself to death. Wasn't this the same as what Madeleine had run up against at the Feminist Encampment? The intellectuals against the activists, the radical lesbian separatists against the radical lesbians, and Mothers Against Drunk Driving ("What were they doing there anyway?" he turned to her) versus NOW? Everyone against the housewives?

Madeleine nodded "Yes," sipping slowly.

"I am that housewife," said Stan. "Everyone hates management."

"I still can't believe you're management, man," said Jeff.

"Neither can I," Stan said.

Madeleine leaned over, tipped the bottle to her glass so that the tide line met the red rim of its original volume.

"We can talk union-talk anytime, Jeff," she said. "I want the dish."

"Oh you do, do you? Oh you do, do you?" Jeff spoke like a parrot.

"They're doing animal imitations these days at the Actors Workshop," Stan said.

"You're joking," said Madeleine.

"I'm joking," said Stan. He patted her silk-cropped head. "You know this woman once had hair to her waist?"

he said to Jeff. "Maybe it's time to grow it back," Stan said. "She's so beautiful in the pictures."

"Why did you chop it all off?" said Jeff. "Girls are usually so weird about their hair."

The wine was staining Madeleine's mouth, by the end of the evening her tongue and gums would be black. At this point, her lips looked sunburned.

"Well," she said, thinking. "It was over. I was leaving the farm."

"So?" said Jeff.

"So," said Madeleine.

"What was this, your lesbian phase?" said Jeff.

"No, it was not my lesbian phase," said Madeleine. She shot a look at Stan.

"Jeff," said Stan.

"Sorry," said Jeff.

"At the time, I thought it had something to do with Yoko Ono," said Madeleine. She laughed a little.

"No shit," said Jeff.

"No shit," said Madeleine. "It's some Japanese custom I think, when your husband dies to cut off your hair."

"Say what?" said Stan, but he was smiling.

"You know, an act of solidarity. I guess I was really into John Lennon," said Madeleine, laughing again, but sort of embarrassed. She lifted her left hand to her left shoulder, her arm hung, enfolded like a forgotten wing.

Jeff laughed too.

"Shut up," said Madeleine, laughing still. "Shut up, goon." Her wine spilled a bit so she soaked up the spill with a paper towel. They used paper towels because one or the other of them always forgot to buy napkins. By this time they were all more or less a little drunk. They were happy.

Stan went into the kitchen area to get the food.

"Your hair was long when you were playing hippie with that banker dude in Vermont, isn't that right?" said Jeff.

"Shut up," said Madeleine, "I want to talk about you."

Stan came with some plates and silverware, a couple of extra brews, then he boomeranged back toward the kitchen.

"You mean you want to talk about my women," said Jeff.

"That too," said Madeleine, "that too." She was beginning to echo, which happened sometimes when she drank wine.

Stan thought that it was cute. "That too, that too," he yodeled softly, from behind the counter.

Madeleine ignored him. "Tell," she said to Jeff, her voice rising. "Tell," she said.

"Tell, tell," went the voice from behind the counter.

"Shut up," she said, so loud she scared herself. No one seemed to notice. Perhaps drinking made her hearing more sensitive. She decided to wonder about that later.

"What do you think about a splash of wine in the mussel broth?" called Stan.

"No," said Madeleine. "No, I don't think that would be good." The fingers of her right hand rested on the base of the bottle.

"So, I thought you guys wanted to talk about me?" said Jeff. He said it with hope. Being around him so much, for Madeleine, was like living in the woods. Most of the time, you are not all that aware of your surroundings. Once in a while though, a person is bound to look up. That's when you notice that the mountain in the distance is a deep and perfect blue. That's when she noticed that Jeff was beautiful.

Madeleine looked up.

Stan came over carrying bowls for discarded shells. He went back to the counter and brought back a big pot of pasta, grated cheese still in the plastic container and a pepper mill. Neither Madeleine nor Jeff moved a muscle.

"*Bon appetit,*" said Stan.

It was every man for himself. The guys dove in with gusto. Madeleine sat back; she needed more time. She poured herself another. Jeff had sauce on his chin, already.

"I love food," Jeff said.

Madeleine took one look at him and giggled.

"What?" said Jeff, "what?" He seemed injured.

Stan leaned over and wiped him down. That's the kind of man Stan was. Matter-of-fact. These things didn't bother him. He could tell a stranger that there was something hanging from his nose without being too insulting. This was a quality Madeleine admired.

"Well, about me," Jeff began again. "I got a postcard from Begonia."

"And," primed Madeleine.

"And," said Jeff, "it sounds like Swedish Massage School was a bust."

"*Quelle surprise,*" said Madeleine.

"Hmmm," said Stan, his mouth full of noodles, the tips sliding in.

"She's decided to give regional theater another shot," said Jeff. "She wants me to go with her."

"And," said Madeleine.

"And," said Jeff, "I'm getting tired of breaking up. I'm old," he said.

"Have some wine," said Madeleine. She stood up too quickly. She swayed and rocked. "Whoa," she said. Then she went to the cabinet and brought out two more glasses. "Wine or beer?" she called to Stan.

"I'm fine," he said. Madeleine brought out a couple of

more bottles of beer just in case. When she sat down again she sat across from her husband. She looked at him. She was so used to looking at him that she did not know his face. She closed her eyes to picture him better. There was a blank spot in her mind's eye, right around his mouth. She opened up again, and looked hard in order to correctly capture the portrait-without for the portrait-within. Either way, his lips were too thin. I married a thin-lipped, balding, union man, thought Madeleine. She giggled.

"I take it that you are going with Begonia?" said Stan.

"Yeah, well, why the hell not," said Jeff. "I'm terminally unemployed here anyway."

"You love her," said Stan.

"That too," Jeff said.

"That too," echoed Madeleine. She wondered if she had echolalia. "Stan, do you think I have echolalia?" she said. It occurred to her to do a piece on echolalia for that rag she wrote for (it was the kind of thing they adored, bizarre disorders) if there really was such a thing to report on, if "echolalia" didn't turn out to be just another word she made up in her head.

"I think you need to eat some food," Stan said.

Madeleine picked up a mussel with her fingers. The shell was a black-and-blue beak. The meat inside looked like a tongue. The color of the tongue was mustard. She put it down.

"Mmm," she said. "So," she said, "that's what happened to the soon-to-be-ex."

"Begonia," said Jeff glumly. "She exed her out." He drew a big X in the air with his index finger.

"But isn't that a form of breaking up?" said Madeleine, her own finger slicing a crooked X through the now leaning air. For some reason she wasn't sure of, she wanted to give Jeff a hard time.

"Naw," said Jeff. "There wasn't enough blood."

"Do you think there will be blood when we break up?" Madeleine said to Stan.

Stan ignored her.

"I thought that's why you got married, so you wouldn't have to," said Jeff. "I'd even marry Begonia, if it meant I didn't have to break up with her again," he said.

Madeleine guessed that this was part of it, although she had never quite thought of it that way before. Her own mother said she got married so she wouldn't have to worry about having a date for Saturday night. You get married when you're ready to get married, thought Madeleine, it really doesn't have a whole lot to do with greatest love. You marry when it's time.

Jeff went on. "God, Stan, remember when you broke up with Lizzie—could you go through *that* again?"

Stan shot him a look. There were things he and Madeleine agreed not to discuss.

"You guys are so weird," said Jeff.

"Go ahead, I can take it," said Madeleine.

"You *did* break up on your birthday," said Jeff.

"What?" said Madeleine. "What?"

"So, she threw me a party," said Stan. He looked uncomfortable.

"They had this big fight at the end of the night and he walked out on her," said Jeff. "She was so pissed off she started throwing things at him." He turned to Stan, "Remember you guys had that porch—I could hear glasses crashing all the way on State Street." Jeff laughed. "I'll never forget her shouting: 'I guess you got your party. I guess you got what you wanted.' I mean it was brutal," Jeff said.

Madeleine looked at Stan.

Stan looked at the floor. "I didn't love her," Stan said.

"What about you, Jeff?" she said. Wine made her feel wicked. "What was your worst romantic moment?"

"Oh God," said Jeff, "I'm a bastard."

"You are a bastard," said Stan.

"It was when *I* was going out with Lizzie . . ."

"You went out with Lizzie?" Madeleine said.

"Only kidding," Jeff said.

"You are a bastard," Stan said.

It occurred to Madeleine at that moment that they had a language that she was locked out of, that there were things that they shared that she could never know. Even her husband, half a stranger.

"Naw," said Jeff, "I was on the rebound. It was awful, really, I was going out with this little bricklike girl . . ."

"Bricklike?" Madeleine laughed.

"I remember her," Stan snorted.

"Bricklike?" Madeleine repeated herself.

They were all laughing now.

"Yeah," said Jeff, "I'm a cad. I mean I went over to her parents' house for dinner, impressed the shit out of them, I might add . . ."

Madeleine and Stan looked at each other and cracked up.

". . . went home, banged her, rolled over and got up."

"Why are we laughing?" said Madeleine to Stan.

"I don't know," he laughed back at her.

"And she said, 'Wa-where are you go-going?' " Jeff was having trouble speaking now, he was laughing so hard, between syllables. "And I said, 'Well, I guess I just don't like you that much.' "

The room was silent for their laughter. Stan's eyes were streaming.

"It gets worse," Jeff crowed.

Madeleine was barely breathing, her stomach hurt. She felt blind and doubled up.

Jeff went on. "She started crying, so I said, 'What's wrong?' "

"How sensitive," Madeleine choked.

Stan chortled high. He sounded like a wild animal.

Jeff continued. "She said: 'No one ever rejected me before,' and I said, God can you believe this—I said, I said, you know what I said?"

"Say it already," said Madeleine.

"I said, I said," Jeff was past being able to talk. He was gasping. In fact, he looked a little blue. He looked like he was turning. "Oh, God," said Jeff.

"What?" said Madeleine. "What?"

"Okay," said Jeff, breathing deeply. "Okay."

"Goddamn it, what did you say already?" screamed Madeleine.

"I said, 'Welcome to the club!' " Jeff screamed back at her.

Their laughter was like machine-gun fire. They laughed until they were too tired to laugh any longer.

Then it got quiet.

"That wasn't very funny," said Madeleine, which sent them all tumbling again—only this time weaker, shorter.

"What about you, Mad?" said Jeff.

"Don't call her that," said Stan, "it makes her mad."

"Shut up," said Madeleine.

"I wish you luck with getting anything out of her," Stan said. He was smiling, but he was sober.

"Madeleine," said Jeff, taking a breath for emphasis. "What was your worst breakup?"

Madeleine thought for a moment. It surprised her that she wanted to talk at all.

"I failed someone when he needed me most," said Madeleine.

"Failed? Like in a course?" Jeff laughed.

"No," said Madeleine. "No." By then, she didn't want
to talk about it any longer.

Stan loved to cook, but he hated to clean up. The apartment was a disaster. It was times like these that
Madeleine felt she awoke officially transformed into her
mother. Only Madeleine's mother never had a hangover
in her life, and Madeleine felt hopelessly, eternally hung-
over. She made a sound like she was going to retch, which
even she found unpleasant, and which furthered her own
rising swell of nausea. She had passed out in the hammock, probably in the middle of the conversation. All the
lights were still burning. Outside the window the world
was gray, which didn't tell her much. The world always
looked gray from her window, which faced an alley. Stan
was sleeping on the floor. The sound of his gentle snoring
was reassuring. For all those mussel carcasses, something
in the room was still living; the stubborn bleating of Stan's
breath was proof, and the slow thump-thump of his heart.
Madeleine could hear Stan's heart beating in her temples.
Jeff was gone. He must have left hours before. The clock
read 3:30. The front door was slightly open.
    She sat up. The weight of her head propelled her for-
ward. Her feet hit the floor. Why do I do this to myself,
Madeleine wondered. Why?
    She stood up. Her arms and legs were webbed, felt
connected by sticky strings. They worked in tandem like
a puppet. She surveyed the ruins of supper. She started
to clear things up, bringing bowls and silver into the
kitchen. Stan stirred. She could hear him, but the effort
it would take to turn her head seemed impossible to mus-
ter, it was as far from her grasp as the moon was. She
had slept in her jeans so her legs felt like they had been

inside a cast for months, white and damp as a squid. The outer skin of her brain felt seared to the inner lining of her skull.

"Oh," she said. "Oh."

"Doug," said Madeleine.

Out of the sky, out of her mouth.

What do I do with the shells? she thought. Madeleine put them back into the pot they were cooked in. Some mussels were left uneaten. Their mouths were open, a nest of hungry baby birds. She covered the pot and left it on the stovetop. Then Madeleine stopped up the sink, squirted in some lemon-stuff, and turned on the hot water, very hot. Those familiar clouds of bubbles rose up pressing their lemony fragrance closer and closer to her nose, until she tasted its perfume in the back of her throat. She felt sure she would be sick. Madeleine always felt sure she would be sick, but she never was. Madeleine had developed into a good drinker.

The hot, hot water felt nice on her hands and arms as she drowned the bowls down to the sink bottom. She heard Stan get up and shut the door.

"The door was open," Stan said.

"Yes," said Madeleine. "I know."

Her fingers slipped around the greasy water for the silver. When she found a piece she would wipe it off with a rag, then rinse it in the second sink and put it in the rack. It was slow work, but at least it was work. There was progress.

Stan came up behind her. He slung his arms around her waist, underneath her breasts. He rested his forehead, like a puzzle piece, where her shoulder met her neck. She felt both in and outside of her own body. Madeleine wanted to see his face then, but she was afraid to turn her head, she was even afraid to *try* to turn her head. She

117

felt dense and yet surprisingly precarious. Stan leaned into her, his warm breath moistening a little patch of her hair. It felt cool, his breath, her hair. Him, her, both of them barely standing. There.

"Stan," she said, "do you ever think of having a baby?"

"We can't afford to have a baby," Stan said.

He rocked against her.

Madeleine was beginning to sweat. The heat of the water steamed her. She pushed a bit of bang off her forehead with the heel of a wet palm. She swayed a little.

Stan stayed put, his lips melting against her.

"How come," said Madeleine, "teenage mothers can afford to have babies, poor people can afford to have babies, even Union people can afford to have babies?"

"They can't afford them either," Stan said. "It's just that they're not aware that they can't afford them."

His body pressed against her body, his front curving into the S of her back. Madeleine out front, Stan behind her.

They did the dishes together.

"I used to have such pretty hair, didn't I, Stan?" said Madeleine.

"Yes," said Stan.

He was practically asleep. It was neither night nor day. The sink was full.

"Stan?" asked Madeleine.

"Pretty," said Stan.

"Stan?" asked Madeleine. "Do you like me? Do you like me, Stan?" asked Madeleine.

The Runner

HANNAH and Jack were fighting. That's all they did, they fought and fought all weekend. The baby was in his crib. He was lucky. A baby could sleep through anything. Besides, he was used to this, the background hum of his parents' constant bicker, the build of their silent treatments, the crescendo of their shouts. Doug was gone. He was old enough to escape. He slammed out of the house two hours before. He said "Fucking assholes," and he shook his fist as he went through the back door, where no one could hear him because they were fighting so loud in the front of the house.

They were fighting because they had problems. All married people fought, had problems. They fought because they cared. This is what they told their children. Later on, when the kids were older, Hannah and Jack wouldn't fight at all.

Now they were still loud, so loud their words made Cara's ears bleed. She covered them up with her fists, but the shouting leaked through, twisted its way into her head where it went off like fireworks. She was four, then. She was in the laundry room, curled up in the laundry basket. Dirty sheets and underwear buried her, but still words dribbled into her head, words she didn't know. "Niggardly." "Capitalist." "Whore." Cara was all alone down there, her parents' words raining, pouring, soaking. Kenny was nowhere to be found, which made things worse for her.

The laundry room was Cara's favorite part of the house. It was a treat just to go there, in the basement, which was off-limits to her without a parent or an older brother around to watch her descent down those steep stairs. It was cool and damp and delicious, then, in the summer when it was hot. It was steamy and warm in the winter. The basement was always the reversible of what was outside the house, just like Cara's rain slicker, which was yellow plastic on the outside, red cotton when she wore it inside out. All the time the basement smelled like mold and wood rotting, which suited Cara to a T. She was one of those predetermined people. She was born liking mess and musk, the breakdown of things. She was born allergic to the sound of her parents arguing. Her mother's sobs washed over her, the laundry basket her cradle, her mother's gulp gulp for breath, the ebb and flow of a gentle tide, the yearnings of a sad, sad ocean. She nestled down deep beneath the socks, the towels, the sheets, beneath all the soiled and colored garments, Cara hid herself as well as she could, fully expecting someone to come searching after her.

What were they fighting about, Jack and Hannah? Who could even remember? Whatever, the weekend was ruined, truly ruined, Hannah had cried this out, about three and a half hours, before. Now, she was all cried out. Her breath came in bubbles, little mewings sounded in the back of her throat. She was a lovely girl, and the sight of her—her curly hair as unironed as her dress, her knees crumpled to her chin as she curled pealike, a small globe, up upon the sofa—still weakened him.

That their marriage was a mistake was clear and unclear, that Jack felt for her, that he felt strongly, that at this point he wouldn't know love if it rapped him in the face, were the few truths that Jack was still aware of. He was not a dishonest man. He was a man who was going to change the world. A man who provided for his family. A lawyer. And he was still young, young enough to feel his youth wasting out from under him, young enough to wake up each morning his heart pounding, his internal arms outstretched, reaching for the day that just passed, willing it back to him. That Jack was trapped— as just a few years before, maybe ten, maybe eleven, he had sworn he would never be—by four kids and by car and house payments and by this nagging, crumpled, lovely wife who always, always wanted more from him, of all Jack's truths this was the most self-evident.

And so, in this rare moment of calm (each spouse had to catch their breath) when the sight of Hannah, the silver threads weaving prematurely throughout the wind and turn of her hair, the silver bringing to his stubborn mind the fact that she too had given some things up, it touched a place at the back of his spine. When it touched something somewhere else inside of him, so that it even, just a little bit, turned him on, that was the moment Jack had to lash out at her. "Whore," said Jack. The word itself spat out of him.

The smell of Jack's armpit was the most reassuring smell in the laundry basket. Cara had struck pay dirt, her nose was buried in the City College sweatshirt that Jack wore when he worked in the yard. Her second favorite smell was the baby's smell, the talc and sweetly spiced dew of his perspiration, the fragrance of his soft, damp head. The baby was fine, the baby was okay, the baby was, after all, only a baby. This was a theory that Cara would carry around her whole life: everyone else could age, grow significant, this little brother would always be just short of a person.

She had yet to discover that she started out as a similarly sleepy little bundle, although she was acutely aware of the fact that she had evolved. Cara was a complicated net of emotions, a collection of extremes, without a wax or wane in her entire being, convinced that she was permanently more sophisticated than her baby brother. According to this theory, she was also perpetually inferior to Kenny, which was all right with Cara since she worshipped him, and who in their right mind would worship someone as lowly as themselves?

Doug was different. She never liked him. She hated him, in fact, although Cara's first experience with naming hatred was the baby who she couldn't care less about. It was early one morning when she came upon them, her mother wrapped up in something diaphanous, something that looked like a curtain, an angel wing, with the baby snapped tight to her breast, that it became clear. This little guinea pig chewing on the pink rosette of her mother's nipple was the same baby that slept in the hard nut of her belly just a few weeks before. The baby within had become the baby without. Cara looked at her mother and her brother thus interlocked and said: "I hate you."

Cara's simple statement, sung out loud and clear, delighted Hannah. Wasn't sibling rivalry after all a healthy, natural, normal response? With Doug it was different. Cara had no name for it, no definition for the wild emotion that rooted in her heart. Doug counted. After all, he was older.

Doug took his bicycle. He ran with it, out of the garage and down the driveway. When he neared the curb, he threw his weight and leapt on to it, so that his body propelled the bike, and pushed it off the curb. There was a moment of suspension. Then impact! Doug's feet pedaling furiously before he hit the ground. This way there was a reservoir of speed for Doug to draw from. The pedals turned so fast they forced his feet, his thighs pumping like pistons, his breath coming in shots. He was the fastest kid in the neighborhood. So fast, the wind dried his tears into streaks. His skin felt tight, painted, like a warrior. He would bike and bike and bike until he wore himself out. He would bike all afternoon at full blast. He was like a rocket, Doug. Shooting as far away from home as he could. He didn't need them. They didn't need him. No one in the family needed each other.

There was a lull upstairs. A hush hovered over the house. Cara shifted around in the clothes pile like a gentle cycle. Where was Kenny? It was not like him not to come after her. All of a sudden the smells of the laundry basket overwhelmed her. The inside of her itched. Cara exploded out of the laundry basket. She surprised herself. The silence remained. Perhaps it was finally safe, safe enough to cry, get a little attention. Cara lifted one chubby leg after the other, up those steep steps, her arms wide-flung as a glider as she defiantly avoided the banister. No way would she grab on even if she knew she was falling. If she died, her parents would deserve it.

Where was Kenny? Where he should be. In his room, the room he shared with Doug. Kenny was in his room from the start. When he heard the warning notes, the preliminary bicker, the suppressed shout, he shut his door, vaulted himself up to the top bunk, Doug's bunk, put a pillow over his head (Doug's pillow) and started reading. So far he was three-quarters of the way through Doug's collection of *Mad* magazines. Kenny loved *Mad* magazine. *Mad* saved his life.

Jack was smoking. Hannah hated when Jack smoked in the house. This was Jack's house, he paid for it, Jack would smoke wherever he goddamned pleased. Hannah was quiet. She sat quietly on the couch, hugging her knees, breathing in Jack's smoke. The only thing the couple shared was air.

The door to the basement opened. Cara had ascended, plump as a cherub. She was looking for trouble.

For a moment Jack and Hannah stared at Cara. They stared with the stare of horror that comes from being a parent who realizes that just seconds before their child could have been burned, or lost, or drowned. Their child might have fallen down a flight of stairs and broken her neck. This came after the fact, when a parent could afford to look horrified. If the unspeakable happened, there would have been no time to arrange a face.

Cara took one glance at her parents and she burst into tears. They scared her. This was the starting gun. Everyone sprung into action.

"What in the hell kind of mother are you?" Jack said. He rushed toward a screaming Cara.

"You're scaring her," said Hannah.

Jack swooped down to pick up his daughter. "Just what in the hell kind of mother are you?" said Jack. He turned his eyes up like high-beams, beaming down at Hannah. He was upset, Jack, he wasn't paying attention. He yanked his child up into his arms. The burning head of his cigarette touched the fat pad of her elbow. It was an accident, but Jack burned his tiny daughter.

Cara screamed. Her father burned her.

"On my God," said Hannah. "Oh my God." She rushed from the couch to Cara flailing in Jack's arms. "What kind of mother am I?" said Hannah. "What kind of mother am I? My God," said Hannah, "you burned her."

Cara was lunging toward her, reaching for her mother. Hannah took the little girl—rather, Cara dove, Hannah caught her.

"What kind of a mother am I?" said Hannah. Cara wriggled in her grasp. She was sobbing wildly.

Jack's arms were empty. He stood there in his own house in front of his own wife and daughter, Jack stood there like a criminal, like he was nothing.

That's when the boys' door slammed. That's when Kenny flew down the stairs, sprinted out of the shadows, butt-naked, gleaming in the light. Kenny. Kenny with his seven-and-a-half-year-old body, his skinny, long little body, his arms and legs going, his smooth chest heaving, his breath shooting out like dragon-fire. He streaked. Kenny streaked the living room, running like his life depended on it, his knees practically chin high. He ran through the kitchen, came out behind his Mom and Dad and Cara, circled back in front so that they got one last glimpse of his little white butt; then, Kenny was out of there.

Hannah laughed first. It took her a moment to catch her breath, but then she laughed and laughed. The sound of her laughter was the most beautiful sound in the world. Cara laughed too, because her mother was laughing, because she had gotten to see Kenny's naked butt. Hannah was laughing so hard she sort of sagged against Jack, she was weak with release, so Jack took the child out of her arms. He hugged her to him and Cara allowed it, she allowed herself to be hugged. Jack pressed his lips to her forehead.

"Daddy," said Cara.

Outside, Doug rode his bike without hands, around the trail that surrounded Beebee Lake. He leaned his head back, showed his throat to the sun. Doug knew that road. He didn't have to look where he was going.

In his room, on Doug's bunk, his head buried under Doug's pillow, Kenny lay naked and still.

In the crib the baby grabbed his toes, happily.

Boy Girl, Boy Girl

HANNAH has a date.

The phones were ringing. West Village to East, East Village to Burlington, Vermont. The lines were tied. Her children, grown now as they'd ever be, were talking, miracle of miracles, no holiday or catastrophe, nothing mentioned of borrowed money. They were on the horn night and day of their own free will.

Jeremy—the only kid who regularly bothered to visit his mother—got the dish first, since he was home on a weekend while Hannah was out shopping and he was too lazy to get up so he screened her calls. When the message hit, so '50s—This is Jim, I'll pick you up around eight—(Jim!) Jeremy was dialing before the tape could rewind. Cara, screening herself, picked up with a high-fidelity screech mid-ramble. "Jim," she shrieked. "Who the fuck is that motherfucker?" And since Ken, her favorite brother, was long dead and buried she had no choice but to ring up Doug, the oldest and weirdest of all. She hoped against hope to get his airy sweet wife, Kitsie the practiced simultaneous interpreter, who could pass along the necessary info without risk of another sibling war. So it was Cara to Doug via Kitsie Doug's wife, Cara drawling out the particulars as if she was reciting vital signs. "Well, she's still breathing," Cara drawled across the wire, "I guess this is proof the old bird's alive."

"Cara, Cara," Kitsie clucked, at a kind loss for words. Then, over her shoulder to her husband, "Cara says your mother has never been better," which everyone knew was a lie.

Hannah, at the Mall, looking for, of all things, a new slip, a bra, would have been delighted to know that among her offspring there still existed some form of communication. But she was wandering into the Better Dresses department at Lord & Taylor's and would not be aware of the length of her children's chatter until the bill came the following month—Cara, terminal child that she was, still felt an inalienable right to charge her long-distance to her mother whenever she got the urge.

Hannah has a date. Is this possible? Surely, her husband left her long enough ago. There's been time for multiple remarriages. That first year of being a bachelorette had cured her, once and for all, from even thinking of a man in a fanciful way. Blind dates are awful enough when you are young, but a full-blooded wrestle in a tenement doorway back then at least posed a healthy challenge. Now with the sag of this, the heft of that, the fact that with her husband she'd been for all practical purposes a virgin, and before that a cold fish, Hannah found the sexual politics of the eighties too daunting, those few brief forays into fleshly foreign lands too humiliating to warrant further experimentation. The truth was that inside Hannah still felt like a young girl, and wanted to be treated as such, gently, gently, like something fragile, something beloved, when all the men, even the ones who assumed she'd been around the block, opted to treat her like somebody's mother. So Hannah cried: Enough. Enough already. Life was too short and painful to be spent making a fool of yourself. She had other things to tend to: her rotten kids, her determination to keep herself in a constant state of mourning. Her boy was dead. Ever vigilant, she picked at scabs, sawed away at open sores—the tree, the car, Kenny, over and over in her mind like a botched recording. For pleasure, she'd allow herself to visualize the skid marks—proof that her child had pressed down on that brake pedal, proof that his intention was to save his skin and continue onward with the increasing burden of daily living. No one, not even his mother, could deny how hard it was to be a person.

This is what Hannah told herself and argued with her offspring in those long heated battles, in a frequency only a dog could hear. Soundless wars filled their rare family gatherings. As hard as it was to speak of such things— the road was clear, the night bright and illuminating, the kid drug-free—the not-speaking was what got alarming. Cara turning redder and redder, sputtering with anger, Doug shaking his head with sorrow, with fury. Hannah herself, like a veteran of foreign wars, immobilized by the constant reenactment in her head. If she stopped and got on with it (Just *stop*, Ma, said Douglas), somewhere inside her, Hannah was sure she'd be less of a mother.

This "less-of-a-mother business" was Abigail's theory. Abigail, her oldest, dearest, most intrusive friend. Abigail who set up those initial nightmare dates, who oversaw that horrible episode with the personals (*DWJF mother of*

*four, zaftig but nice, looking for someone with a social conscience,
likes gardening, once in a while he should read a book . . .*) when
not one balding pauncher responded. Abigail, who after
giving up on Hannah years ago, invited her to a dinner
party as an even number, just to round things out (boy
girl, boy girl). Two straight middle-aged marriages, Abigail
and Fred her husband, an older gay couple—Sid and
Stanley, Sid a fellow social worker who was at the Jewish
Home for the Blind a hundred years ago when Abigail
still commuted—and Jim, Jim Weinstein, the widower,
whom Abigail invited out of loyalty to his dead wife. Ruth
had been Abigail's old friend from the League of Women
Voters; Ruth had helped Abigail to establish their local
chapter of NOW. Hannah was an afterthought. Abigail
just liked symmetry at her table.

"You could have knocked me over with a feather,"
Abigail said, later that night in bed with her husband.
"He liked her." And it was true, Jim talked to Hannah a
whole night, about what, about this and that, his eldest
boy's troubled marriage, the fact that Jim needed a new
carburetor. He talked to her about the state of the schools
(Jim was an educator, a principal) he talked about what
it felt like to walk by Beebee Lake past dusk, which he
had done night after night since his wife died. "It almost
makes her death make sense," he said, that he should be
free to walk around the lake at night. Although the death
was horrible, first one breast then the other, the surgeons
chipping away at her from the outside, her own maddened
cells eating away from within. Jim tried this one on
Hannah tentatively, the way Hannah would test out a hot
iron. And she understood, Hannah understood him, or
sort of, in her own psychology, her own language. "Within
loss, there are newfound freedoms—you have to fill the

absence with something," she said. "It speaks well of you to fill it with moonlight."

"Did you see them, gabbing away, head to head, like that?" said Abigail. And Fred nodded, although he was title-glancing *The New York Times*. "Do you think I should feel guilty?" asked Abigail, sitting up. "Poor Ruth," said Abigail. "Accch."

"Ruth's dead," said Fred.

The truth was the only thing that could hush Abigail up. So she sat quietly, fiddling with her glasses, not-reading her book, that new L.B.J. biography. They'd known Hannah for years, the two couples met on their honeymoons, celebrating in the same restaurant in Havana. Jack, Hannah's ex, and Fred had hit it off. Jack was in law school, Fred a storefront "community" attorney. In fact, they were still friends of a sort, which suddenly occurred to Abigail. "Don't breathe a word of this to Jack," she said. "I won't," said Fred, "I won't." Hannah had won Abigail and Fred in the divorce. There had been no question about Abigail's loyalty; she had a lifetime of things in common with Hannah—social work, political activism, a desire to remain semiurban in the suburbs, a child or two who was good-for-nothing—and Jack had grown up to be a real self-centered shmuck. He'd been such a sexy, exciting kid, what a waste Jack was. He was a caricature of his type—a radical, a revolutionary, who grew up to be a fat cat with a much younger second wife. Rumors spread among his youngest children that he recently voted Republican—Abigail got this info from Hannah, who got it from Cara, who got it from Jeremy, who on a rare visit to his Dad's saw his small stepsister play with a suspicious campaign button involving a local Connecticut louse and his lousy local election.

Out of Time

"Can you imagine what it would be like to sleep with her now," said Abigail. "She hasn't had sex in years."
Fred could imagine. He always had a thing for Hannah. "Read your book, Abby," said Fred. "You're making me crazy." So Abigail obliged, although a mere five minutes later she said: "How did this crook become president?" And then, "God help me, I voted for him."

Hannah has a date. And if it were up to Hannah, she wouldn't tell a soul. Not Jeremy, who was waiting shyly, but expectantly, on the couch for her return and for an explanation. Not Cara, who spent the better part of her collect-call an hour later grilling her mother for information. Not Douglas, who rang Hannah up out of the blue that evening to inquire about her health and well-being, about refinancing her mortgage, waiting for her to say something, say anything. Not Abigail, who when she dropped by later that afternoon to pass on the materials for voter registration, said in a loud voice, in Hannah's own kitchen: "Nu? Are you going to shtup him?" The question made Jeremy blush and leave the room, which made Hannah want to die. Even puberty hadn't been this well-monitored, this painful.

Out, out, if only Hannah could have cried. Out, Abigail, you nut, you well-intentioned busybody, you meddlesome best buddy, former partner in crime! Out, Douglas, you disappointing banker, you noncommunicative, repressed Republican, out, child who makes your own mother feel like you're the parent and *she* is the child! Out, Cara, out, Miss Narcissistic, Miss Draining, Miss Jappy Suffering Vulnerable Mess with your shrink bills, and your food bills, and your clothes bills and your phone bills! Out, Jack, and all memories of Jack, and middle

132

age, out, all time and circumstance that moved Hannah away, away from girlhood and beginnings and hope, away from those precious years when Ken was alive, away from the ever-loving arms of her own mother.

In the play room, Jeremy sat quiet as a cat. He was the only one left that Hannah could stand to be with. Eventually Hannah would get rid of Abigail, and Jeremy would have time alone with her. In this riot of scene-stealers, Jeremy was the patient one.

"They had a good marriage, didn't they?" Hannah asked Abigail. She poured her a mug of coffee and set it next to the Entenmann's blueberry-cheese coffee cake, still in the box, that Abigail was already forking away at.

"Lovebirds," said Abigail, her teeth flashing blue. She took a long sip of the coffee. "Hannah Gold, you make the worst coffee in Connecticut." She continued with her cake.

"Oh, Abigail," said Hannah, "maybe I'm too old for this. Maybe this is a mistake."

"Mistake-shmake," said Abigail. "Live a little, why don't you?"

Live a little, Hannah Schwartz Gold. Pretend, at least, to still be kicking. What harm would it do for you to get on with your life?

An hour away by car, an hour and a half by the Metro North, Cara was rifling through her phone book. It was Saturday, soon to be Saturday night. She could, of course, call Enrique, although she had told Ilana she would go with her to some opening—Ilana always had a crush on one "emerging" loser artist or another—and Cara had promised never to speak to Enrique again, anyway. She promised Ilana, that is, and her therapist. She had threatened Enrique himself: "That's a promise," she said. Then there was that dentist, the one her mother would really like. She'd recently met him at a party, and although she had no memory of him, no memory to speak of, he insisted that he had known her all her life, that they had gone to the same schools and everything. That he always had a crush on her. And, he had played Little League for a while with Ken, her older brother. The dentist was boring, but kind. He even produced a linen handkerchief when the mention of Ken made her cry—oh that name, that name still brought on tears, whether it referred to her brother, to a character on a soap, or even to the boyfriend of a Barbie doll. Yes, Cara could, for once, take a positive, healthy action. She could call up this nice and decent guy. Even Hannah had a date for Saturday night. Cara picked up the phone and dialed. She was not about to be beaten out by her own mother.

"Here's a tip," said Abigail. "After the Mondale defeat, Ruth, may she rest in peace, and I went to The Golden Buddha to tie one on. You know those funny drinks they had there in those plastic volcanoes? And she told me Jim liked to do it from behind." She sipped the last sip from her mug. "Like a dog," said Abigail.

"Abigail," said Hannah, "shut up."

Abigail stood up and gathered her papers together. She had eighteen errands to do before dinnertime. Tonight, they'd have takeout. Fred would be so tired he'd believe her when she told him the moo goo gai pan came from a recipe of his mother's.

"Do us all a favor," said Abigail. "Get lucky."

Hannah has a date. The cosmos has altered. In Vermont, Kitsie switched gears, put the roast back in the freezer, called up the baby-sitter. Doug's favorite jazz guitarist was playing over at the college. Kitsie herself had a new silk blouse Doug had her pick out for her birthday. They'd go to the concert and then maybe drive into Middlebury for a late dinner at Kitsie's favorite restaurant, and if it wasn't too chilly, they'd eat their fettucine on the porch that hung over the rushing stream that was high that year on snowmelt.

In the city, Cara struggled into a new black mini and a new set of black leggings, she powdered her cheeks, outlined her lips in carnelian red. The dentist had sounded happy to hear from her. He had mentioned dinner and a movie, or perhaps some live reggae. He loved music. Maybe he wasn't so nerdy after all. Cara could come out of this with a real boyfriend, the kind that called when he'd said he'd call, the kind a girl could confide in. She dressed carefully. She shimmered with anticipation. She radiated hope.

Even Fred had the fever. Another Saturday at the office. He spent the whole morning staring past his contracts out the window over the harbor of New York, dreaming of Hannah's creamy thighs. In Cuba, she'd worn skorts, those skirt-short combinations. Later, at the club, while struggling at tennis (a skill that seems easily acquired only by the young and suburban-born—his privileged offspring) Hannah's thighs in their tennis whites were marbled like a high-quality Stilton. The blue-on-white, like fancy stitchwork, was that much more attractive to Fred simply because the veins were brought about by pregnancy (he knew this from his own wife) and he'd always found fertility to be sexy. As a young man he had followed pregnant women on the street. As for Abigail, he had never loved her better than the three six-month stretches (for they had three children) he'd had to ski down the slope of her belly to get where he wanted to go. And then there had been that episode in the seventies when Hannah got wind of another instance of Jack's philandering, and Fred and Hannah made a pathetic attempt at an affair of their own. Hannah had been a tender, erotic disaster, she'd stripped down as far as her panties before collapsing into tears. The closest to sex Fred got was the swing of her breasts against his chest when he took her into his arms to comfort her.

Hannah has a date, thought Fred, all morning and through his afternoon meeting. It was like the first song of the day on the radio; he couldn't get it out of his head. By the time he got home that night, his sole goal in life was to make Abigail scream out with forgotten pleasure. He went straight to the upstairs bathroom and poured on the eau de cologne.

"Ma, you have a date," said Jeremy. He said it with delight. Jeremy was a kid who loved his mother. "What will you wear?"

"What will you wear, Mother?" said Cara on her fourth call of the night.

"I hope your mother wears that scarf we bought her for Christmas," said Kitsie to Doug, as they stopped at an intersection, waiting for a light. "What scarf?" said

Doug. "The teal-colored silk you liked so much," said Kitsie. "The teal-colored silk *you* liked so much," said Doug, and he leaned over to kiss his wife. A car honked its horn, but Doug paid no mind; he hung in there a little longer, which was nice.

What should I wear? thought Hannah, in bra and hose standing before the open closets. What? she thought, shifting her gaze toward the mirror. What? The bed was littered with outfits, the room looked like it belonged to a teenager, nothing she had tried on was right.

Hannah was in tears. She slipped on her robe, padded out into the hall, stood outside Jeremy's door and knocked.

"What should I wear?" said Hannah.

Jeremy opened the door to find an unhappy mother. Jeremy was getting used to things a person should never get used to.

"How about the sea-green silk scarf Doug got you for Christmas?"

"I'm Jewish," sobbed Hannah.

"I know," said Jeremy, softly. "How about the green silk scarf and your mustard-colored sweater?"

"Cara hates that scarf," said Hannah.

"Cara hates anything with color," said Jeremy. "Trust me, Ma," he said to her.

A long time ago Hannah had placed her trust in Jeremy. Why should this night be different? Hannah listened to him. She wore the bluish-green silk scarf and the mustard sweater and when Jim picked her up at her front door at eight o'clock sharp, he said: "What a beautiful color." Hannah thought Jim meant the scarf. Jeremy, hiding in the foyer, was sure Jim meant the color of Hannah's eyes.

*   *   *

They were blue, Hannah's eyes, blue bursting with yellow, as if the iris were a deep well that one dove into and the yellow was the resultant splash of water glinting in the light. They were blue, Hannah's lips, in the movie theater, although no one could tell because of course it was dark, the projectionist had turned out the lights.

On the screen was a madcap comedy, about a funny family, children who caused their parents nothing but strife, but who were loved and loved in turn, with a velocity that broke all the rules of physical science. Hannah and Jim couldn't help but laugh now and then in recognition, although the movie was profoundly depressing. Hannah was especially cold and miserable—the AC turned the theater the temperature of a frozen foods department. Her teeth chattered, so Jim passed her his jacket. It had been a long time since a man's jacket graced Hannah's shoulders, and she drowned herself in the comfort of his worn, professorial tweed. The owner of this jacket was a teacher, a principal. This fact tempered Hannah's misery. Anything to take her mind off the fairy tale unfolding in front of her.

The end of the picture was happy, but stupid. Parents and various children were all pregnant and beaming at the same time. The solution to the problems of the disintegrated nuclear family seemed clearly to be the production of more offspring. Hannah wept at this, she wept at their simple smiling faces, she wept with jealousy over the celluloid mothers who got to watch their children raise children of their own. She wept into the tweedy collar of Jim's jacket. What a dumb ending, thought Hannah. She hated that movie like poison.

What did Jeremy do as he sat at home, waiting up for his mother? He made phone calls, updates to his siblings. He pulled the extension cord from the kitchen into the dining room. He sat at the dining room table, because from there he could look through the glass doors and see outside. Outside was the yard, a collage of dark and darker shadows. Inside was Jeremy's reflection in the mirror of the glass.

At Doug's, Jeremy got the sitter; his brother and sister-in-law had already left the house.

Cara, who, courtesy of the cat, had a run in her legging, picked up the phone in a panic, screaming: "What the hell do you want?" After some fraternal calming, she asked for his advice: "Should I poke runs through both legs, or what?" Jeremy voted for the runny look.

Then he rang up Steven, his roommate, his heart. Jeremy had "come out" slowly, the way he would enter a cold ocean. He immersed himself in his friends' and family's reactions by degrees; he let them get used to him. By the time he had the courage to confront Hannah directly, she'd rehearsed the interaction many times in her head. Perhaps there was an element of disappointment, she meant to say, Jeremy *you* would make a wonderful father, although, "this" of course doesn't rule "that" out (Hannah would be trying), but I am always proud of you. Hannah wanted so much to be *there* for this child. The actual moment had gone somewhat differently: "I love Steven, Ma," said Jeremy, and Hannah burst into tears. And there they were again, Hannah dissolving in her chair, Jeremy at her feet, patting her hand, always ready to comfort her. They'd come a long way from that day; now Hannah sent Steven chicken soup when he got sick, she attended all of his acting workshop's performances.

"Give me the dirt," said Steven, "what was the old guy like?"

Jeremy dished Jim as best as he could, after all Jeremy

had only glimpsed the guy from the foyer. "He seemed nice," said Jeremy. "He seemed nice." The repetition was to reassure himself.

"Come home, already," said Steven. "Jeremy, I miss your guts."

But Jeremy couldn't leave Hannah like that, with no one to come back to. He promised to be home by Sunday, brunch.

Then Jeremy did something completely out of character. He hung up from Steven and dialed his father. He stood up to do this, moving the phone waist-high up onto Hannah's ironing board. He could see his reflection in the glass doors; it looked like he was standing at an espresso bar. The phone rang three times before Jack picked up. Jack had been balancing his checkbook.

"Dad?" said Jeremy, although he knew full well who Jack was.

"Ken?" said Jack. "Son?"

"Jeremy," said Jeremy.

"Jeremy," said Jack. "Of course. Jeremy." He said this as if he were reminding himself of something. "Jeremy. Everything all right?"

"Everything's fine," said Jeremy.

"Good," said Jack, "very good. I'm very glad to hear that, Jeremy."

They went on this way a little longer, before Jack passed the phone to Mags, Jack's stepdaughter.

"Come over and draw my picture," Mags said. Jeremy was an artist, so he promised.

"Next week," said Jeremy.

"Come over and draw my picture now," said Mags.

"*When*, Miss Maggie?" said Jeremy.

"Next week?" said Mags. She said it with hope.

When Jeremy hung up the phone he stood where he

was for a while. He imagined Hannah ironing. He imagined Hannah looking out those glass doors for something. He imagined Hannah looking at those glass doors and only seeing herself, ironing. He went into the playroom and turned on the television. A long lonely night stretched out before him, but Jeremy would wait up for her.

They ate at the new Italian restaurant, Jim and Hannah, the new one that Hannah thought might be part of a chain, that Pasta and Something. They ordered Chinese-style, Jim's idea, sharing some of everything, antipasto hot and cold, pasta puttanesca and frutti di mare. At first Hannah felt shy, but soon she wandered plate to plate with her fork, the way she had done for years in restaurants with her four children. Between bites, they argued over a local referendum. Hannah took the position that the referendum had only to do with its writer's penis size. As she spoke, Hannah wondered if she should be saying this. Jim laughed—he'd been in the locker room at the Health Club with this referendum-guy, and he thought Hannah just might be right. Jim laughed again, and said it probably wasn't fair to judge, without his glasses, Jim was legally blind. Hannah told Jim that as a teenager she had lied during her eye examination—she had hoped glasses would make her look smart. That's when Jim told Hannah it would be a shame to have anything come between a man and those beautiful blue eyes.

There was a wonderful silence.

Who knows who started gabbing again, but a few minutes later one or the other realized that in the sixties they had both worked in the same school system. And Hannah remembered aloud—how could she forget this—that Ruth, Jim's wife, had been Douglas's Social Studies teacher, that she had been marvelous with him, marvelous. This allowed Jim to talk, he talked about his wife with pride.

While he spoke—color heightened, eyes shining—Hannah thought about what Abigail had said, about Jim and Ruth, about doing it from behind. What had seemed intimidating hours before was now a little exciting. Hannah smiled. It pleased her that Jim had had good sex with his wife. Hannah felt happy that he had loved her. Wasn't that the trick in life? If you had it once, you could have it again. The ones who were in trouble were the ones who never got that close to anybody.

Jim caught Hannah's eye. "Why are you smiling?" said Jim. "Do I have sauce on my face?" And he did, which made Hannah smile more widely. This man, this Jim, he made things easy for her. Jim looked at his reflection in his water glass and laughed aloud. Then he wiped his cheek off. Hannah decided that Jim was very good-looking, just not in an obvious way. His face was long, but it had character. Behind his glasses, his eyes were sunk deep beneath his brow, but they were nice eyes, they were hazel. All her life Hannah had wondered what hazel eyes really looked like, but now she knew—it wasn't the color, it was that the irises looked rich, the consistency of hazelnut butter. And the lines—from eye to temple, cradling his mouth and chin like a child's string game, scored across his forehead—they made Jim look as if he had lived through something, as if he had bothered to experience life. Hannah liked that.

"Some comedy," said Jim. They were back to talking about the movie.

"As if having children could possibly be the solution to anything," said Hannah.

Jim nodded. He had a mouthful of garlic bread. He took a healthy slug of wine.

"That's when the tragedy starts," said Jim.

Hannah nodded with her heart.

"I heard about your boy," said Jim. "A thing like that shouldn't happen to anyone, but especially someone as good and kind as you."

A tear slipped out Hannah's eye. Jim touched the tear with his finger. He held it near to the candlelight. Hannah's tear, it looked as precious as a diamond.

"No more tears," said Jim. "Between the two of us there have been enough tears around here to last a lifetime."

But those tears kept coming. And the words, words she did not speak to anyone. Did he kill himself? Was her child a suicide? She couldn't stop herself. The window to her soul was open. Hannah was alive.

Jeremy was watching *Showtime at the Apollo* when he heard Jim's car pull into the drive. Jeremy watched this show every Saturday night he spent at his mother's. He liked the Apollo dancers with their feathered fans, he liked their spangled headdresses. They were campy, sure, but they were also a pretty sight. They reminded him that somewhere out in the world people were having a good time. Hannah fumbled with her house keys, Hannah always fumbled with her house keys, but Jim's car didn't pull away until Hannah unlocked the door and was safely inside. Jeremy stayed put where he was, in the playroom, on the sleeper couch, wrapped up in the old boat blanket.

Hannah tiptoed in.

"Hi, kid," she said. "You shouldn't have waited up."

"The Apollo dancers," said Jeremy. He pointed toward the television.

Hannah kicked off her shoes, she stretched her toes within the webbing of her stockings. She got on the couch next to Jeremy, so he threw her some of his covers. They both rested their feet on the same ottoman.

"The girl on the left looks a little fatter than last time," said Hannah.

"I know," said Jeremy, gravely.

They watched together for a while.

"Did you have a good time, Ma?" asked Jeremy.

"I did have a good time," said Hannah. "I really had a good time."

"So he said he'd call, he'll call," said Steven. Steven was trying to reassure him. Also, Steven wanted Jeremy home. "Jeremy, you can't wait with her by the phone." It was Sunday noon and past brunch. "Get your butt back here," said Steven; he was getting a little bit ticked off. "I'll be back by *60 Minutes*," Jeremy promised him.

"Of course he'll call," said Kitsie. She was working the waffle iron. "You called me when you said you'd call," Kitsie said to Douglas.

"So did he call her yet?" asked Fred. He was hanging over his wife's shoulder; Abigail was on the phone with Hannah, tying up the line. "Shhh," hissed Abigail. "Give him time."

"He'll call, Ma," said Jeremy. "I'm not leaving until he calls you." On Monday, Jeremy called in sick to the restaurant where he worked. He said to Hannah, "I'm sure he'll call by Wednesday." On Wednesday, Jeremy predicted Thursday night. By Friday, Jeremy wasn't talking. He took the 11:00 train back into Manhattan.

Sunday afternoon, over a week later, Abigail dropped by for coffee. Hannah had stopped picking up the phone, she let the answering machine do her answering—wasn't that what she paid good money for? She had Abigail worried. "You could call him too, you know," said Abigail. She took a sip from her mug. "You and your mourning. He's had enough of that, Jim. I bet you scared the wits out of him." She took another sip and considered it. "I hope you didn't feed him any of this coffee."

Fred took on a new client. He spent the whole weekend at the firm. He called Hannah once on Sunday evening, although he had no clue what he would say to her. He hung up in relief when he got her recording.

"There are other fish in the sea," said Kitsie, brightly, on the phone to Hannah. Douglas was working late in his home office and didn't have time to talk.

In the middle of the night, Steven woke Jeremy. "Promise that we'll never break up," said Steven. "Promise that I'll never have to go out there. I don't want to be alone." Jeremy was so tired he promised Steven what could not be promised by anyone.

"Sure, he'll call," said Cara. "Where have I heard that before? Christ, a confirmed date for Saturday night is only even money. There should be a law that they have to put down a deposit on your time. 'I'll call you.' Hunh. Fucking asshole. What a line. Jim. Hunh. What kind of name is that anyway? Jerk. Well, you can forget it, Ma, he'll never call. They never call," said Cara.

The dentist had been a dolt. Cara had been too much for him. Any way you sliced it, he never asked her out a second time. Cara waited two weeks before pronouncing him bald *and* boring.

As for Jim, what happened to him? Who knows? He got a little scared, maybe Abigail was right. He had enough of his own troubles. He meant to call Hannah, but it kept slipping his mind. He ran into an old girlfriend from high school, who had been a close friend of his wife. There was no scheme to this; he didn't plan to disappoint Hannah. He wouldn't have known why he didn't call himself, if someone had bothered to ask him. How was he to know how much was riding on this date? He'd liked her, Hannah, he'd had a good enough time. Not everything in life can be analyzed.

They met again three months later at the supermarket. Jim was browsing through the deli counter. Hannah caught his eye.

"Hannah," said Jim, a little bit surprised. "So nice to see you." He sounded like he meant it.

"Likewise," said Hannah.

"I've been meaning to call," he said. "Maybe sometime we could take in another picture?"

"I'm too busy," said Hannah, as if she'd be busy the rest of her life.

And it was true, from then on in Hannah was too busy, too busy with her garden, too busy with her children, too busy with her ironing. Jim's first pass through her life was at a fleeting and perfect time, in the same way that the planets crossed and shared their paths during that harmonic convergence Cara made so much noise about. Circumstance like this—Hannah open, the stars aligned— occur about once every other century. Hannah's window. She could only afford to reach through it and touch the sexy, messy land of the living this one last time. She wasn't made of metal. So Hannah'd risked and lost— wasn't that the story of her life? Better now to console herself with old and familiar pain, the rules she knew, the safety of her practiced suffering. Here, Hannah could count on performing well. She'd stand at her ironing board, look out into the yard and watch the months fly, each day taking her that much further away from Kenny. Instead of counting the years toward death, she counted the years away from his life, away from the feel of his touch (light), the smell of his breath (yeasty, like beer), his skin (baked bread), his hair (the precious sweat, the oil and salt of his exertion). At night she lay in bed immersing herself in the accident, replay after instant replay, so that when she dreamed, her dreams would be full of Kenny; she'd risk nightmare after nightmare in hope of resurrection. Often, Hannah awakened herself by screaming. The car, the tree, her son. Impact. It all seemed so real as she broke through the threshold of sleep, as if it were actually happening; her heartbeat would smash against her breath. This was the moment she was after, connecting one world with another, life and afterlife merging briefly, violently, like the fleeting prelude to a nuclear reaction. It was the closest she could get to her boy; his reach, his cry, his blood.

Could any Jim ever bring her as high as that?

Hannah had a date, a last one. And it was pale, pale beside the rapture of her grief.

This Is the Life

HERE we are.

Ilana's as oiled up as a girl can be without slipping off the chaise lounge, and I'm diving into my second Pisco Sour.

I love my husband. It's just that I like to get away every once and a while. He and I have a kind and gentle life. The first time I heard that phrase, I was kicked back and watching the TV. The screen was red, white and blue everything, and I thought, well isn't that the truth. Kind and gentle. Me and John, we entered our marriage the way you might enter a bath. Even now, five years later, we're both careful to not stir up the waters. And we like it that way—we're the type of couple who spends Saturday evenings in two big easy chairs each reading different copies of the same book. Sunday mornings, over coffee, we'll discuss it. John and I are the envy of all our friends; they can only describe us with good adjectives. But that's neither here nor there.

Me and Ilana, we're on a Caribbean beach, and John,

he's back in Westchester, probably fixing the garage door and listening to Mozart.

This morning I painted my toenails red for good luck. I have never painted them anything before. As a girl gets older, she understands the need for paint. When we unpacked, Ilana had seventeen little glass bottles; most of them for the skin, and under the eyes. I toyed with one or two, dabbing out the creams, spreading them thin across the back of my hands. The surface was smooth, but my skin looked just as cracked and dry underneath, like a painting under glass. Ilana said I could use some highlighter; in her mother's voice she said that I was looking "ghostly," so she rubbed peach onto my cheeks, something sticky on my lips, the sheerest blue above my eyes.

"No more granola-girl, Sylvie," said Ilana. "Now we're out for drama."

"Well, make me over," I said, and sat before her portable makeup mirror. I said, "This is why I came."

The water is sea-foam green, the sand is beach-colored. The pool back at the hotel is the color of ice, Ilana's contacts. My drink is pink. Everything here is light, light, light.

We do this once a year, Ilana and I, we go on an all-girl adventure. Last year we went to New Orleans, sucked down oysters and hurricanes, toured the swamps and plotted Ilana's way out of a relationship. This year the topic is Ilana's wedding.

The guy is the same guy, Pierre, the "emerging artist." His real name is Peter and he comes from Ohio, but he has been in the East Village long enough to qualify, to weasel his way into Ilana's large and fickle heart.

The island is Saint Martin. An hour and half ago we paid some local guy good money to transport us and our belongings (Ilana's lotions and potions, the hotel's towels, our rented snorkeling gear, two chaise lounges and a couple of thick, glossy *Bride's* magazines) out to a small, neighboring island. The boat was a speedboat. Our driver, a beautiful young man wearing nothing but a bright lavender thong. The other passengers were a topless Dutch lady (sort of heavy) and her three dachshunds. The Dutch lady is the driver's business partner—aside from boat rides and renting out snorkeling equipment, the two of them run a snack bar on the beach. The Dutch lady wore a pair of Ray Bans open on a cord around her neck. Her body was just pink, lightly seared by the sun. As we hit wave after wave broadside, and the boat shot through the spray, her breasts bounced, her sunglasses bounced, and I was sure her dogs, those little sausages, would fly off. I crouched down and clung to the seat for dear life. Ilana went white—and closed her eyes. The dachshunds sunned themselves on the prow of the boat like this quaking ocean was their own backyard.

The first all-girl adventure was to the Catskills. The purpose—to have a goof. It had been two years since my college boyfriend died, and I hadn't yet cheered up. Sometimes I think I still haven't. I met Ilana at his funeral. Isn't that funny, funny-weird, to meet your dearest friend at your boyfriend's funeral? It was August. The heat was limitless. The chapel, located in an outdoor mall in Connecticut. I was eighteen. The boy was twenty. We were officially broken up when he died. He had spent the last six months of his life cheating on me with every girl in sight, so for the summer, I gave him the boot. I figured I'd teach him a lesson—he humiliated me, and after he'd sleazed around with that first batch of freshman girls, I'd toughened toward him. I figured a couple of weeks without me and that jerk would come back crawling on all fours.

At the funeral I was a pariah. I had broken his heart, see. A dead boy. I told him to take a hike during his last four weeks. I think his mother blamed me. It was a single car accident. He was an impulsive kid, highly reactive, so I don't have to tell you what was on everybody's mind. Now, well over a decade later, I still wake up some nights thinking about what I did to help drive him to it.

I sat at the back of the chapel in a pew full of strangers like a scarlet woman. I was eighteen and I wasn't a widow. I carried the burden of being the romantic sum total of his short and dashing life. Up front Scott and Jake and Rip and Doc were the pallbearers. They looked so old, those boys in their suits and ties. They were the only ones I recognized besides his family, and I only knew his mother and his brothers, Cara his sister, slightly, from a Spring Break when we were fighting, from a Spring Break when the boyfriend brought me home. Ilana, thank God for Ilana. Ilana came to my rescue. Cara had pointed me out to her like a found object. Ilana sat beside me and said, "This must really suck for you," and the gratitude I felt at that moment put me into debt to her for the rest of my life.

Ilana spent the better part of the next few years reassuring me that I did nothing wrong. Over and over again, "You did nothing wrong, Syl," that was Ilana's theme song.

Ilana knew the boy forever; Cara was her best friend from childhood. Ilana even had a crush on him for a little while, although she spent most of her preadolescence mooning over Douglas, the eldest, handsomest, most fucked-up brother. She'd always liked the middle one fine, Ilana said, but she never quite understood why Cara was so nuts for him. Cara really believed he was God. To Ilana, he was just another geeky older brother who was

151

always doing crazy stuff, getting into trouble. She says her best memory of him was when he threw some neighborhood kid's fat mother into a pool. The mother had refused to let Cara's brother ride his bike off her diving board, ostensibly on to the other side—this was during the age of Evil Knievel. After he threw the mother in, the kid felt so badly, he brought her roses every day for a week. That was my old boyfriend. A real brat. A regular charmer.

On the first all-girl adventure we took Cara to the Catskills with us, which was an act of insanity, Cara has never forgiven me for being naked with her brother. It was one of those Borscht Belt places, with a lot of food and a lot of horny doctors and lawyers. The second night in, Cara slit her wrists. Ilana found her drunk and bloody in the bathroom. The cuts weren't deep enough to kill her, thank God, but they were deep enough to send her to her second round of loony bins, deep enough to mark Cara a nut-case for life.

I don't know why Ilana and I kept up the tradition after that disaster, but the next year we went camping in Vermont. We spent one trip in the airport Hilton in Phoenix; we never left the hotel room, just lounged around watching pay TV, reading magazines and tarot cards. Our best trip so far was a couple of years ago in Acapulco. I had been teaching Cheever's *The Swimmer*, I was getting my degree at Columbia, and Ilana (being semiliterary—she works in layout at one of those downtown magazines) and I decided to do a reenactment. We snuck into hotel after hotel along the coast, swam the length of each of their pools—if they had a length; some were heart-shaped, whale-shaped, one had Mickey Mouse ears—and we drank cocktails at each pool bar. By the end of the run it was sundown and I was drunker than I had ever been in my life. I puked my guts up into an azure sea. That's when I told Ilana that I was officially over Cara's brother, since I never knew for certain how I felt about him in the first place, the bastard; that's when I decided to marry my husband.

John is the kindest man I have ever known. He is an Art History professor. We met in grad school. I teach at SUNY Purchase, he teaches at Sarah Lawrence. There is nothing unusual about our story. You can fill in the blanks yourself.

He's probably out on the back porch, procrastinating on his research, sipping sun-tea and reading the *Sunday Times*.

John.

Ilana and I, we are lying on this "remote" beach, on chaise lounges, drinking Pisco Sours we got at the beach bar. A shack really, with two huge coolers filled with Coronas and a battery-operated blender. This is the life.

Ilana wants me to talk her out of marrying Pierre, the subtext to our journey. Last year in Louisiana, she wanted me to encourage her to stick with it, make things work. She likes to use me as a counterbalance, and I don't mind. Pierre is fine for Ilana, for now, for the next ten years. He's talented, and he is endearingly shy, but not a real mover-and-a-shaker. If Ilana gets a child or two out of this and a couple of paintings, she'll have done all right. When it comes to marriage, it makes sense to be practical. Right now, Ilana wants an "artistic" life, and Ilana's no artist. Eventually, I suppose, Ilana is going to return to the suburbs. Then, when she wants economic stability, maybe she'll need another man. Me, I wanted someone that I could stay married to, someone I could count on. So I'm for it, Ilana's marriage, and I'm not for it, I'm neutral, I'm kind.

"He's a nice guy," I say this sincerely to Ilana.

"Who wants nice?" says Ilana. "I want excitement."

"John is nice," I say, "You-know-who was exciting."
It's true, *he* was exciting. In college he snowed a local
pilot into taking us for a spin in his tiny plane; the
smoothie even talked the pilot into allowing him to take
over the wheel for a while. He steered us toward campus,
flying so low over the Arts Quad I thought I could pick
out my friends from the kids hanging out on the lawn.
We made love in all of our classrooms, we even did it
during a History lecture, in the back of a giant hall. Once,
when I was depressed (about God-knows-what back then,
the effect of depleted ozone on the environment?), so
depressed that I couldn't eat or sleep, the boy "borrowed"
one of his professor's cars and drove me out into the country to look at sheep. Sheep! That may not sound exciting,
but it was the most exciting afternoon of my life, he and
I in a field of sheep-and-more-sheep, holding hands, being
quiet, feeling shy.

A year and a half ago Ilana and I invoked a morato-
rium on the dead boy's name. Enough was enough
already; it was time to get on with our lives. Besides, Ilana
gets it all the time from Cara, who is obsessed beyond
belief with her dead brother.

Which reminds me. "Lana," I say, "is Cara going to
be your maid of honor?"

Ilana shoots me a look.

"If you don't mind." She says it like a statement.

I don't mind. I hate weddings. It's bad enough that I
have to *go* to Ilana's; I'm grateful not to have to get too
involved. I think weddings are acts of hostility against
your friends. First the gifts: wedding, engagement, bache-
lor party, bridal shower. Then if you are in the bridal
party it's an ugly costly dress and an uncomfortable pair
of shoes in a completely unuseful color; plus, you've usu-

ally got to travel. The food's bad, the band is awful. You spent the whole afternoon sitting at a table full of people you couldn't stand in school, trying to make uncontroversial conversation.

With John and me, it was a justice of the peace. His parents, my mother. Private. Ilana stood up for me.

"Did I tell you Cara met a dentist?" Ilana sits. She re-oils her arms, her naked breasts. Me, in an ancient Grateful Dead tee shirt over my swimsuit, I'm still covered up.

I laugh. "About sixteen times," I say.

"A dentist! I can't get over it," says Ilana. She flops back down again.

I love her when she's snobby.

Ilana thumbs through her stack of magazines. She says, "How can I wear white?"

"You just do it," I say. "Spend enough on a dress and you won't be able to back out."

"Cara's wearing black," Ilana says. She flips her hair, Cara-style, slides over to her side. She purrs: " 'It's my signature color.' " No one can mimic like Ilana.

This time we smirk together. Cara plans to be in mourning her whole life. At least this is what Ilana tells me, I haven't seen Cara in years (it's not allowed, I "upset" her) but Ilana keeps me updated. The truth is I am a little obsessed with being updated on Cara; I am constantly taking her emotional temperature from afar. Why? Maybe some weird loyalty-thing to her brother (who adored her); maybe because she is the closest thing to him that is still alive. Maybe because in her own crazy way she interests me—this beautiful, neurotic kid who's determined to do nothing with her life. She's a dabbler, in all those things it's easy to dabble in—acting classes, design school, fiction writing—for a while she even wanted to be a therapist. She's a course-taker, Cara; she never produces anything. Not true, I take it back. Cara is an endless producer of grief.

In India, it used to be that a woman would throw herself on her husband's funeral pyre. Sati. The death of a husband—the end of his wife's life. Over the years Cara has gradually turned herself into her brother's ancient Indian widow.

I listen to Ilana patter. All she needs is some encouragement, an occasional nod. We go over all the details of the wedding—it's going to be in the East Village bar where they met, her brother's band will play, Cara's mother will do the flowers.

"Wait a minute," I say. "Are all the Golds coming to the wedding?"

Ilana flips over like a fish. She plants her head in the opposite direction.

"Un-hunh," she says.

I am silent for a moment.

"You'll have John," she says.

I'll have John. My life is geared so that always, I will have John.

All of a sudden I can't bear to sit still. I stand up too quickly and the earth rocks, the water rocks, the sand rushes up toward my eyes so that everything shines gold—a hot, blinding light.

"Water," I say, and stumble toward the bright blue smear that stretches out before me.

Within seconds, I am in. A shiver shoots through my body and I am free. The water is releasing. My God, the sea is wonderful. I feel suspended in the lightest syrup; to stay afloat I barely have to move my arms. When we first got to the island, we did a little snorkeling. Ilana is braver than me, so I got her to hold my hand. The fish, neon against the clear blue—that's so blue it's green when you are submerged in it—darted around like butterflies. What I liked best were the jelly-weeds, the stringy sea creatures that I admit I'm not sure were plants or fish. They swayed to the winds of the water. As corny as it sounds, time seemed to stop down there, it was romantic, mysterious; Ilana's hand in mine, the two of us breezing through the sea like mermaids, waving around like we were the ocean's arms.

"Sylvie!" Ilana calls to me.

I stand up, blink the salt out of my eyes. The dachshunds are back from their run around the island; the Dutch lady went snailing, and here she comes down the beach with a mesh bag full of their curly black shells. Ilana is sitting up, she is laughing and pointing, because the dogs, in some weird birdlike formation, are headed toward me, shooting across the sand like little missiles. A small wave breaks, but this does nothing to deter them; they zoom torpedolike out into the ocean. I feel like a sitting duck.

I go under. From beneath the topskin of the water I can feel the dogs' little legs, like mutant thumbs, wheel and paddle by. One even touches my head with his paw, as if I were buried underground.

The air in my lungs shoots me up like a geyser. The dogs have waddled their way past me—and now it's clear: I was not their destination. The dachshunds spotted the speedboat; our driver is back from spear-fishing which he does, responsibly, from the other side of the island. Here, there are too many snorkelers, too many swimmers who assume that they are the focus of everyone's attention; it would be too dangerous for him to let one of his silver spears fly.

"Robert," I wave to him. He is dark, the thong so

157

bright it hurts the eyes. This young man really is quite
beautiful, the muscles in his back, his arms, his legs, ravel-
ing and unraveling as he bends over the side of the boat,
scooping the dogs up out of the water. Once safely aboard,
the dachshunds scamper back to the prow, into the warm
island sun. They are animals: they rest when they are
tired, eat when they are hungry, they know exactly what
to do to be happy.

"Would you like a drink?" Robert asks me, and he
points to the cooler he has been dipping in and out of since
we boarded earlier this morning. I hesitate only a moment,
some good-girl instinct that my mother successfully installed
like an electronic device when I was still a teenager.

"Sure," I say, my breath sending bubbles through the
water. I do the breaststroke because it allows me to connect the sea and the air, one landscape to another, and
because it's a lazy stroke, enough to keep me going, get
me where I want to go, but not too much energy needs
to be expended. I don't have to give it too much thought,
and I am lazy here on the island. I'm lazy at home, lazy
at life. Which is fine with me, and with John. He's a little
sleepyheaded himself, my husband. We live safely in the
suburbs without risks: we have a lightning rod on the top
of our house and one on the top of our garage. We plug
up our electrical outlets. We always wear our seat belts.
And twenty-four hours a day a radio in every room is
tuned into the same classical station. Like me, John likes
the dreamy, gentle smooth spots, the ease, the grace of
our safe life.

Oh, John, who may or may not be sitting by the phone
waiting for me to call him. John, who considers all-girl
adventures (and Ilana) a necessary evil in our marriage.
Who hates anything at all that connects me to the dead
boy and that vanished, youthful life.

Robert lends me an arm like he is throwing out a life-line. He reels me up and out of the water. I shake the wet out of my hair and sparks fly, like lightning bugs and daylight. We laugh at nothing, the way people sometimes do at the beach. I laugh because I am outside the fabric of my day-to-day; Robert laughs because he has managed to have his day-to-day exist outside of time. Now and now and now. There is no past, no future, floating out here on the Caribbean hammock of weaving water.

Again, the roof of the cooler swings back, Robert's hand plunges into its glassy, icy depth—he fishes out two Coronas. "I even have limes," says Robert, and he works his knife like a sushi-chef, flashing out green slices, stuffing them into the bottle's long throat. We click the lips of the beers and then down them hard—salt air makes you thirsty. I kick back and lie on one of the boat seat's inflatable cushions.

"Oh, God," I say. "God, God, God."

Robert laughs again, and shows his teeth. I close my eyes. From behind my eyelids I can see the sea and sky, only now they are veined and obscured, like I am living inside a leaf.

"God," I say. I sound like a teenager.

Robert's been futzing with the tape deck so now there's music. Jim Morrison's deep throaty voice seems oddly fitting out here although I have no idea why, except that like The Doors, being out here on the boat with Robert reminds me of what I felt like when I was younger. He passes me another beer.

"To us," says Robert, and we click bottles. "To us," I say and drink so fast that my throat clenches and the cold beer hurts going down.

On shore, Ilana waves to us. She is standing, long-muscled and firm. All those aerobics classes have kicked in, her arms are strong and ropey, from up close her stomach is banded, her calves and thighs sharply defined. She is acting out something, like charades, she swings her arms like a cheerleader, and her high, white breasts roll. It's hard to tell exactly what Ilana's miming, but there's some cute, young guy—looks like a college kid—at her side, so I wave her off. I even touch my nose, to indicate that I've got it, whatever message Ilana was trying to send out. They head off down the flat sandy path that cuts from this beach all the way across the island to a rocky cove. I watch Ilana walk from behind, and for a second I like her a little less. In the past two years my skin has begun to sag a bit off my bones.

"To Ilana," I say, and Robert bartends us another round. "To the dogs," says Robert, and he points his bottle at the prow. The dachshunds loll like miniature sea lions, they loll like giant slugs.

"How long have you lived here?" I ask, to be polite, to make conversation.

"Do you want to dance?" Robert says, ignoring me.

Why not, I think, I've always loved The Doors. The sunbathers on the beach are too consumed with their tan lines to focus their binoculars and watch us. They are all half-naked anyway, I'm the one who is covered up. There is nothing here to be self-conscious about.

Robert gives me a gorgeous smile.

"Sure," I say to Robert.

Dusk comes to the islands in shades of pinks and oranges. Even Robert has taken on a rosy tone. A half hour ago, the Dutch lady got tired of waiting for Ilana, and hitched a ride back to the main island with a passing yacht.

Robert and I agreed to take custody of the dogs. We've switched from beers to wine, from Jim Morrison to Frank Sinatra. We lie legs entwined on the bottom of the boat.

"To my husband," I say as Robert passes me the bottle. The wine is as dark and dry as blood. I swig, and click my teeth against the glass. Robert holds the bottle up into the dying light. "To both my wives," says Robert, and we explode into fits of giggles.

Here's what we've learned about each other in the passing hours of what I now suppose is Ilana's "last fling": Robert was born and raised on the main island. His first wife was his island wife; his second, the one he got in the States where he went for two years to make his fortune. He came back to Saint Martin simply because it is heaven on earth, and he was busted broke in California. Here, he collects conch, spear-fishes, entertains lonely tourists on his speedboat, brings them to beaches like this for snorkeling. He makes out fine. His second wife, a Californian surfer-chick, lasted a year and a half and then felt compelled to return to "real life." "Why," asked Robert, "can't real life be full of pleasure?"

Why?

What Robert knows about me is more than I know. He knows my secrets because Robert has read my palm. Like him, I will have more than one spouse—a thought that both intrigues and frightens me—and many, many lovers. When I made a fist for Robert, he translated the side of my hand into his prediction: that I will one day have twins—daughters. But the section of my hand that made Robert sad, the section that brought tears to his caramel eyes, is somewhere near my thumb. Robert patted the spot, and looked up at me, his eyes a swirling melt.

161

It broke his heart what he read: that my one true love had died. That's when we pressed our lips together in a first kiss, that's when we broke out the wine.

Where oh where is Ilana? Why oh why don't I swim back ashore and go after her? How come the dachshunds never get tired of sleeping on the rocking nose of the boat? Could they be narcoleptic, or dead? Could they be lying in a collective canine coma?

The sea is awash with mysteries. Robert's face speaks nothing of his soul. His hands reveal nothing of his heart. His skin is a curtain, his lips the only connection to whatever demons rattle around inside him. He speaks of his own lost love, the California girl, the one who went back home after a whopping eighteen months on the island in order to make it big in the movies. He alludes to some terrifying episode—drug smuggling, some scam involving tourists, a murder? my mind reels—the prelude to her departure. What makes this island man tick? Is he dangerous or just sexy or both? Where is Ilana? What is my lonely husband doing at home? If I left him for good, as Robert seems to think I will do soon, where would dear John go?

Right now I can live with all these questions.

I'm in Robert's arms. I could care less about John, about Ilana. We tangle up, sip our wine from each other's bottle, the way lovers sip champagne in those old movies. Some spills down my neck and Robert cleans me off with his soft, patois-speaking tongue. I experience momentary panic.

"Ilana. John." I say their names out loud to anchor me. "Ilana. John."

Robert repeats them out loud, soft as an echo, light as the ocean air. "Tell me, darling, about your dead young man." He talks like a sweet, silly love song.

So I tell. Out here there is nothing to lose.

*   *   *

Last year, after the jaunt to New Orleans, I had a dream. Dreams are boring I know, especially other people's dreams. It always seems like the dreamer is a liar, editing the story here and there, spicing up the Freudian stuff. But God as my witness, I am telling the truth.

I dreamed that I was lying on a boulder in the swamp. The rock below me began to squirm. Then, in typical dreamlike fashion the rock was no longer a rock at all, but an alligator camouflaged to look like a rock to lure me. The creature opened its long jaw and bit out all my reproductive organs. When some locals happened upon me, not bleeding—just hollow, curled empty on my side—a man said in his Cajun accent: "How did she let it happen—the gal's been around 'gators her whole life."

I woke up to one honest sentence.

Ilana never reappears at the shoreline. Perhaps all that earlier prancing around was to say that she would go back to the hotel on that college boy's boat. Perhaps he is a serial rapist or a murderer. Perhaps the both of them have drowned. I am a little worried, but too headachey to give it too much thought.

Robert wipes himself off. He bounces up, steps back into his thong. Then he uncorks the last bottle of wine.

"One more for the road," says Robert.

The dogs yip and yap. They scramble down to the floor of the boat, so I get up and adjust myself. Those poor puppies must be hungry. The moon slides a white path across the water. The big island looks like it is strung up with Christmas lights.

I am crying.

"What's wrong?" asks Robert. He looks tired.

I say: "If Ken hadn't died I bet my whole life would have been different."

I believe this to be true.

"Who?" says Robert. "Oh, that boy you were lovers with at school?"

"Yes," I say.

"To *Ben,* then," says Robert, and he raises the bottle high.

"To *Ben,*" I say, when Robert passes me the wine. He bends over to start the motor. The boat coughs against a few small waves and then takes off at a steady clip. Inside, everything—towels, puppies, empty bottles—flies. We follow the moon's walk across the water.

The night air crackles with jeopardy. It's as if the starshine were whispers of lightning. Wherever the lights, from the stars, from the boats, from the shore, hit the water they hiss—the darkness steams, it radiates energy.

Ahead is the main island, most likely Ilana, and a message at the switchboard from my husband.

"Ilana," I say out loud. "John."

"Ken." I cry his name. The ocean is black. The air is warm. The sky is star-light.

"I love my husband," I say. Robert is busy with the motor. I am not sure if he hears me. Wave after wave slaps the boat aside.

We rocket toward the harbor.

Back at the hotel room, Ilana is furious.

"Where the hell have you been?" she says. "I was scared out of my mind. What was I supposed to say to John?"

The college boy took her back on his boat, my husband

left five frantic messages. They passed the test; Ilana and John performed exactly as I hoped they would.

I sit on the edge of my double bed and shake.

Ilana comes up with something witty and original. "You look like you've seen a ghost," she says.

When I was young I thought everything that happened to me was just practice, preparation; I kept waiting for my real life to start.

"This is my real life?" I ask Ilana.

Ilana sits down next to me on the bed. She pats my hand. "Sure it is honey," she says. "Now, you'd better call John. He's worried and he's going out at nine."

The first Sunday night of every month is our Town Council meeting. Sunday is also the night John always forgets to put out our recyclables for collection.

I pick up the phone, engage the switchboard. I tell the operator I have to make a collect, person-to-person call to the States, although there is nobody else who could answer our phone at home. The operator patches me through. The phone barely rings and then, the miracle of my life, the miracle I have grown to count on. The phone rings, and John picks up. "Hello," he says. "Are you all right?"

Oh God, I love my husband.

"Honey," I say. "I'm fine." I say, "Did you remember to put out the garbage?"

And in this manner, we begin again.

Nephews

OUTSIDE, something was wrong with the Milky Way. It was warped. Like a record. And it had wavy edges, ridged like a chip or fries. That's what Evan said and he knew, he knew from reading the newspaper. Also it was cold outside, really cold, the kind of cold where your eyelashes could stick together and you could go blind, one of those freak spring storms. Even from inside, looking out through the window, the cold made everything go watery, steamy, almost the same as with smoke, with fire. And it was dark, a very bright, very white dark beyond the house, the snow looming like ghosts in big glowing heaps, misted with night air charged by snowlight.

Inside wasn't a whole lot less frightening. Kenneth Gordon Gold II was being held hostage. On the couch. After having broken his ankle the week before in a game of touch football (in the parlor), his older brother Evan had the nerve one very long half hour ago to make away with Kenneth's crutches and leave him helpless and pitiful in the living room. Mom was at the store seeing what she could do about dinner and cheering the boys up. Dad was far away at Grandma's because Aunt Cara was having another one of her nervous collapses. Kenneth was at Evan's mercy.

Evan hated him, always had, always would. This is what Kenneth had to believe in, it was his constant, his measuring device. How much Tommy Lieber liked him was about half of Evan's hatred. Mom's love was close to equal. Dad's seemed sort of far away, linked to another place and time. Even among these givens, there was room for fluctuation. Dad floating in and out—paying him special attention. Mom when she was mad, even then, never close to Evan. Evan himself, intensifying, hating Kenneth more and more as the minutes of his short little life ticked past.

As far as Evan could go, that's how far he went, now. Kenneth knew this from the set of Evan's teeth, sort of crooked and fangy. He knew it because one short half an hour ago Evan had swung that crutch down hard onto the special spot on Kenneth's neck where even if you barely touched it, you were instantly a dead man.

Kenneth was not a dead man. Of this he was positive. Dead men weren't nearly as hungry as he was marooned out on the couch that way—although after the wood had fallen he had expected to see stars at least, or some fat little angel babies. What he had seen was Evan all scared and crying, believing himself that this secret neck spot was the way once and for all to get rid of his brother. Evan was crying for fear of what was done to boys who knocked off their siblings, Kenneth was sure. He was sure Evan was already concocting some scheme to prove how it wasn't really Evan's fault, how Kenneth *made* Evan kill him. At first Kenneth had lain there stunned, holding his breath, trying to milk the moment, but Evan was smart, everyone said so, and he saw Kenneth's eyes flicker instead of staring, so he knew that Kenneth was just a faker and lousy at it. That's when Evan took the crutch away again, and went off into his own room. Probably to read a science book, if Kenneth knew him, and he knew him all right, knew that he wouldn't emerge, come to his rescue unless he, Kenneth, the baby, begged him.

His begging days were over.

In Connecticut, Cara was sleeping upstairs, or what was equivalent to sleep, lost in a narcotic haze of fitful patterns. Hannah, her mother, had turned the room, still outfitted with Cara's girlie furniture—the pink shag, the canopy bed, about a million Barbies—into a bower, as if the blossoms themselves could give her color, as if their scent would billow her up to some happy height. Flowers could not, would not, do the trick, and Hannah knew this, having unfortunately been down this road before. But since the accident that took her middle son and was the convenient excuse for Cara's constant state of collapse, Hannah had learned to find pleasure in gardening, the scramble of mulch, of soil, the tiny, perfect seeds, the surprising yield of living things, the squirmy creatures that tunneled through the rich, moist earth.

Even now, in the cold of early spring, when she entered the greenhouse, to plant and prune, train and weed and pull, Hannah was amazed by the smell of it, the steam of it, sexier than sex had been, thank God. For although there was loneliness, loneliness so familiar it kept company, Hannah didn't believe she could ever let go of herself that way again for fear of falling, falling out of her body into some unending hole—of what?—of being? Now, many years after the accident, years after her divorce, several dating experiences that could scar a teenager for life (experiences that still made her want to run, hide, whenever they came to her, in flashbacks, reruns) she traded in her king-size for a single bed. Bought new sheets and comforters, a brass headboard, and relaxed. So many things would go undecided, left to the fates. Not this one.

But in the greenhouse, she'd let go gladly, losing herself to herself, forgetting time and space, the inescapable fact that she was a mother. In a world clearly bereft of miracles, a true miracle: things wanted to live. These things that wanted to live struggled determinedly and rose from the decay of leaves and plants and other flowers before them. The soil was electric with the elements that rained down as the result of the death of distant stars. One of her kids—who could remember which—suffering through high school astronomy had passed on this amazing fact, casually, probably over pizza, or fast food, a beer tossed back so matter-of-factly its drinker hoped she would not notice he was drinking at all. Hannah was shocked with the way he shrugged it off, the beer drinker and his amazing fact (he, for she knew it was a son, she never mistook Cara's actions for anyone else's as they were so plainly, so decidedly, Cara's), this precious information that informed the rest of her thinking about what lived and died, what the cycle itself was all about. So much death in all of it.

After what had happened in the past few years Hannah was weary. Even with Cara, she was weary of the weakness of her daughter. In effect, Hannah had developed an odd, cynical edge, with which she surprised herself. Hannah was supposed to be supportive, kind, giving. Hannah. The one who was sure to *understand*. This had been changing, no gentle shifting of climate, but rather

her own exponential rise of temperature, her very own greenhouse effect. It snuck up on them all, born from the steady stream of destruction that was the collective history of their family, and then descended all at once. Hannah, sweet, good, *motherly* Hannah striking out in odd strikes of anger, of sarcasm, savaging random as bolt lightning.

In the garden it was different. Pure. Simply, she liked to watch things grow.

Hannah poured coffee. The kids had chipped in for her Hanukkah gift, or Winter Solstice gift, as they now celebrated the holiday, her shamefully assimilated brood. They had gone to the infrequent trouble of contacting one another, Cara probably the ringleader after Doug called to remind Cara into action. Hannah knew her children.

She could see it, Doug carrying out the practical, the responsible role; Cara, thus programmed, and in a tizzy, searching out the most expensive, most "perfect" gift she could charge. Then Cara, ever Cara, upon discovering that charging indeed led to bills and bill collectors, declaring to her brothers that they would have to lend her the funds (Hannah was sure of this, not realizing that she herself had been the one to lend those very same funds to Cara) to buy this terribly complicated, and as far as Hannah could tell, useless machine. Sure, it espressoed and cappuccinoed, blew fluff into glasses of warm milk. But who wanted fluffy milk? Wasn't the pleasure of fancy coffee going out to a fancy place to order it?

That machine ground its own coffee beans, leaving its owner with that much more time on her hands. And then an alarm could be set, days ahead even, so that when one woke, one found a full pot steaming fresh.

Hannah despised that machine, it lacked humanity. If she were to disappear during the night it would happily continue on without her, wasting a pot of good coffee, with no one left to drink it. This is what she hated most: the waste of it all. Her flowers for instance, the big, empty house, the money she set aside toward Ken's college and (prayerfully) even graduate school. Herself as a mother, full and brimming, readied to pour.

Her child was dead.

And this other one, this Cara, hovering over the edge of life: the only activity she had proven to be any good at, an expert, Cara, at threatening to fall. So when Hannah brought out *her* pot—Old Reliable—the coffee cups from her wedding, some of those Mallomar cookies the kids (even though it would be a joke to call them kids any longer) were so hot for, she held her breath for a second, and sure enough, Doug opened up with his signature manly scold.

"Ma," Doug said, "I wish you'd use that coffee machine we bought you."

"Oh," said Hannah, "I do, I do," like an overeager bride. "But tonight, since it's just us," Hannah continued, "I wanted to use the old stuff." Which didn't make a whole lot of logical sense, but was just enough clucking, Hannah knew, to appease him.

He was her firstborn and clearly the handsomest of her children, the most tense of her children, the most restricted, the most responsible. So far he was the only one to have kids of his own, the only one to marry, even, and not too well, Hannah thought. On this subject she and her ex-husband finally had something on which they agreed: Doug's marriage as a disappointment. Her daughter-in-law was all right, one of those blandly pretty shiksa princesses, always in headbands and short skirts. Nothing was exactly wrong with her, she was just so airy, in conversation you passed through her like a jet through a cloud. Kitsie was sweet and kind and all, Hannah would give her that, but she had the personality of a throw pillow.

"Ma," said Doug, "something has to be done about Cara."

"And just what would you have me do?" said Hannah. "She's too old to be given up."

On the couch, with the coldest cold there ever was looming beyond the window, twisting its way through the trees to freeze you stiff as a dead bird, Kenneth resolved once and for all to stand up to Evan, even though without his crutches he could not stand up at all. He'd show Evan who was the boss around here, tell him to get out of this house until Evan could behave himself, act mature. Mom said Kenneth had to learn to fight his own battles, and Dad, Dad seemed never to believe him when he came crying about the things Evan had done. That Evan was smart all right, he would lure Kenneth in, invite him to play a game and Evan's games could be fun, they could be adventures, so Kenneth was bound to say sure, become a willing victim, even when he expected the worst.

The funny thing was that they would have fun at first, the boys would, like tonight for instance, when they played private detective before Mom went out for the groceries and Evan changed the game on him. "I proclaim that now the game is: I get to beat you up for a dollar," said Evan. And when Kenneth said, "No way," Evan said, "Okay, I keep the dollar," which is how Kenneth ended up almost dead and crutchless and Evan got to work on his science project which would surely get an A.

It was unfair. It was unfair that Evan was crueler and smarter and stronger and cleverer. It was unfair that everyone liked Kenneth best. There were two sides to this story, Kenneth could see that much, but was it his fault after all, that he was the favorite? He didn't ask to be born second. When Mom explained it, this is what it was all about. Not the favorite part, Mom would never say that, but the coming in last, being the baby. Sibling Rivalry, Mom said. It was a burden. And then the fact that Kenneth was named after Dad's dead younger brother, which made him, Kenneth, special, more chosen. He would sit on the floor by Dad's side while Dad read the newspaper, and when he was very still, Dad's hand would pass back and forth over his head, lightly, lightly, like he was a puppy. After, when Kenneth looked in the mirror, his hair looked extra shiny, and it lay quiet, which never happened when he or Mom combed it, then it wheeled out in a spiral, the center like a bull's-eye, Dad's bald spot. Evan, well Dad never petted Evan that way, but then again Evan never had the patience to sit still. As Mom said, you have to look at something from all angles, which effectively disarmed him, Kenneth, because when he looked at things from all angles, usually Evan had a point.

Not this time.

Kenneth needed strategy. When Dad figured something out in business he divided things up, where he was weak and where he was strong. Kenneth, on the couch, crippled, was actionless, but he could "reason" with him, with Evan, he could "negotiate," and then when Evan was unaware . . . ZOPPO!—he'd be an easy victim. The lamp crashing down on Evan's skull. The letter opener through his heart like a vampire, sure to die. He could trip him, Kenneth could, so Evan's head would crack open and his brains would ooze out. Or he could make him drink one of his own science experiments, poison him,

Evan, burn his throat, eat through the walls of his guts.
Kenneth had options.

"Evan."

He called out to his brother.

Right after the accident, Hannah noticed that people
stopped asking about her children. Years later, they pre-
tended that Kenny did not exist, that he was never alive.
They just skipped over him, asked Doug this, asked
Jeremy that, asked voice hushed, eyes lidded about Cara.
And then, thank God, she had grandchildren, grandchildren everyone could ask freely about, could crow over for
godssake, when Hannah fished out her most recent pho-
tos. But during the first few years after the accident—
what a word! An accident was spilled milk, a broken vase,
wetting the bed, that was an accident—no one showed an
ounce of curiosity, human interest. At the supermarket, at
the middle school where she worked, at the pool, they
stopped asking. It was as if her children were all little
dominoes, one falling, knocking down the other—which
was the way it was in life really, one fell, knocking the
others down. Only in her most private moments did
Hannah stop blaming her dead young son for whatever
present family crises she was in the midst of, and recognize, for his sake, that the family had been in trouble
before. His accident, a convenience really, when it came
time to assign blame.

After all these years, nothing had returned to normal,
not even with her closest friends, her confidantes. A new
normal took its place, a "post-Ken" reality, Cara called
it. So Hannah was grateful, really grateful, when she ran
into an old high school chum at the ballet at Lincoln
Center a few months back, a girlfriend from so long ago

she didn't even know if Hannah had children at all. The woman talked on and on about her own son, her daughter having turned out well enough. She was heartbroken. Her son was a Republican lawyer who went to Bhopal for Union Carbide. Hannah comforted her. "There are mysterious things beyond our control," Hannah told her, "there are reasons for the un-understandable." And when the woman got around to asking Hannah about herself, Hannah declared rather blithely that she had never married. She was one of those free spirits. No offspring.

Looking at Doug now, she wondered if he, too, had voted Republican. He was such a conservative sort. How did he come from me, thought Hannah. As a teenager he had worn his hair as long as the rest of them, and he had done the whole Vermont farm bit, so she'd had a surprise when years after college he opted for B-school, a shock, when he brought that girl of his home. The one before her had been quite lovely, a bright girl, a girl with a mind of her own—not one of those spineless females who just doted on him—and consequently she broke his heart quite heartlessly which led almost instantly, Hannah thought, to this present disaster, this Kitsie. Putty really, yes putty, hair putty-colored, neither red nor yellow, but putty-pink, silly putty that he could fashion into whatever he desired her to be.

Cara said: "She's like New Age music," and while Hannah wasn't quite sure what New Age was, she got her drift, so to speak. That was one of the few delightful things about her, about Cara, her ability to sum things up. And as much as Cara adored the brother she lost, worshiped him even, even more, that was as much as she despised this oldest son. Doug. Wound tight as a spring.

"Sexist," said Cara. "An emotional fascist. The truth is," said Cara, "Doug is psychically bald."

Hannah looked at her psychically bald son. Her Reagan-supporting progeny, her middle-aged child. And remembered. Remembered how responsible, how dutiful, how economically solvent Doug was. Hannah remembered how much she relied on him.

"What would you have me do?" said Hannah. Calmly.

"Kitsie and I want her to come and live with the boys and us," said Doug.

Hannah was speechless.

"She needs a change," said Doug, "new beginnings. A real stable family setting."

Cara in Vermont? Cara and cows? Cara and pasture?

"You must recognize by now that you have no control over her," said Doug.

"She's a grown-up, Douglas," said Hannah. "I am not supposed to have control over her."

"She's a mess," said Doug. "What she needs is a little discipline, a little continuity, a little structure. Fresh air, Ma," he said, "grass and trees."

"You make her sound like a poster child," said Hannah.

And then, a moment or two later, "Besides, Cara can't stand that wife of yours."

Hannah did an imitation. She stretched out on the sofa Cara-style (which was paradoxically languid and loose, and nervous and brittle, as if she were a figurine of graceful glass anxiously waiting to crack), she flipped her head back, ran a fan of nervous fingers through her hair.

"*Mother*," she drawled, "with Kitsie, there's no there there."

Doug stiffened. "It was Kitsie's idea," he said, "and it was a good one. A Christian one," he added.

Hannah shot him a look.

"I mean it in the sense of the Judeo-Christian ethic," Doug said, "and you know it. Ma. Don't give me that look."

There was silence.

"Just what the hell kind of a name is Kitsie, anyway?" said Hannah.

Upstairs, Cara, flanneled in a pair of her dead brother's old pajamas, tossed in and out of sleep, trying to guide her dreams. It had been a tough week. She had succeeded, finally, in destroying everything, simply everything she touched. No more Enrique, no more Neighborhood Performing Workshop, no more rent money. A final breach with Ilana. And then running up that phone bill of hers again, with her hateful rants, with her threats and predictions, her promises, crying, crying, slamming down the phone, picking it up and dialing again, any number that she could remember, camp friends, old lovers, her mother, hanging up before a voice came on. Hannah had called the police in to restrain her, which was embarrassing really. Cara inconsolable, answering the door outfitted in those very same pajamas that she refused, then and now, and whenever else she was collapsing, to take off. Cara, feeling very skinny and pathetic, sobbing at the Boys in Blue—and one of them pretty okay-looking—to go stop a murder or something, didn't they have anything better to do, play in traffic even, just please fucking leave her alone.

Hannah arrived one long hour and a half later, in a flurry of fear and anger, took one look at her, at Cara, and then she led Cara out to the car like a halfwit, bundled her up in the backseat, swaddled her in the old boat blanket like she was barely two years old. And took her home. A mother has no options. Cara counted on this. Cara the child was taken home.

Kitsie was at the market. White light glazed the fruits, the vegetables, huge and oversized, laid out in a palette of irrational color. The eggplants were white, the peppers yellow and red and black-purple. The cauliflower was the color of carrots and the carrots, vice versa. Displayed were red-leaf lettuce heads and pink-dotted beans and apple-green, hard little tomatoes, bouncy-tough as rubber. Here, nothing was as it should be, none of it local but produce flown in from faroff and distant countries, and from Florida, from California, and yet everything was prized, for being foreign and unexpected, for being not as you were raised to think they should be. Kitsie liked it. She liked the colors, the shapes, the vitamins jam-packed behind the thick and thinner skins of the fruits and veggies she handpicked and laid in her basket for her family. Here was reprieve really, no kids, no husband, no immediate needs to be attended to. Just pretty fruit. So she was careful with her selections, with her inspections. Kitsie took her time.

Could it be, thought Hannah, that finally I am old?

Doug was looking at her that way again, that fleeting blink of a look, fast as a camera's shutter, that captured everything, from the knuckles that were beginning to lean in opposing directions, to the light, frecklelike brown spots that were beginning to adorn them, to the whitening of her silver hair. Lately, she had seen this look, as quick as it was, flash from child to child. Cara, typical Cara, had burst forth last month over lunch with—"Oh God,

Mother, you look old enough to die." It had struck her as funny, even then, that Cara still believed in a childish age:life ratio, as if youth had ever protected anyone, as if a certain amount of years was something you were entitled to. But with Doug it was different. He knew better than to give her the once-over. So she chose to stare him down.

"Forgive me, Ma," said Doug, in a rare moment of insight.

He was her son.

Hannah sighed. "How are the boys?" she said.

"The boys are fine, Ma, just fine," Doug said, and then, "You know how much Cara adores them," which was true and not true; Cara liked to think that Cara adored them. She liked to kneel down when they were little, talk to them from their own diminutive height, but only when she had an audience, someone to document the prettiness of the sight. Cara in a skirt—when she still wore the long billowy kind, before everything went black, got narrow, glovelike—hooping around her like a cloud, the boys whispering in her ears, Kenneth on tiptoe, their faces facing high. For Cara was pretty; neurotic, thin, but still incredibly pleasing to the eye. And Hannah knew her well enough to know that the whole time she was on her knees, curly head bent kid-level, face inclined, she was thinking about how she appeared from the outside.

Now that the boys were older, "real people," Cara said, she was both more and less interested. The cuteness factor was fading, preadolescent gawk was setting in, but they captured her attention; Evan with his incisive wandering mind, and especially the baby, little Kenneth, because of his sunny side, yes, but mostly because he was the namesake of the one person Cara truly put before herself, her brother that died. And this little guy having practically the same exact birthday—Kenny I born on the fourth, Kenneth II the sixth of November—thus she imbued him with Kenny's spirit, turned him from boy to instant treasure, a recipient of her aborted emotions, a toy substitute, a human sponge. There wasn't anything Cara wouldn't have done for either of them, her brother or her nephew. Or at any rate, that's the way Cara would like to have it remembered—Cara truly putting someone before Cara, a Cara who was unselfish, a Cara who loved.

Hannah hated herself.

"How's Evan's science project coming along?" said Hannah.

"He's a whiz, that kid," Doug said. "Kitsie tells me his teachers are amazed by him."

"And little Kenneth," said Hannah, "how is my sweet boy?"

"Just terrific, Ma," Doug said. And then, "Ma" (pause) "let me broach the subject with Cara. It would be good for her, I know it, it would be good for Kitsie and me and the boys."

"Douglas, your guilt is showing," said Hannah.

"Ma, just try and support me on this one," Doug said, sounding a whole lot like his father, the man who always asked for support, but never seemed to want any at all.

Hannah looked at the floor, the table, the wall. Her eyes were swimming.

He doesn't even like her, she thought.

"Douglas," said Hannah, "she's all yours."

He lured him in, Evan. He volunteered to play his way. "Evan," Kenneth called out, "I'll play Jelly-on-the-Feet, I'll play Boot Camp." But Evan wasn't so easily won over. "You are physically incapable of playing either one," said

Evan, "plus, you are a hopeless coward." "I'll play Master-Slave," said Kenneth, which was about as brave as he could get and therefore turned out to be the clincher that drew Evan out of the bedroom and into a position where Kenneth could finally take some vitally important but still unknown action.

So Evan was there, smart Evan with his long face and sharp chin, with his red hair, Mom's hair, and his lips and eyelids, all his skin, covered with freckles. Evan was there, bratty and smart and strong and frightening and incapable of brotherly love. Evan pale. Evan pale-eyed. Evan's pale blue eyes narrowed down to two hard shafts of blue, ballpoints.

"You don't really want to play," said Evan, Evan with his ESP, "you just want to trick me." He had X-ray vision. He was a closed-circuit monitor. He could loop the tapes that ran through Kenneth's head, rewire them.

"You never want to play to the end," said Evan.

He was a boy full of God. Powerful, frightening.

"Will too," said Kenneth, "I'll play to the end." Not stopping to figure out why now, tables turned, he was begging him.

"You are bad," said Evan, "bad boys have to be punished." He stood poised at the edge of the couch. And then . . . shot out of a cannon, Evan, Evan running the room, leaping from overstuffed chair to overstuffed chair, from coffee table to end table to loveseat cushion. Evan in motion, flying, around and around the room, bridging each gap like an extra syllable. It was the chair-and-Evan, alive, an animal, a beast. Evan-and-the-coffee-table. He breathed life into a whole new species of creature, Evan-and, Evan-and, the room rearing and bucking, windswept by the beating of Evan's new creatures' new wings.

And he didn't have time, Kenneth, to think really. He had no time to put any half-baked plan into action. He was marooned, without flight, and Evan was airbound, spinning and spinning, cushions aloft, carpets tangled, books and pillows skidding sharply around him. The living room was a twister. Kenneth was dizzy. It was as if he were the one turning, turning; Evan-and, Evan-and, the room, the books, the cushions, the pillows, staying still in a circle around him. He was a whirlpool Kenneth, spiraling inward toward his collapsing center of self, surrounded on all sides by his brother.

"He died, so you'll die," sang Evan. He sang out loud, angry, his cold smart voice rising up and out, ringing.

"All Kenneth Golds will die young."

And Kenneth was turning and spinning, circling in closer and closer to the long-ended funnel that led deep past where his throat was, where his stomach was, into the dark catacombs of his heart.

"Dad named you Kenneth so you would die young." Evan's voice rang out.

And Kenneth a top, tunneling in, burrowing in like a screw at high speed, like a snail shell gone backwards, around and in, around and in, until he was hyperventilating, couldn't breathe, trying to think, pant, trying to think, pant, losing ground, going in, losing ground to Evan, until at last, chest heaving, tears streaming, snot so hot it was liquid sliding like bubble juice over and around his chin, so that whatever air he had was trapped, held back as if by plastic, leaving him with one clear thought, before he began to drown, go under.

I was chosen, thought Kenneth, Dad chose me.

Then the wave of anxiety overtook, tumbled him without air, without foothold, hands flailing, head tucked, body wrapped up in his body until he was tight as a fist, until the attack reduced him to nothing but the crashing surf, the soaring tide, to what felt like the incessant pounding of his very life fluid, as if it were muscling its way through the doors of his young soul and flooding his little-boy lungs.

Assimilation

ALL the boys loved Hannah, and Hannah couldn't love. Isn't there always a girl like that? One a boy could die for. She was lovely, or so I'm told, but not lovely enough to warrant all that mass undying devotion. She was a little too tall, maybe. A little too sharp around the edges. She straightened her long dark hair, so there was always something remotely chemical to the touch. Not that it was touched often, a boy could consider himself lucky to brush by Hannah's hair in the corridors at City College, to stand behind her—fingers tentative, but outstretched—in the line for coffee at the Settlement House. Chance encounters. A boy's fingers, the dark wheat of her hair—a shuddering feeling, a current, knowing that finger, that hair, could easily turn to dust.

She was twenty, my mother, the girl who grew up to be my mother. She wore black skirts, black character shoes. White blouses buttoned up to the collar. Revolutionary's glasses. Little round wire frames and glass that she probably didn't need, but when set against her nose that way, that strong, frank sensual nose of hers, they made those light, light, light-blue eyes gray, her gray eyes slanted like a white Chinese. Those glasses made Hannah look smart. And she was quiet. Boys who like girls, smart boys who like girls, always go for a girl who is quiet. They like mystery, girls they cannot reach. Later when they are men, they go after the simplest dish they can find, one who spends her life puzzling *them* out; but early on, a boy still likes a challenge.

My mother was a determined girl. The daughter of European Jewish refugees. Her father had been a Trotskyite, now he ran a grocery. He was a worker, and the first president of the Grocery Workers' Union. Hannah was proud of him, she adored him, which may or may not have had anything to do with the fact that she could or couldn't love. Raised the way I was, on a simplistic blend of post-Freudian theory and mock-Jewish guilt, I find it hard to step away from these things, from analysis, from shrinking the life out of everyone. Her major was English Literature, but she already knew what she wanted to do. The work of the world—Hannah was going to be a caseworker. She'd go back to the ghetto from which she came and teach the people simple skills that would organize their complicated lives. Day care. Literacy programs. English as a second language. So much needed to be set in motion. There was no time for romance. "Love, shmove," said Hannah, "it's all a false business." She had a way with words.

I am the youngest child of the woman this girl grew into, the woman like an overcoat bought a size or two too big, waiting patiently in the closet for time to add years like pounds to the girl's slender frame. I am Jeremy, the third and final son. I came in last in the race. By nights I'm a painter, by days I'm a graphic artist. And I am Hannah's homosexual child. When you have four, you should expect one of everything. One of everything is what Hannah got. Would it help to know I have a banker for a brother? The eldest, a fallen hippie, a family man; Doug, the spitting image of our father. Would you get the picture if I told you about my sister, Cara, my flickering, painful light? That Cara, with her dark, staccato beauty, her fingers going, going, ripping at the label on the beer bottle, tearing the napkin to shreds, splitting her own split ends; that Cara, my constantly collapsing, exciting, pathologically honest, nut-job of a sister, has always been my favorite one? She may be extreme, but Cara feels so deeply that the loudness of her emotions reverberates through my reserve. She has so much excess pain I feel like I can funnel my own aches through her. But even Cara, my closest connection, my deepest tie, in fact all my siblings exist out of my reach, like circling planets, and I am as distant from them as the moon, say, from the sun. Up close they have been known to eclipse me, Doug solidly blocking my stream of light, Cara a frenetic strobe with her dramatic twists and turns; Ken, a permanent fixture, now, in our galaxy, a black hole, a vacuum, sucking up all that glows. It is a testament to our internal structure, the laws of our universe, to my own inability to shine, that I can only see them clearly from this distance.

I have a dead brother. How strange, to possess a person who is no longer a person, to *have* him, to still be responsible. The middle one. Died at the tippy-top of his teens, still climbing the stairs of his spine toward his full and perfect height. Died a stranger to me, really. As a sibling, Ken was clear. The linchpin of our family, the necessary one. I was grateful to him for being the glue, what kept the cracked plate of this family together. He was vital as a brother. It's knowing Ken as a person, that's where I got robbed. I have absolutely no idea at all who he was. Therefore, I suspect, I am clueless to his death, what with no insight into the life behind it.

There are nights where I am visited by his ghost. At first he came to me in different forms, handwriting on the misted windows, swirls of meaningful characters on the rug. At times I saw him in my food, in cereal for godssakes, in the cream in my coffee. He patterned out the stories of our lives, things I needed to know, in pictures, in the handwriting of my mind. Still, he never revealed *himself* to me. What did he do to get all those girls so crazy about him? Did he make himself indispensable on purpose? What was on his mind that August night when impulse set him free?

What's a thinking person to think? Sober, Ken drove his car into a tree on a moonlit night on an empty road he knew like the back of his hand.

What's a thinking person to think.

It wasn't until a week after the fact (the funeral came first, there was a week of sitting shivah) that Hannah and I came on the scene of the accident. Me, crawling through the door they had to blowtorch just to get him out of there, me crawling across that wreck's cracked leather, looking for artifacts (a pipe, a comb, some rolling papers?) of the extinct tribe of my brother, his dried blood lifting in flakes, swirling around me like fingerprints. I am constantly amazed that even though none of us was there, *she* can see the accident, Hannah, in her mind's eye, so clearly, the car, the tree, the car, the tree, Kenny . . . that the moment her imagination reaches impact Hannah can find herself flung forward, on the bed, off the couch, or worse yet, lying on the playroom floor in front of the TV, it's Hannah practically levitating in anticipation, then falling, falling when there is no space to fall, just as Ken, the car, the tree, pitched forward, forward, when there was no forward, no future, no place to go. Chilling: they hurtle themselves, Mom and Ken, at nothing, not space, not time.

Would it have helped her then, Hannah, when her heart was ice and she could not love and she worried about herself and all of her womanly capacities (was she frigid, was she heartless, would she ever care for anybody?) to know that one day she would be dissolved like fizzy powder by her love for her son?

(Although you and I, you and I, clever as we are, way past twenty as we are, know that she could not help but love, that she loved so indiscriminately, her sky-eyes seeing everything, no wonder she wore those glasses, to blur the vision, slow the image as it traveled pupil to retina to excitable imagination, that there was no choice but to shut down, turn off.)

I daresay the singularity of her present focus, on lost child, on family—lost (poor Hannah, obsessed with the death of her son, unable to recognize the living life that surrounds her), that all-consuming focus would have seemed incomprehensible then when her mind was expanding in so many varied and startling directions she would grow giddy from the joy of it. The world of ideas was news for Hannah. Marxist philosophy, Freud and his reinterpretation of Oedipus the King, the first hints of feminism. "To each according to his ability, to each according to *her* need." Hannah would repeat this over and over in her head like a mantra, waiting impatiently for insight.

At times she had no control over, on the train to school when the overhead lights would flash on and off from some blip in the electricity, her heart would beat double-time and pound up into her throat; and her head would swim with ideas and plans and dreams, as if she, Hannah, were a composer and a symphony hit her all at once. Sitting on the john, even, the buttons on those black Capezios winking up at her like co-conspirators, the tiles on the floor would pitch and toss in waves like water, the room would spin; the sink, the tub, the shower, would whirl around Hannah, Hannah the apex, the vortex, spinning and sinking, funneling down into the abyss that was the center of her adolescent hungering self, drunk on the first few gulps of self-knowledge. If you knew her then, you couldn't have helped but like her.

Marilyn was in love. Marilyn was Hannah's Puerto Rican roommate. Sure "all this" would lead to Hannah's having Puerto Rican boyfriends, Hannah's mother cried when Hannah moved out of the house. The two girls met at the Settlement House. They worked there days: counseling adolescents, organizing hootenannies, supervising community outreach programs. Hannah went to school at night. Brooklyn was just too far, too far far away, "spiritually," for Hannah. Her life's goal was to get over the Bridge.

Marilyn had an apartment in the East Village, a one-bedroom, but money slipped through her fingers like a string of false pearls, and Marilyn, she had plans. She was out to catch a husband sure, she was out for a little excitement. She dreamed of trips to Europe, a beautiful home, two cars, etc.; and it took nice clothes, a couple of a good pieces of jewelry—money, to get a man. Clearly, someone was needed to pay the rent. And they liked each other, these girls did, Marilyn from her middle-class Chicago family, Hannah and her Woody Allen nightmare-fantasy, growing up under the El, living behind the grocery, her own mother stirring vats of soup and colored clothing side by side in the back of the stove; Marilyn and Hannah liked to talk to each other, they liked to confide. Marilyn would buy a straw-skirted bottle of Chianti, pour the hooch into a juice jar, stick a candle in the bottle, light up, sip the red stuff, and while Hannah watched the wax reassign itself, its shape, its texture, its color, Marilyn would entertain her with stories of the size and shape of her various lovers' various members.

Poor Hannah, for all her admirers, there had been a Sheldon Pinkowitz, but what is a Sheldon Pinkowitz? He amounted to not much more than an intellectual experiment. M & H, now they had a good time. So Hannah squeezed in her own twin bed from her mother's apartment, she squeezed in some of her childhood furniture—a bureau, a child's desk, that little ballerina lamp that still sits in Cara's old room at home—and a pile of books. And she paid fifty dollars a month, which was, in those days, "a small fortune."

What did she read, my mother? All those books in piles by her bed. All those books tucked behind the living room sofa where Hannah spent her nights, while on the mismatched twins shoved into one deliciously illicit king-size Marilyn was entertaining Norman "Jack" Goldblatt (my father), the one she was currently in love with. If Hannah's mother only knew that Marilyn, warm and soft and pliant, was "spread like a stain" across Hannah's mother's white sheets . . .

I suspect during those long nights of Marilyn and Jack

weaving and interweaving like a living braid in the next room, Hannah read *Lady Chatterley's Lover.* Marx, Emily Dickinson, E.E. Cummings. Any newspaper she could get her hands on. Tennessee Williams. If she were born later, if she were born later but was still younger, say sixteen, she would have been a Sylvia Plath lover. (Would it be too cornball to admit that if she were born thirty years later I could have counted her as a friend?) If she knew enough, she would have read Virginia Woolf. She probably avoided Pound like the plague. She was incapable of separating the political. She is incapable still. It is her most salient, profound and unattractive feature; she's ethical Hannah, and she's judgmental.

Our family, according to Hannah: Cara is too frivolous, our father an unforgivable adulterer, my past sojourns into the night meaningless physical trespasses upon the holy temples of men's bodies. Doug is a materialist, capitalist pig—although there, Hannah might be on the money. Ken ducked out, abandoned his family, his mother, when she needed him most. All her children could have been saved from their American yuppied-out, selfish and tormented existence, if she, Hannah, had been some kind of mother. What Jewish matriarch doesn't believe that *she* is the source of all ills, of all pleasures?

She can be a righteous, vainglorious, quiet pain-in-the-ass.

And she was home, Friday night, Saturday night, reading, avoiding the multitudes who adored her, listening carefully to the grunts of her future husband as he pounded away at her roommate on her own childhood bed—Hannah actively rejecting the life of the body, for the life of the mind.

Hannah. What was it like to be you? The girls at City College, the girls at the Settlement House, wondered cattily as they raked you over the coals while they sneaked Lucky Strikes in the ladies' bathroom. And the Sheldons, and the Bernies, the Mymans, and the Stanleys, boasting that with one roll in the hay each would be the one to melt your frigid, polar cap. Is there nothing so desirable as an object unattainable? Hannah. With your rallies and your youth groups and your crush on Paul Robeson, with that awestruck, slightly dazed way you slid down the halls, swayed to the rocking of the El—your lack of overt sexuality the sexiest thing about you. Oh the severity of your smile; you were the closest thing in two boroughs to a goddess.

And you knew this to be true, and you didn't know this, which was half the charm, the not-knowing; the other half was the obvious—you suspected. Once so exalted and desired, how impossible to actually succumb to being held, to press lips to lips, to meld the body of your soul with Myman's or Stanley's or Irwin's; it would have been ruinous to your image. How could you let down your pants? Your chastity, your ice-princesshood, was an insulating, deifying and most precious possession.

Marilyn loved Jack. She adored him. And Hannah, for the life of her, couldn't see why. He knocked on their window at 2:00 in the morning (they were on the ground floor, the building in the back, the apartment so dark and airless it smelled like a mouth), and Hannah begged her not to let him in. "Self-respect," hissed Hannah, even as she bundled up her sheets and blankets around her nightclothes and headed out to the couch.

When Jack entered the apartment—a tall, windblown young man, in need of a shave, a haircut—Hannah wouldn't even look at him, give him the time of day.

"Jack," she'd say, with just a hint of royal acknowledgment, out of the side of her mouth. More often than not, he was a little drunk. More often than not, he was wildly excited about some ideas he had for organizing the University support staff, or petitioning for radical changes in the curriculum, for proving, finally and without a shadow of a doubt the innocence of the Rosenbergs, Sacco & Vanzetti; he'd be flying high from some underground political meeting he attended, drunk on the exhilaration of possessing Marilyn herself, his educated, middle-class Hot Tamale, his mother's potential heart attack. And Marilyn fussed some but she let him in, she let him in. She wanted him for her husband, and like the rest of us, in her all-out wanting she drove him away. But let's be real. Jack was a kid. A louse. A renegade in his hard-biting liberal phase, and Marilyn was an accoutrement, a trophy. Brown sugar. What can I say?

He is my father.

Jack was older than the Mymans and the Sheldons. He was in law school on the GI Bill. He hadn't exactly been in battle—he was in Intelligence, and had worked on some project that led to a piece of our earth being torn to shreds, a project that he will not talk about to this day. This subject is an agreed-upon family silence. He was sufficiently tortured, but not hopelessly damaged, which for girls like Hannah, was the fatal combination. Sexy. Someone to mend, to tend to, to nurse back to health. He was mean and sarcastic and smarter than hell. He was hell-bent on changing the world. A regular dreamboat. Hannah was a little too pinched for his taste. Too caught up by conventional morality. Too often dateless and home, when he wanted the apartment and Marilyn to himself.

When Hannah and Jack spoke, which was not often,

they spoke coldly or they argued. While Marilyn applied her lipstick, touched up her hair, rolled a dark, silky stocking up a dark, silky leg in the bedroom, Hannah and Jack fought over methods of spiritual enlightenment, over Freud, over the judicial system and solutions to poverty, hunger and social injustice. Jack's rhetoric was a confounding intertextual blend of unrelenting idealism and the bitterest cynicism. Hannah has always been simpler; she was still fired by her own inner power, by what was and was not right. This fatal combination lead to my incubation; like an organism and a petri dish, together my future parents were positively viral.

"I don't understand how you can defend a guilty person," said Hannah. She told the truth; she was guileless. She couldn't understand it.

"Everyone is entitled to a proper defense, that's the law, don't you believe in law, Hannah Schwartz? Don't you believe in democracy?" Jack was on the lookout for whatever it was that would trigger the rise in color (she pinkened pig-white), heighten the slant behind the glasses, in those academic blue eyes.

This argument, or ones like it, we have all heard before. Haven't I, too, known love? Steven and I, in our youth, arguing over Keats and truth, over Heidegger, over William Burroughs and Edmund White. Steven and I, unlovers, years later at his bedside while he died, that cruel and slow procedure where we raced against time, arguing over what had led to our unloving, arguing about the purpose of this short and cheated life. The arbitrariness of it all is astounding—no matter what decade one lives in, what school one attends, what profession one agonizingly chooses to go into, there will always be some perfect somebody awaiting you, destined to savage your gossamer, tender heart.

*   *   *

Freud be damned, I love my mother. I love her worn-out, spiritless shell, the face that she wears badly, her open palms, reaching for all that's lost to her. I will talk to her on the phone. I will attend her at the Ballet, the Opera. I will argue with her about the latest editorial in the local, I will be her foil, her devil's advocate. I will help her drag Cara from shrink to shrink. I will help her entertain the grandchildren. I will *not* tell her to date, snap to it, get on with her life. I will not tell her to stop digging in the dirt: oy Hannah, the flowers, everywhere the flowers, in the greenhouse, in the yard, in the playroom under can-cer-causing blue lights, as if through all that planting she could plant back a son, that he would spring like fruit from among her blossoms, that she could pick him whole, serve him up to her fractured progeny, that all their many wounds would be healed by just one bite. I will not tell her that I am HIV positive. How could I? Could you?

In every family there is "a good child." Ken, my brother, was the propper-upper. The entertainer. The sac-rificer. Trigger-happy. Impulsive. He was the only one who could make my mother laugh.

I will be the understudy, Hannah's partner in her dance of grief, I will accompany her eternal whirl of mourning.

How did it come to pass that Hannah moved in and Marilyn moved out of the slots on Jack's dance card? Was it that Marilyn took too much time with her makeup, too much time in the shower? Or did she finally get wise to the fact that she was being taken, that she would never be invited home for Shabbes, much less to meet mishpoche?

Whatever, she was a girl who knew that she had her whole life ahead of her, she was a girl who knew that her life was slipping away by the hour. She borrowed two hundred dollars from Jack (God knows where he got the money) and she went to Paris. And that was that: Marilyn, the two hundred, were lost and chalked up to youthful inexperience. She was washed from their lives, like silt, the finest, darkest powder. No one even bothered to find out what became of her.

So why is it Marilyn who has often been spotlighted in my mind's eye? Since childhood I have pictured her in a beaded dress. She leans against a piano in a nightclub in Paris, surrounded, yes, by swirling blue smoke, her voice, her laugh sounding like she is underwater. I blame you, Marilyn, for skipping town, for your expatriate performance, for blithely setting into motion the ruination of so many lives. In my dreams you are sassy and fat and luscious, unlike the wasting sagging Hannah, you, Mar, remain forever juicy. And like my brother Ken, you will always be young.

Marilyn, come clean: was it not your fault that Hannah and Jack . . . that fatal combination? My scarred childhood, their divorce, Kenny and the car (I suspect) he so willfully plowed into a tree?

Your life has been Brie and brioche, jazz musicians, made-to-order hand-tailored brassieres, Hermès scarves. But what about my mother, with her empty house and her empty cunt and her empty arms? What did she do to you to deserve this treatment?

The way Jack tells it, he was used to going to the apartment in the back. It was force of habit. Cara swears Hannah told her once, right after the divorce, that Hannah loved him the minute she laid eyes on him, that her heart skipped beats and all that hoo-ha, that her heart landed in her throat. That all this couldn't-love business was to keep her from going on an endless string of dates that were nothing but an awful waste of time. After Sheldon Pinkowitz, sex held only the vaguest of attractions. Why, she would have jumped Jack's bones immediately (Cara said this: jumped Jack's bones) was she not so scared to death of him, was she not so misled by Sheldon. And then there was all that untouchable-image stuff, so Hannah held onto *it,* her virtue, her ice. Who knows what is true at the beginning when you look back at it from the end, with hindsight? After Ken died, my mother swore she could never remember loving my father. It was as if Ken sucked up the total sum of emotions allotted toward this lifetime.

It's not necessary, the gory details. Why recount the biweekly fights over bowls of spaghetti? Still, I'd like to focus on Hannah's face, not quite as pretty as Cara's, never that pretty, that glittery, that insane; but still handsome and intelligent and alive, as she leaned toward the candlelight at Il Bambino, or Minetta's Tavern or Forlini's, when she wanted to make a point. But who needs to go over word-for-word the arguments that mutated into the soundtrack of my childhood? What is important is that months passed, and so did Hannah's resolve, lack of interest being the prime seducer; but even when she came around Jack couldn't seem to kiss her. And when he did, the kisses were short and dry. He ran his fingers through the snarls of her hair, and said it was late, he was tired, and then he picked another fight. All the boys loved Hannah, but Jack. Jack just did not desire her.

How do I know this? Who knows how I know, their

history is recorded in my blood, my bones, like years in the rings of a tree; my grandmother told me, is how I know; I know because I've surmised it. And then there are Ken's visitations, nights when he comes to me as if in a dream with the knowledge of the dead. These days he comes like a newscaster, standing straight before me as he delivers the blow-by-blow.

i.e.: I am in the bathroom shaving, I am looking into the mirror. Behind me is another medicine chest, that I do not use; it's stuffed with shoe polish, Milk of Magnesia, styptic pencils. Out of the corner of my eye, I see him, Ken, in the other mirror, I look at the reflection of his reflection, his graying hair still long, his left ear earringed, love beads across his throat, hopelessly out of date, out of time—exactly the hippy-dippy twenty-year-old he was when he died. He stares straight ahead, as if he is reading a cue card, he won't allow me the privilege of meeting him eye to eye. He recounts events in the most painful manner possible.

Ken says: They stopped sleeping together when you were four, in the seventies they once tried spouse-swapping with Abigail and Fred, Jack cheated three weeks into the marriage with Selma Blodgett.

In other words, Ken tells me all the things I would not want to know.

You prick, I say. Look what you've left me with. Get the hell out of my bathroom.

So what does he do? He melts. That's the trouble with Ken. He goes away.

There is always some special someone who will make a girl tear her hair out, even a girl who cannot love. Hannah took this literally, she literally pulled the hair out of her head. Nothing so dramatic as to yank it out in clumps, rather a steady twist and tug, one at a time, the ping of exit from the hair shaft reminding her that there were other pains besides Jack-pain, that she was supposed to be doing the work of the world, not devoting her precious life to some sexy screwed-up postadolescent. Had this gone on long enough, this not-lovemaking, she might have baldened herself, plucking her hair like grass.

Marilyn was history, and Hannah's other girlfriends were just girlfriends, they weren't fellow caretakers of the heart. Hannah was upset, upset enough to confide in her mother, which must have been plenty upset, if you ask me.

The hair. The heart. Jack's lack of the old interest. All this, my grandmother, Lillian, told me when we first found out about Em, Jack's present wife.

"Hannah, she couldn't get him to touch her." Pause. "That playboy," said Lillian.

"Everyone likes me except the one I like," Hannah told her mother. "But if he doesn't like me, why does he keep coming around to fight?"

Why indeed. Why? How funny that in our family fighting was always a sign of connection, even affection, our personal language, native tongue. Could it be that back then Jack possessed some insight. Perhaps he was touched by the chill of warning. Perhaps on some level he knew: ahead lay disaster. A failed marriage, a dead child, a homosexual son. Jack, where were you when your bones were speaking? Why did you not heed the outcries of your gut?

I'm in the shower. It is late and I have just spent an hour examining my body. This is a waiting game—I wait for the sores to emerge. I have been through this twice before, with Steven, with my cousin John. I am twenty-seven years old and I have buried sixteen friends, a cousin, a brother, and the man I loved, the man who would have been my husband if we hadn't fucked ourselves up. In the art of death, at twenty-seven, I am an old hand. The strange thing is that I know I am dying, yet I still physically feel fine. The fun part is ahead of me. I have already turned the page, the page where everything changes, physics-shmysics—the page from where time, clichéd or not, irretrievably marches on. I let the hot water pound and steam all my liquids free. Infections leak out of me. This is the 1990s.

Ken, you bastard. First, you had to be the center of attention. Then you fucking died. Now, you go and rob me of my inalienable rights to my illness. Who could look to Ma, for help, for comfort, to be a mother for godssake, after you?

The prince. He makes his appearance. The mirror—Ken. The whole thing is like out of a bad B movie. His eyes are locked on something outside of himself. He rattles on, starting in midsentence.

(This is how the dead spend their time? I ask you.)

Out of Ken's mouth, into my head: She wanted him, but she couldn't get wet.

Ken, I say. Ken. I say his name. Out loud.

He couldn't get it up, Ken says.

(My parents, those cripples.)

Wait, I say. How did they get into bed anyway? I say this, inside my head, outside my head. I want to know.

But Ken won't hear me. He just rattles on.

He had pimples on his back, there were dark hairs far down her thighs, he hated the taste of her, his lips felt like rubber, he couldn't roll the condom on . . . my dead brother reads me the more-than-thirty-year-old tragic report.

(Wasn't there someone who could have saved them?)

Shut up, I say, but I am interested.

I stand naked in the jet stream.

It could have been night or day, it is hard to tell in that dark apartment. Hannah was at home, as usual, not-reading, tearing her hair out of her head. She was wearing a pair of black Capri pants, and a man's shirt—probably her father's, what other man was there to lend her a shirt, she had a sister, no brothers. Then again, it could have been a trophy Marilyn left behind. Clearly, I do not know everything.

Hannah had not heard from Jack in weeks, a month maybe, strings and strings of days, yards of them. He had not answered her notes, her calls. Her notes: Call me, Jack. Her calls: Tell him at least to write me. The windows were open, the air damp. That little back apartment smelled of dirt, springtime, I guess, of possibility, mold and plants growing, of mud and spoil, the breakdown of things. One way and the other, coexisting, sharing time.

Hannah: not-reading, tearing.

Jack at the door.

(Why couldn't he have been hit by a bus?)

She had a moment of hesitation, a wrestle with her better, stronger self, and then the slide of resignation as she turned the bolt. The door cracked open, his handsome face there in the opening, his knee spreading the opening wider. Hannah, filling like a vessel, Hannah sodden with hope.

Jack in the doorframe. "We need to talk," he said.

(Who among us has not heard that phrase before. Is

it not always accompanied by some internal movie score, clueing us in, the inner thump-thump, the solid beat of the approaching assassin, the imminent arrival of the circling shark?)

"So talk," said Hannah. Hannah of a thousand words.

"Can I sit down?" asked Jack.

"Sit," said Hannah. "Make yourself at home."

Her hand swept toward the red chair, the red chair that became the "climbing chair" when my eldest brother was four and Ken was born. The red chair that became a fort, before Cara wielded power. The red chair that she and I turned over so that we could play cave, and jail, and boat.

Jack sat down on the couch. I wish I inherited an ounce of his confidence.

Hannah sat down on the red chair, miles away from him.

"I've never felt this way before," Jack said to her.

And Hannah, in her head, silently: You think I've felt like this? You think I like to spend my life systematically destroying my looks, hair by processed hair, ignoring my classes, ignoring my work, you shithead, you self-centered, arrogant bastard?

Or was it me, thirty-some-odd years later, thinking these thoughts for her? Where does she stop, Hannah, where does Jeremy begin again? Why is it I can only think in questions?

And Hannah, aloud: "Talk straight, Jack, it's late, I'm tired."

So it was night, perhaps a sleepless night, perhaps a sleepless night edging on early morning. How adolescent of them.

"I feel the need to explain myself," Jack said. "My actions." He too, had completed Psych 101. He ran his fingers through his hair.

"So, explain," said Hannah, giving an inch, not giving an inch.

"Hannah," said Jack. Then he waited. "You're not being fair."

Her jaw set, but she kept quiet. You see there was still some reason to hope. After all, he was there, Jack, on her couch, at 3:30 in the morning.

Jack looked at the floor. He looked up at Hannah. There was a smudge of ink on her lower lip where a pen had rested earlier. I imagine Jack imagined Hannah, the pen, her mouth, her lip. "There's ink on your lip," he said, "Hannah."

Her hand fluttered up to her mouth. She bit her lip, rolled back her tongue. She looked like she might cry, then. "Well, go on," said Hannah.

"I guess I'm a little bit afraid of you," Jack said.

"Afraid," screamed Hannah. "For godssake what is there to be afraid of?"

A look of panic streaked across Jack's face. He thought to flee, I'm sure of it, but he had come this far, he was in it for the duration.

"I met, I mean I was dating this older woman," Jack began again.

"Older?" said Hannah, loud but not screaming. "Does that mean married? What would she want with you? Does that mean old enough to be your mother?" The tears began to roll.

"Not that old," Jack said. Then he smiled. It was as if her crying released him. Jack smiled sheepishly at Hannah whose lips trembled through the liquid lace of her tears. "Why not," he said, "they might as well get us guys when our bodies are still good. Obviously we don't get much more mature."

Jack grinned. Hannah, weak, lovesick Hannah, she

smiled back at him. And as if this gave him courage, Jack forged on. "I love you, Hannah."

He caught her like a camera catches an image. He caught her unaware. He was a time-defier. Everything stopped inside her.

"There, I said it," said Jack. "I said what I came here to say, so there's no point in my staying." Jack looked at the floor, he looked up at Hannah, frozen in her moment. Jack made no moves to leave her.

"Jack," said Hannah, and in an instant he was kneeling by her side. He took her hand to his lips, he smoothed the stray hair away from her face, he stroked her cheek with one finger.

He was perfect.

"I love you, Hannah Schwartz," Jack said. "I love you." And with that last heartfelt admission, he began to tremble, and then his tear ducts, too, began to go.

"Jack," said Hannah. She got off the chair and onto the floor, to hold him. "Shhh, Jack," said Hannah. And then she was kissing him, Hannah crying, Jack crying, kissing, kissing, both of them in need of a Kleenex perhaps, liquids flowing heedlessly, but dizzy, dizzy with the danger of touching, the danger of being touched.

"I love you, Jack," said Hannah.

"I love you, Hannah," said Jack.

"There is nothing, nothing to be afraid of," said Hannah.

"Nothing." Jack kissed this back to her.

And that was that. It was all over for all of us. We were promised to each other.

The Hard Summer

IT TOOK the old cat's dying to make Douglas cry. He did *not* cry when his parents divorced, when his favorite brother died, when his one true love up and ditched him. He did not cry at his own wedding, although Kitsie, his wife-to-be, she cried buckets. And when his boys were born, Evan first and Kenneth last, Douglas never shed a tear. The theory held by his primary family, Hannah Gold, Cara Gold, Jeremy Gold—a group of loud scene-stealing criers themselves, real wailers—was that once Douglas got started, he probably would never stop. And if Kenny had lived, lived longer than his second year at college, if he had been a little bit more careful one night well over a decade ago when driving home from a date, if he hadn't hit that fucking tree, doubtlessly Kenny would have agreed with them. Obstinate as Douglas was, this time he proved his family right—he cried like there was no tomorrow.

It wasn't as if Doug even liked that cat, it was fat and lazy, and for the past eight years it had lain inert on his sister Cara's torn-up couch. But when it died, finally, after living longer than any cat had lived before—"if you could call that living," said Jeremy—when Cara found it folded and stiff inside the inside corner of the single closet in her tenement apartment, well from that point onward, everything changed. Doug oozed tears day and night.

After the cat died, Cara packed her bags, got a summer sublet, and headed up to Vermont, to Doug's home and hearth, to recuperate, to "heal" herself. Although she had started this round of falling apart last spring with a breakup with her boyfriend, a huge fight with her best friend Ilana, the cat was her final disaster. Cara said that it was the last cat that would ever know Kenny, although the cat probably didn't know anything, it was senile and half-blind and for humanitarian reasons should have been put to sleep ages ago. After it died, Cara had stopped eating, sleeping, even combing her hair. Hannah, her ever-loving but completely worn-out mother, had given Cara three options. Cara could: (1) go through another bout of intensive therapy, (2) spend several wholesome months with her oldest brother's family up in the country, or (3) finally, finally became a grown-up and get a real job. Cara opted for greener pastures.

Doug and Kitsie and Evan and Kenneth made up the upstairs study for her. The boys swept it out. Kitsie sewed a new bedspread and hand-hemmed a batch of antique eyelit curtains. Doug got out a pair of old jeans and painted the walls the sunniest Easter-chick yellow he could find. As he worked Doug's tears thinned out the paint, the turpentine.

Douglas cried, he cried all the time. He cried when his mother, Hannah, told the cat-news to him over the phone. He cried when he relayed this news on to his children and his wife—upsetting her so, really Kitsie was extremely sensitive, that she went quietly into the downstairs bathroom to shed a few tears herself.

When anyone precious to Kitsie was hurt—for example if one of the older boys teased her littlest, Kenneth—Kitsie took it straight to her heart. She epitomized "empathetic." When over drinks one night a friend recounted the emergency appendectomy recently performed on his wife, Kitsie fell into a faint. She could not help herself from experiencing pain alongside her loved ones. Once, when Evan was to present a project at the local science fair, she stayed up all night rehearsing his speech in her head. Evan, being Evan, the sturdy, smart sort, slept like a baby and still won the blue ribbons hands down—he was a genius. Kitsie trembled throughout the entire awards ceremony, even after it was announced that Evan took first prize.

So Kitsie suffered as Douglas cried. He cried when he picked Cara up at the bus stop in Burlington, spotting her a block away from inside his car as Cara was the only departing passenger dressed in black, head to toe, in the heat of summer. That night, after a tense and silent supper, Doug cried over his boys' sleeping bodies when he went down the hall to check on them, because he couldn't sleep himself—he spent the better part of the night crying in and out of Kitsie's arms in their big sleigh bed, in that old, restored house that he worked so hard to pay for. It was exhausting, all that crying. He was a wreck, Douglas.

Cara was a wreck too, of course, but everyone was used to this. Even Kitsie had a callused spot for Cara in her soft and tender heart. Cara haunted their house like a ghost-girl. She barely ate the nutritious meals that Kitsie prepared for her, just used her fork to mash her cigarette ashes together with whatever else was on her plate. She wandered the halls of that big, beautiful house in her black outfits, smoking her Gauloises, stinking up the drapes and the thick rugs that Kitsie had haggled over at estate auctions. Privately, Cara reminded Kitsie of some fallen star out of a silent movie. She seemed to dare any-one to speak to her, and if someone (that someone usually being Kitsie) ventured a kind or loving word, Cara would either freeze her or burst into tears herself. Then there would be two full-grown Golds, a sister and a brother, up in their rooms, flung out on their beds, sobbing their poor hearts out. This was a new turn on sibling rivalry: who could cry the longest, the loudest.

It was a wonder anyone had any time or energy to get any work done with all that weeping and wailing, but life went on. Doug rose early every day, showered and shaved and headed out to the bank. There, the demands of his demanding job, his career, pretty much kept his head above water. It was only at rare moments that he had to shut his door, lie flat on his carpeted office floor, and cry the hard cry that comes without noise or tears. Kitsie, too, continued onward, making her way around Cara as she did her chores, cleaned the house. The boys spent every day but Sunday nine-to-five at Day Camp, and Kitsie had looked forward all year to free afternoons filled with shopping and long walks, baking, working in her garden. She'd hoped to get Cara to share in these simple pleasures, but an invitation out to lunch with Kitsie and some of the other-mothers was only met with scorn.

As for Evan and Kenneth, after initially being burned from an overture or two, they kept out of Cara's hair. This was especially painful for Kenneth, the baby, because he had been Cara's favorite. And even smart, exacting Evan had always been intrigued by Cara. When they were little she had made it a point to play with them, pose for their paintings, hang up their drawings on her refrigerator. She

used to spend hours with the boys, telling funny-sad stories about their dead uncle, Kenneth's namesake.

Now, when Cara wandered the halls and Kenneth was
playing quietly in some corner the way he liked to, or was
singing to himself in a patch of sunshine by one of the
window seats, Cara would reach out and grab him to
her, hugging the breath out of his body, scaring the boy
dumbstruck. These "monster hugs," as Kenneth referred
to them to his mom, later when he was complaining, only
lasted a few seconds. Then Cara released him, leaving
Kenneth feeling as spent and used as a used Kleenex,
while she continued with her pacing.

Evan she completely ignored, even when he wanted to
point out all the poisonous mushrooms and leaves that
grew in the woods at the back of the house, a proposition
the old Cara would have eagerly jumped at. What was
clear to anyone who ever knew her was even clearer to her
nephews, the forever teetering Cara had finally wigged out.

"Just stay out of her way," Kitsie advised, "until she's
feeling better," so the boys pretty much kept to themselves. Sometimes, Evan would bring a group of friends
to watch Cara through the windows—she was a sight, her
curly black hair tangled practically into dreadlocks, often
wearing what looked like a long-sleeved black body stocking, smoking and stalking and talking to herself. While
Cara provided some entertainment in the monotony of
Evan's summer, she terrified little Kenneth.

So it was Kitsie who got stuck with Cara—Doug too
weak from weeping, too practiced in his older-brother
indifference, too much a stranger to give his sister anything she could use. True, it had been his idea to bring
Cara here. Or rather Kitsie let him think it was his idea;
she had thought a reconciliation with Cara would be best
for him. But after bullying Hannah for months into

encouraging Cara to come stay with them, when Doug had finally won the battle, his energy ran out. Once Cara arrived, he'd had no idea what to do with her.

Originally, Doug had had some vague notions about the two of them talking, but about what, he wasn't sure. He'd pictured Cara in some pretty peasanty thing, as if she were a girl again, playing with his children. He'd figured he'd give her career guidance, set her up with her own clothing line, help her get started with a store. Maybe, he'd introduce her to her husband. This was Doug's way of thinking until Cara first stepped off the Greyhound bus looking like a shrouded corpse. Still, he had faith that just the act of taking her in would be enough to right all that had gone wrong between them. Doug had not thought past this, past some half-baked theory that harkened back to his hippie days—that the green hills of Vermont could magically heal anyone.

Doug and Cara had been enemies their whole lives. They had nothing in common, these two dark, unhappy siblings, except that they both loved their dead young brother. When he went, what was left to link them? Kitsie had convinced Doug that it was time to make amends. "You two are family," said Kitsie, "you need each other." Their parents were getting older, and Jeremy, the youngest Gold kid, well, with Steven, his old boyfriend, dying, who knew what would happen to Jeremy over time.

"How is your brother?" Kitsie ventured to Cara. Doug was at work, the boys at camp, the sisters-in-law were sitting at the table in the kitchen. Waffles hardened and turned to rubber on Cara's plate. The freshly squeezed juice had begun to separate like the three-layered Jell-O that Hannah used to make on special occasions. Kitsie helped herself to another corn muffin and some of her own strawberry jam. Cara was sipping the same stale cup of black coffee and smoking away again.

"Do you mean, does he have AIDS?" said Cara. "He says no. So I believe him. Don't you believe him, Kitsie? Are you calling my brother a liar?"

A silence followed Cara's outburst.

"I pray that he's all right," said Kitsie.

Jeremy was a talented painter, he was sensitive to other people's feelings, and he was extremely supportive to his mother—Kitsie knew all this and she was grateful for him. Plus, Jeremy was the only Gold who had ever done anything to usher Kitsie into the family. From all these things, Jeremy earned Kitsie's affection and respect, even if she didn't exactly know what to say when she was alone and face to face with him. Besides, his brother was dead too, and his old boyfriend, and just thinking about pain like that was enough to make Kitsie's eyes well up.

So it was true, Kitsie did pray for Jeremy. She couldn't bear the thought of what would happen to this family if anything were to happen to him.

Cara hooted. "You're a real trip, honey, you know that? Keep on praying, Kitsie, maybe you'll bring Kenny back to life."

Then Cara got up and with a hint of her old drama, stormed proudly out of the room.

Kitsie stared at the space that Cara had most recently inhabited. She looked at Cara's dish aswirl with a gray paste of ash and syrup and mashed-up waffle. All that waste made her sick. Kitsie reached over and threw the dish at the wall near the sink. The plate shattered on impact, just like her husband's family had shattered when Kenny hit that stupid tree, now so many years ago. Kitsie's anger scared her. When Cara poked her head back in the room, Kitsie was still standing, frozen by her action.

"Way to go," said Cara. She was no stranger to plate throwing herself. "I didn't know you had it in you."

Kitsie inhaled sharply. Her arms were rigid, her hands in fists. "You have everyone turning cartwheels, don't you," said Kitsie. "You're nothing but a lazy little princess!"

Cara's head disappeared, again. In a moment, Kitsie could hear the sound of Cara's feet thudding on the staircase, the slamming of Cara's door as she rushed into her room, and then the squeaking of the bedsprings when Cara flung herself across the mattress, where she would probably cry all morning and afternoon.

So it went, Douglas, overwhelmed and distant, buried in his work. The boys doing boys' things: avoiding their weeping, scary father, avoiding their creepy, scary aunt. Cara was continually provocative and Kitsie quicker to anger, speaking up in a way she had never done before in her life.

The house ached with sadness.

Kitsie tried not to complain too much on the phone to Hannah, but then again, Cara *was* ruining their lives.

"I hate to say I told you so, but I told you so," said Hannah. And then, "Why don't you have Douglas drive her home?"

Why not? It wasn't as if the idea had never occurred to her. But there was something at stake here, Kitsie was sure of it—her husband's happiness. She had to help him smooth the jagged edges of his family, put the shattered plate back together again. She resigned herself to sticking the summer out.

"Doug," she said that night in bed, the two of them

wrapped up in a summer-weight feather comforter. "Can't you talk to Cara?"

Doug leaned his handsome, weary head on his wife's chest. "Ken was the only one who knew what to say to her," he said.

"What would Ken have said to her, then?" asked Kitsie.

"It's been a long time," said Doug. "Sometimes he's hard to remember." And he began to cry again, little trickles, no sounds.

"Try, honey," said Kitsie. She had never met Ken; she wanted to know.

Doug rolled over onto his back. He wiped his eyes with his pajama sleeve. He thought for a moment. He reached his arm up and with his finger traced an invisible picture against the backdrop of the ceiling.

"He would have said something like: 'Cara, you are too great a person to waste so much time being such a jerk.' Something like that," Doug said.

"Something like that," echoed Kitsie. She reached her hand up around her husband's wrist and traced his invisible picture along with him. If one of their children, en route to the bathroom or going after a drink of water, had passed their open door just then, the boy might have thought that his Mom and Dad were pointing out the stars.

The next day Kitsie planned to use what she thought of as "Ken's line" on Cara. "You are too great a person to waste so much time being such a jerk." She practiced it over and over in her head while scrambling the scrambled eggs, but Cara didn't make it down to breakfast at all that morning.

Later, at midday, after both her husband and her boys had left, when Cara did venture down the stairs, she looked so pathetic and waiflike, so very frail that Kitsie wouldn't have had the heart to whip out Ken's line, even if Cara had done something typically awful to deserve it.

Cara didn't do anything awful. In fact, she was uncharacteristically subdued, which seemed somehow worse than when she was rude and angry. At least then, there was something attractive about her spark. But as Cara wandered over to the window seat dressed in another one of her black body-things, her hair so matted and brittle that it didn't even resemble hair any longer, Cara reminded Kitsie of one of those kids with that accelerated aging disease that once in a while she saw on the nightly news. Cara looked like an old child. She spent most of the day staring out a living room window. Kitsie urged her to go outside, after all . . . summer in Vermont, lakes, hikes, wasn't that what it was all about, but Cara just said no thank you, which made Kitsie fear the worst.

When the boys came home from camp that afternoon Cara was still at the window seat, folded up on her perch. Evan said that he was going over to Nate's house and Kitsie said why don't you take your brother, and Evan said do I have to, and Kenneth overheard him and said that he didn't want to go anyway, so Kitsie asked if he was sure. Kenneth said, sure I'm sure, and Kitsie said, okay then scoot to Evan who ran off fast before anyone could change his or her mind. Then Kenneth told Kitsie that he had passed yet another swimming test at camp that day and now was a deep-water diver which made Kitsie proud but also a little bit concerned. Then Kenneth went to play in the yard and he looked so sweet out there, digging and playing with his army men and singing to himself, that Kitsie didn't want to disturb him. She had to do some marketing before she started cooking supper. So Kitsie went into the living room and asked Cara if she wanted anything special at the store, to which Cara didn't even bother to nod "no." And then Kitsie headed out, feeling like she left her sister-in-law, her house and her son in a fairly harmonic moment.

When Kenneth bounded up the backstairs some fifteen minutes later and went into the kitchen to get himself something to drink, he expected to find his mother there. Kenneth was at that age when there was nothing worse than expecting to find your mother somewhere and not having her be there. Nothing worse, that is, than being left alone in the house with his Aunt Cara.

And he *was* alone with her, this Kenneth quickly realized. He had first sung out his mother's name, "Mom, Mom," but when she didn't come to his side immediately, as she usually did, he became more tentative. He walked as quietly through the house as he could. "Mom," Kenneth whispered, like a kitten mewing. When he came upon Cara curled up on the window seat exactly as he had left her, when he whispered "Mom" and his mother did not magically appear as usual, when Cara did not even turn around and acknowledge that Kenneth was standing there—that's when he thought Cara was dead, or worse. That's when he thought she was "undead," or so he explained to his mother later, when he was crying so hard that he couldn't catch his breath and the veins in his neck stood out.

Evan had told him about the undead at night when Evan thought it would be scariest, but Evan was wrong, the scariest time to think about the undead was when Kenneth and Cara were alone. The undead were half-dead, half-living, caught between two worlds. Usually, they were dead people who weren't ready to go to heaven

215

or hell because they were in love with somebody still living, or they had to right a wrong, or even a score first, here on earth. Cara was the rare type of undead who wanted to "go" before her time; she wanted to be with her dead brother. If she were really undead, as Evan claimed at night when he sneaked into Kenneth's room to frighten him, Cara had the power to mark anyone she chose as the next in line to die. And if Evan was right— and Evan was always right, Evan was a genius—all Kenneth Golds would die young. This would be a perfect time for Cara to get him, Kenneth Gordon Gold II, the pale-by-comparison sequel to his godlike uncle.

Kenneth was so frightened of his aunt that when Kitsie came back from the store and was unpacking some of her groceries, she found him hiding in one of the cabinets in the pantry. He was curled up in a little ball and his chest was heaving, heaving, hyperventilating, his fear like a vise across his lungs.

"My God," said Kitsie, after opening the cabinet door. For a brief second she thought Kenneth had been forced into that position by a robber or an intruder. But Kenneth had been prone to these attacks before. Immediately, she was on the floor scooping him out, and he was in her arms, her little boy, tremors shuddering through him like a series of aftershocks.

"Sh-sh-sh, baby," said Kitsie, her lips pressing against his head, fragrant and damp with sweat. "It's all right, honey," she crooned as she tried to soothe him, but the arms of his anxiety were shaking him so hard from within that he twitched and moved against her.

"Mom, please," said Kenneth, gasping. His little chest was heaving, his words staccato, issued out in gulps. "Please, Mom," he managed.

"Anything, my love," said Kitsie. She was trying to

hold on to him, to wrap her body around him, to bring him back inside her where he was safe once. "Anything."

"Mom, don't leave me alone with Cara," said Kenneth.

"Never, never again, my love," said Kitsie. She pulled him tighter toward her. Her hand glanced against his bent knee, and the leg shot out in a kick, his reflexes heightened by his anxiety.

The independent movement startled both of them. Kenneth asked, "What happened?" coughing through his tears.

"It must be your reflexes," said Kitsie. Without thinking, she reached out and gently karate-chopped his knee again. The leg threw itself away from its hinge like a newly written checkmark.

"Wow," gurgled Kenneth.

"Wow," said Kitsie.

And then they both giggled a little. Kenneth hit at his knee with the back of his hand, and again the leg kicked out.

"Double-wow," he said. He was still red-faced, but now smiling.

"Double-wow," said Kitsie. She sat back, cross-legged on the floor. "Now do you want to tell me what happened?" Kenneth told her about the undead and Evan's predictions about his own oncoming demise. Kitsie held him to her. Not anything or anyone would ever hurt her child. She would die first.

"Don't listen to any of that bullshit," said Kitsie, and Kenneth's eyes got wide. He'd never heard his mother curse before, but her anger reassured him, and he felt better. He looked better too, his breathing and his color had almost come back to normal. He felt a little pleased, even, to think of the hell Evan would catch when he got home.

"Hey, Mom?" said Kenneth. He rubbed his right index

finger against the grain of the hardwood floor. "Why did you and Dad name me after Uncle Ken, instead of Evan?"

Kitsie looked at the boy's bent head. "When Evan was born, Daddy just wasn't ready to be reminded yet. By the time you came around, he was able to remember happier times. Does that make sense?"

Kenneth nodded, still with his eyes to the floor. "Mom," he said. "What was so great about Uncle Ken?"

There was a rasping sound in the doorway, followed by a hacking cough. Kenneth and Kitsie looked up. Cara was standing in the entry; it was obvious that she'd been listening.

"He was fun," said Cara. She coughed again.

There was no way to tell how long Cara had been in the room, but from the look on her face, Kitsie judged she'd been standing there long enough. Cara was smoking, but she seemed less twittery than usual. She leaned against the doorframe and slid down until she was resting on her heels. She took a drag from her cigarette, bent her head back and exhaled a column of smoke. Then she brought her eyes back to Kenneth's level.

"I'm sorry that I scared you, kid," said Cara. Her voice was tough, but her face wasn't.

Kenneth stared at his crazy aunt. Then he glanced over at his mother. Kitsie gave him a reassuring look.

Cara slid farther down so that she, too, was on the ground. Now Kenneth and Kitsie and Cara were all on the pantry floor, sitting Indian-style. To Kenneth, they looked like the kids at camp when the counselors called a powwow. He wanted to say this, but he wasn't really ready to talk yet.

"I've been a real pig," said Cara, in the same measured tone. "I promise to work harder."

Kenneth nodded.

Kitsie had no idea how to react to this, but she ventured to try. "Cara, how was Kenny fun? Kenneth needs to know."

Cara dragged again. "He was always into something. He'd switch gears when you least expected it. I don't know. He was just exciting." She finished her cigarette, but she didn't know what to do with it. She rubbed some of the ashes into her pants leg, then she swiveled her head around in search of an ashtray. A few red embers fell to the floor. Cara wet her thumb and pressed them out. She nervously fingered the dead butt until the floor was sprinkled with tobacco crumbs.

"Leave it there for now. It's all right," said Kitsie.

Cara looked at the cabinets. She reached out and twisted a hand-carved knob. Then she turned to Kenneth. She said: "You know what was so great about your uncle? He liked me. Kenny really liked me a lot." The voice was steady, but her eyes were not.

Still, in the relative calm of the moment, Kitsie could see, finally, why everyone always talked about how beautiful Cara was. Not that she looked beautiful, she looked a mess, with that crazy, filthy hair of hers, that skin so pale that aside from the heavy black brow and lashes, she could have passed for an albino. She was so bony that her arms and legs looked like giant, dried-out stalks. No, Cara wasn't beautiful now, but Kitsie could see the beauty in her, perhaps the way an art restorer can see the beauty in a painting before he goes to work, or the way she herself had seen the grace in this big old house before they put in the new windows, reshingled, spackled and painted, before they redid the floors, the garden and the yard. Cara just needed tending to. She looked like she'd been deprived.

Kenneth was quiet. He knew how important it was to be liked. Evan, his own brother, didn't even like him.

"Got it, kid?" asked Cara.

And Kenneth nodded, he got it. And Kitsie got it, too.

Cara turned to Kitsie. For the first time in her life she talked to Kitsie like a person. "I tried to kill myself once, you know," said Cara.

"Yes," said Kitsie, "I know."

"That's scary," said little Kenneth.

Kitsie lay her palm across his thigh.

"It is scary, you're right," said Cara. "But you know what scares me most?" she continued, and for this she closed her eyes. "What if Kenny didn't die? I mean, what if he didn't die and I was still the same? I mean, what if I was the same as I am now and Kenny was still alive?" Cara opened them. Her eyes were her mother's shade of blue.

Kitsie took a minute to respond. She had to think this one over. It was hard for her to imagine Cara without her grief—grief seemed to define her; no wonder it was so hard for Cara to give up.

Kitsie said: "You would be the same, but you'd be different." Kitsie told her sister-in-law the truth.

"That's what I figured," said Cara, and she reached into her sleeve, pulled out her pack and tapped out another cigarette.

When Douglas got home that evening, he found Evan running wild in the yard with a couple of his buddies. They had gotten ahold of some of the neighbors' laundry—the only people around for miles who still hung out their clothes to dry—and the boys were trying it on for size. Evan himself had a pair of Old Man Hardy's underwear on his head, as billowy as a chef's hat. Doug's presence put an end to all the fun. Just the sight of a father, arriving at this high-pitched and primal moment, would have been enough to quiet the boys down, but when they saw Evan's father's tear-stained face, the mood turned maudlin. After a few words of abrupt apology, Nate Henry's promise to return the stolen goods to the Handys' washline, and a couple of "later, much" 's, the band of eleven-year-olds headed out into the night. It was suppertime. Most of the boys had their own fathers to contend with, and those who didn't, like Carey Crawford, were thanking their lucky stars.

"Evan," said Doug, blowing into his handkerchief, "why aren't you inside helping out your mother?"

"Aww, they're all crazy in there," said Evan. By now he was used to his father's tears; he didn't like it, but he was used to them. "They're hanging out on the pantry floor."

And they were crazy in there, and they were on the pantry floor. Kenneth was drawing pictures of his army men. He'd gotten up long enough to get his pastels and his papers, then returned to the floor to set up shop. None of the groceries were put away, they were still half in the bag, half on the counter the way that Kitsie left them an hour and a half before. But Kitsie was there, there on the floor, a glass of white wine in one hand, a pair of scissors in the other. By her side lay a big red wide-toothed comb. Cara was on her knees, facing away from Kitsie. She was still smoking, but now she had an ashtray in her lap, a large, oval silver ashtray that Douglas had received from the bank after engineering an especially tricky mortgage. The bowl of the ashtray was covered with ashes and lipsticked butts.

Kitsie was cutting Cara's hair. Or trying to. First she had wanted to wash it, but Cara wasn't up for that huge a production. Then Kitsie had attacked the snarls with the comb, but Cara had shrieked too much—that's when

221

Kitsie poured herself that glass of wine. Now, she was going at the larger tangles with a scissors, trying to cut the knots loose. She'd forgotten to spread newspapers; so there was hair everywhere, all over the pantry floor.

"So he goes under, right, and there I am staring at the ice. Then this lady, Mrs. Weiskopf? Weisbord? Who remembers? Her dog's chasing a squirrel, if you can believe it, and he leads her to the lake just as Kenny begins to drown. The timing was perfect . . ." said Cara. "Motherfucker."

Kitsie had pulled at a curl too hard.

Doug stood at the mouth of the pantry and didn't know what to say.

"Did he get sick?" asked Kenneth.

"He almost died," said Cara, "but he didn't get sick."

"Sure he did," said Doug, making his presence known. "He had a whopping case of the flu."

Cara turned to him. "Did not," she said.

"Did too," said Doug. "Don't you remember he had that giant cold sore on his lip?"

"He had it before he fell in the lake," said Cara. "He always had a cold sore." She said it like she was talking to an idiot.

"He did, you're right," said Doug, remembering. "Kenny always had a cold sore."

"Tell about the time he stole the car," said Evan, calling from the other room.

"Grandma was out shopping," said Doug.

"Grandpa and Grandma had just had this big fight," said Cara.

"You tell it," said Doug.

"You," said Cara, but she continued telling the story anyway.

Kitsie glanced down at Kenneth and then up at

Douglas. "Honey," she said, "why don't you order in a couple of pizzas?" Pizza was Kenneth's favorite.

Douglas looked at his wife hard. She looked back at him.

"Sure," said Doug, "why not?" He bent down and tousled Kenneth's head. "What kind of pizza do you want?"

"Pepperoni," yelled Evan. He was in the kitchen, helping himself to a pre-dinner bowl of ice cream.

"Pepperoni," said Kenneth, quietly.

"You sure?" asked Doug. Kenneth said that he was sure.

Douglas looked at Cara. Half her head was a mess, half her head was cropped short. There would be hell to pay when Kitsie finally passed her the mirror. Still, for the moment she seemed calm. She lit up another cigarette and blew.

"What about you?" Doug asked Cara.

"Eggplant and anchovies," said Cara. She picked at some old flaking nail polish on her thumb.

"Gross," yelled Evan.

"Peppers and garlic," whispered Kenneth.

"Fresh tomatoes," added Kitsie.

"Kenneth's a baby," said Evan.

"I am not," said Kenneth.

"How about Chinese takeout?" offered Douglas, which opened up a can of worms. Soon everyone was shouting but Cara, who had become extremely engrossed in the state of her nails. No one could agree on anything. Finally, Doug declared the boys spoiled, and said they couldn't order in after all. Evan went to bed without any supper— he refused to eat, even when his mother brought him up a tray. Kitsie just scrambled together some eggs and onions, and opened a can of soup; and they sat down at the kitchen table. Doug grumbled something about working hard all day and expecting some real food, but he grumbled good-naturedly. Cara didn't manage to eat anything, but she did tell Doug that he sounded exactly like their father. Kenneth fretted quietly, wondering about whatever punishment Evan would dream up for him because once again, without meaning to, Kenneth had gotten his older brother into trouble.

What could anyone do? They were all different people. And wasn't it true, as Cara had said, once, a long time ago, in the middle of an argument with just about everybody, that a family was just a group of strangers forced together by circumstance and need? In bleaker moments, Kitsie could see her point. But then, at the dinner table— her husband eating and talking about his day at work, Kenneth playing with his food, Cara with her new haircut, off in her own world, but her mood a tiny bit improved, Evan ensconced upstairs, probably reading a science book—Kitsie was filled with hope. Clearly, nothing was solved here. She wasn't going to lie to herself; the rest of the summer was sure to be no picnic. But there were reasons to feel good. Her boys were safe, her sister-in-law looked less like a street urchin. And her husband—talking to his nutty sister, drawing out his youngest son—he was a good man.

"Cara," said Doug. "Tell Kenneth the story about when Kenny threw Billy Gallagher's mom into the pool."

So Cara told, and Douglas interrupted. But that was all right too, because somewhere amid all the hullabaloo, things changed in that old house. And when she looked back on that night months later, that thrown-together dinner would seem to Kitsie somehow monumental. It was then that Douglas and Cara first started to talk to one another. Slowly, sure, and with trouble, with effort.

And that night, they talked, long after little Kenneth had been put to bed, after Kitsie herself had fallen asleep on the living room couch. They talked about their dead brother, about their mother and their father, about Jeremy some, too. And it was late when they finally finished, and they weren't exactly feeling great when they headed up to bed. Cara was upset, angry; Douglas, totally exhausted. No, that wasn't the night when the siblings started to feel better. That came later, in fits and starts. This was the night for arguing, for feeling worse first, for beginning what they had to begin, for laying out the groundwork for their survival. Doug and Cara didn't become best friends or anything, that long, hard summer, but they weren't on opposite sides anymore, either.

After August, and Kenny's Yahrzeit—the anniversary of his death—Cara returned to New York City. For what? To continue her daily struggle. And Douglas? He worked at the bank, he played with his kids, he started some carpentry projects that he never got around to completing, he fought a little with his wife about the boys; Evan was getting hard to handle, Kenneth needed to learn how to stand up for himself. In late September, Douglas wrote Jeremy a letter about some things that were on his mind, trying to get to know him; since Douglas was so much older than Jeremy, it was almost like—Douglas wrote— they grew up in different families, in different times. In October, Jeremy wrote a letter back to him, telling Doug about himself, his work, how much he missed Steven, and asking Doug to explain to him a little about his own work, a little about his life.

And Douglas cried. He cried when he noticed how old his mother was getting. He cried after he spoke to his father on the phone. One afternoon at the office he cried because his own true love had dumped him when he was still a kid, and he had never cried about her before. When Kenny's birthday rolled around, in the middle of the day,

Douglas cried silently and furiously for fifteen minutes, like a brief summer storm. And in bed, sometimes when he was making love with his kind wife, Douglas cried into Kitsie's shoulder.

From then on in, Douglas cried, off and on, like most people.

Out of Time

KEN WASN'T going to get lucky. That much was clear. But he really liked this girl "as a person," so Ken hung out in Katiya's basement apartment anyway, eating her food, drinking her wine, looking at her artwork, listening to her talk.

It was around midnight. He was sitting on a big easy chair, dangling his naked feet. Katiya was on the floor massaging them—she had just finished a summer course in reflexology and she needed to practice for her final. On the table sat the remains of the dinner that Katiya had cooked—a tofu-cashew-vegetable stir-fry—Ken's second dinner of the night. He hadn't realized the invitation included eating. He'd come to see her paintings; he'd come to get his feet massaged, to possibly get lucky, to get Sylvie out of his mind. Whatever Katiya was doing, she was doing right; it was working.

On the floor next to Katiya, next to her aromatic oils and her rolling pin, was a still-hot bong and that half-drunk bottle of wine.

Out of Time

This was on a Saturday night during the summer that followed the spring semester of his sophomore year—what F. Scott Fitzgerald proclaimed to be the best time of a person's life; this proclamation hadn't served true for Ken, so he was determined to make up for lost time. He was young, bright, and a certain type of girl found him incredibly good-looking (the type of girl that went for pretty, smooth-talking, granola'd-out guys). So when Ken decided at the last minute to stay up at school for Six-Week Session and fulfill a stupid science requirement—anything not to have to go home to Connecticut—he'd had high hopes for the summer. He'd forgotten to take into account how beat Collegetown could get on a summer Saturday night. The bars were the same boring bars they were all year and the music scene was worse; plus Ken was sick of hanging out with his housemate. However, if he were to stay home alone like he tried to last Wednesday, he'd probably end up bumming over Sylvie, the girl who dumped him last month. Or worse, he'd end up having an existential crisis, worrying about the meaning of life— a subject that was on his mind a lot lately; or worse yet, he'd just end up smoking pot. So it was kind of nice to be hanging out with Katiya, hearing about her theories on art, a relief in a way to spend the evening talking to somebody who was more than happy to do the thinking for the both of them.

Katiya was smart. The more avant-garde Fine Artsies thought that Katiya was the genuine article. She'd walked away with most of the junior prizes and had just shipped an installation to her first group show in New York. She'd made Dean's List all six semesters even though she had managed to piss off most of the faculty. She was known for her revolutionary tactics—she spent a lot of last spring painting canvases with a mixture of oils and her own menstrual blood. News of this leaked out to the local *Times Union,* and the college on the other hill had offered her a solo show. The cattier members of her department swore that if Katiya was a genius at all, her genius lay in self-promotion.

But the truth is that Katiya *was* smart, at art, at other things, she was tactical, practical, she had vision, she had insight. For instance, she had loved Ken now for months, she'd loved him an entire semester, which was smart because all in all, Ken was a good guy. Sure he was awfully hip, but he was also sort of decent and in an old-fashioned way, Katiya thought, he was kind. He couldn't stand to see anyone upset. Katiya's spies said this is why he stayed with the pale, mysterious Sylvie Caplen for so long, because Sylvie was upset about one thing or another most of the time.

When Katiya got that first bad review in the art students' paper, Ken had cut class with her, taken her, Katiya, out for a superexpensive lunch in one of those restaurants you only went to when a parent or two came to town. Between her and Ken they had eight glasses of wine, and an after-dinner cognac, all before 3:00 P.M. Each time they lifted their glasses for a toast, Ken would say "Bungo!" (he'd been reading lots of Hemingway) and they both dissolved into fits of giggles. So she really didn't mind too much when Ken's credit card was rejected when it came time to pay the bill. Katiya wrote a check, and Ken had paid her back weekly in five- and ten-dollar installments; an endearing act, Katiya thought, in and of itself.

Sometimes it seemed unbelievable to Katiya that she and Ken had been inhabiting the same campus for almost two years and she hadn't even seen him until this past semester. When Ken had first walked into their Poetry

section her silent inner voice had cried, "That's him,
that's him," so loud that it embarrassed her and she
turned her head to stare across the room at the broken
clock. As soon as class was over she went back to her
apartment to look him up in the Pig Book. Kenneth
Gordon Gold, Kenneth Gordon Gold, she rolled the words
over her tongue. Under "dislikes," he'd put down "Math
and Disco." Under "likes" he wrote, "Camping and
Life." He was so beautiful. His eyes were blue, real blue,
blue on many levels, not the one-dimensional color that
she squeezed out of a tube. And then there was his hair,
which Katiya really couldn't see that well in the Pig Book
picture, but which she had noticed right away up at
school. It was almost black with a white tuft in the front,
with white mixed in among his right brow and lashes, his
coloring sort of inside out like a photo negative. Everyone
knew he was practically living with Sylvie, but then again
everyone knew that he was sleeping with all the prettiest
girls from this year's freshman class. So how serious could
it be?

And when Ken talked about poetry in their seminar,
rather, when his opinions erupted, poured forth out of his
mouth before he could bother wasting the time to raise
his hand, Katiya wanted to get up and dance. Ken seemed
to *feel* his way through a stanza rather than just sit back
and coldly analyze it, like they encouraged you to in that
dopey English Department. He was as out of place there
as she was in Fine Arts. When she daydreamed, Katiya
thought of the two of them as renegade antiintellectuals,
especially Ken, who seemed incapable of a reaction that
didn't come straight from the gut. They would be so good
together; Katiya knew this in her heart.

So when Katiya heard that Ken was staying up for the
summer, she cancelled the job her stepmother had ar-

ranged for her working as a receptionist in a NoHo gallery in New York, and planned to stay up at school that summer, too. She'd managed to "assist" a couple of courses at the college on the other hill. In May, rumor had it that Sylvie and Ken were on the rocks anyway. And about two weeks after Sylvie went home for the summer, one of the spies told Katiya that Sylvie had finally given Ken the boot. That's when Katiya made her move. She had run into him swimming at the gorge three days before, accidentally on purpose; Katiya hated the gorge in the afternoon—it was so crowded, it reminded her of Jones Beach. When Ken asked politely about her work she'd casually suggested he drop by Saturday night—Saturday night was one of the few times that she took off, she said—to experience her art for himself.

Oh she was clever, Katiya, she was smart. On Saturday night, when she opened her front door, wearing one of those long, loose Indian dresses, Katiya had said right off the bat (sounding to Ken a little like Richard Nixon) that she wanted everything to be perfectly clear, that she hadn't felt sexual in months, and she didn't want to give Ken any wrong ideas. The only intercourse she was into was intellectual; and she wanted to get this out of the way, Katiya repeated herself, before anyone got too comfortable. Then she undid the leather thong that was knotted around her hair and she shook out her long blond braid as if for emphasis, until there were long blond waves riding across her shoulders. She gave Ken a hard green look with her hard green eyes, like she was daring him.

But hey, this was all fine with Ken, Ken who had "borrowed" his housemate's favorite jeans for this special occasion, Ken who had broken out the new guayabera shirt his little sister had sent to him, Ken who had even bothered to pretend to shave. He wasn't so "male" that he couldn't deal with this girl's proclamation, and that's what he told Katiya the artist, Katiya from his Poetry seminar last semester, Katiya who had shocked him, the unshockable, by being so upfront. After going out with Sylvie all that time he kind of liked, he had to admit, Katiya's directness. Sylvie would stew about for weeks in a silent rage never letting him in on what was bothering her, always determined to keep him wondering about what he had done that was so fucked up.

With her ground rules set and acceptable to both parties, Katiya led Ken down the rickety stairs into her studio apartment, half the room cluttered with giant angry canvases, the other half her living area, filled by her big brass bed.

"It was my grandmother's," said Katiya, inclining her head toward the bed. "It cost me a fucking fortune to have it shipped up here."

She was a tough talker and Ken liked that. Sylvie was the softest talker in the world. When she'd broken up with him on the phone (on the phone!) he hadn't been able to make out most of the words. Her monologue came across the wire in a series of whispers and cries. The only point that he heard clearly, and it rang as clearly as a bell, was that Sylvie was sick and tired of Ken cheating on her. Which really upset him, Ken, because he was sick and tired of cheating on her, too.

Was it completely wimp-ass to admit he couldn't seem to help himself? It wasn't that he didn't try; he didn't want to be a jerk. And after he went to bed with some of those girls it didn't even make him feel any better. Sure, it was nice at first, Ken liked to hold a lot, he liked to be held. But after, that's when it got worse, when the girl would be kissing his hand or something, acting as if they were official now, as if the two of them were in love.

Ken wanted Sylvie, period. But there was something about Sylvie that Ken couldn't possess, he couldn't own. She was always so unhappy. And many of those other girls were so nice, so beautiful, so young—wasn't it true you only live once? And wasn't it true that for most of this life Ken felt all alone? And wasn't it true, as his mother said warningly, time and time again, that Ken was especially prone to impulse?

His father was a hopeless philanderer. Was this in the genes, his inheritance? Biological predestination and all that? None of it had anything to do with Sylvie, per se, Ken loved her! This is what he tried to say to her over the phone, but none of the right words came out.

In Katiya's kitchen there was a regular wooden kitchen table and two benches, and that huge, overstuffed easy chair. Ken had followed Katiya in there, although she didn't ask him to—he followed in a trance. Ken had still been a little stunned that Katiya wasn't in a "sexual period," because she had been flirting with him for months. And he was surprised, too, because this hands-off policy of hers didn't seem to bother him that much. In fact, Ken kind of liked having the pressure turned down. This way he could go home alone, unembarrassed and unthreatened. He'd been through too many girls already, this summer. It was nice just to hang out with one like a friend. And now it was possible he could leave as an enlightened male and still feeling a little like a stud. Sometimes, he hated to admit this, even to himself, he threw passes at girls because it was expected of him. But tonight, the onus wasn't on him. How could it be Ken's fault that Katiya didn't want anyone to touch her? She was in a creative period, she said, exceptionally fertile and selfish; she just wasn't in the mood to share herself with anyone.

She was a good-sized girl, Katiya. Her arms were strong from stretching and lifting those huge canvases, from punching out chicken wire, from throwing buckets of industrial paint around and around her large studio. She said that she believed in the physical process. The dress she wore was long, purple and diaphanous, so that as she moved or gestured when she talked—which she did often, gesture and talk—the fabric slid like a spotlight highlighting one voluptuous body part after another. And then there was her hair, her hair! Her hair was extravagant, it was lovely. Sitting behind Katiya in class last semester, Ken had an overwhelming urge to take the end of the great blond braid to his lips, and suck it.

Tonight the braid was loose, and if this had been any other girl, any other set of rules, Ken would make sure he was wrapped up in a sheet of that gorgeous hair by the end of the evening. But tonight, Katiya had reserved herself for herself, which was just as well, which was very smart of her, because Ken had other things on his mind. It had been a hard year. Everything was changing so fast, he had to race to keep up. His dad had remarried, his mom had started the second stage of falling apart—she was mad at everybody. His older brother Doug was lost to him. Doug was busy building his adult life—working his farm, living with his girlfriend Madeleine—in which there were no rooms constructed for Ken or any other members of his family. Jeremy, the baby, there was never that much going on between Ken and Jeremy anyway, Jeremy was so much younger and a real loner—they liked each other fine. But the family was in shambles and his little sister Cara needed him, she had needed him all of her life, and she needed Ken *more* now, because she was seventeen and everything hurt her.

Cara needed him and Ken was too far away at school, too preoccupied with falling in and out of love, with Sylvie, with English Literature, with Oriental Philosophy, with his best buddy Jake, with being a hunter and a gatherer (which only lasted one weird afternoon in which he ate some wild mushrooms and boiled up the wing of a dead bird), and finally, with turning into an ovo-lacto vegetarian. Because Ken was too goddamn busy figuring things out. He was almost twenty-one. His life was about to begin. He needed to *know* himself. He couldn't spend all his time taking care of Cara.

This is what Ken wrote in the letter to his sister in response to her previous letter to him that yelled (the letter so loud he had to keep folding it back into the envelope) about how she couldn't believe that he, Kenny, had deserted her to another suburban summer of hell. "And don't call me Kenny anymore," he had written in his letter.

Tuesday morning Ken burned that return letter before he could post it, called up Cara, listened to her cry (which pained him), then promised to hitchhike home to Connecticut that Saturday and take her into the City to catch some jazz or something. Have a good time. *Kenny* promised her.

But there he was, nowhere near Connecticut, on Saturday night at Katiya's drinking some cheap Chianti, and he hadn't even bothered to call Cara to cancel on her. Why didn't he call her? It's not like he just forgot. He'd meant to call her all day, but he just didn't have the strength to lift the phone off of the receiver. He couldn't bear to disappoint her, to hear the hurt in Cara's voice, and yet he hadn't had the heart, really, to go home and face them all. He hadn't even called his mother in weeks, his dad in months. His mother called him, once in a while, but he had his housemate, Scott, tell her that he was out. Sometimes his mom would grill Scott, and Ken would watch as Scott made faces at him, all the while telling his mother that he, Kenny, was having the time of his life this summer.

Kenny had seen his family, all of them except for Doug, that past Spring Break and those few days had been enough. He'd brought Sylvie home, to a total disaster. His mom nagged him (in front of her!)—he'd neglected to declare a major and the college sent her a note. Whenever Sylvie floated into a room, Cara broke out in hives of jealousy and set out to torture her—she'd even asked Sylvie if she was acting out Ophelia for some play or if she walked around that way in regular life. It was true, Ken had to admit, Sylvie was a little too pale, a little too ethereal, but hadn't that been part of her charm? Everything that week degenerated into a screaming fight, between Kenny and his family, between Ken and his girlfriend. The topper was a strained dinner they had over at his father's when his stepmother asked, very politely, if his mother was finally dating anyone.

Kenny just couldn't take them, his family, at this point in his life. Maybe when he was older. Right now, every single one of them drove him absolutely berserk. They were all so incredibly demanding.

That night at Katiya's, living in the here and now, his family could go take a flying fuck. Ken was actually feeling pretty good, a rarity these days, and he was going to enjoy it.

They'd had a nice, long, leisurely dinner. After, Katiya

worked as she talked; Ken up on the chair, Katiya down on the floor. His feet were like bread dough in her hands. She was trying to explain how one created art. For her it was this way: at first she'd be attracted to an image, an object. Then she'd boil up a pot of tea and take to her big brass bed. She'd get under the covers—naked, said Katiya—and she wouldn't leave that bed until she figured out if she could come up with an intellectual connection or justification for that image, or if she should just discard it. An example: she'd watched their mutual friend Phil fall down some of the rocks at Buttermilk Falls. After first rushing him to the hospital (where, miracle of miracles, she learned he'd only broken an arm and fractured his right femur bone), Katiya got into that big brass bed for fourteen hours straight. She'd been attracted to the rushing water, see, the rushing water eventually got translated into the energy crisis and then into her whirling-dervish approach to throwing paint. It was the thrown-paint "work" that won her junior honors.

Ken groaned. Katiya had found a pressure point.

"And you?" said Katiya, "what is your life's work?"

Katiya had struck a nerve. While he wasn't above squandering time, Ken, while it was true that one of his major activities seemed to be kicking back and getting lazy, he wanted to have a "life's work" already. Lately, every moment, every action, every sentence seemed so vitally important to him. He was in a constant state of trying to figure his stuff out.

"I believe in physical labor," Ken said. It just came out of his mouth. He really had no idea what he was talking about.

"Does that mean you want to build something?" asked Katiya, encouragingly. She put down Ken's left foot. She leaned back on her palms and looked at him.

"Yeah," said Ken. "I want to build something." The statement sounded all right to him.

"What?" asked Katiya.

Kenny thought hard. He had changed his major three or four times already in his head. First it was Environmental Science, then for two weeks Architecture. History had been a useless course of study, so he picked English Literature, because that's what Sylvie was studying, because it was the most useless one of all. He had no idea what to do with his life—his life that was stretching so endlessly broad before him. His dad was a lawyer. Kenny couldn't picture himself inside an office. His mom said she saw him doing something public service–oriented— like being a teacher—but that's how she saw everyone. The truth was, Kenny knew, that he'd need much more money than that. He was sure that by the time he was really grown-up he'd be doing *something*—everybody ended up doing something. Most able-bodied, educated people had a job, if they wanted one—though Ken wasn't sure, even, if he really wanted one. All those photojournalists for example, those television anchormen, they didn't all know exactly what they were going to do before they turned twenty-one, either, Ken would bet on it. He wished he could call one of them up for confirmation, and ask them how they had got to where they were; it seemed so impossible to get to where they were from where he was.

In the meantime there was the Park Service, the Peace Corps, the possibility of bumming around Europe—all, Ken was well aware, were delaying tactics. Those, and his two more years of school. He had no clue what his life's work was going to be. He was born passionate, but without a single passion. He figured that so far, this was his biggest curse.

"I don't know yet," said Ken. "I guess I'm lost."

He said this simply, like a fact.

"You are lost, aren't you?" said Katiya. "I noticed that." She wanted him to be aware of her insight. She wanted to help him. She wanted him to be grateful, to know that she, Katiya, was the only one who *understood.*

What was this bitch's problem? All of a sudden Ken felt uncomfortable. He felt the difference in their altitudes; and instead of being empowered by towering over Katiya, he felt diminished, like he was a child sitting in a highchair. He slid off the cushions and got on the floor beside her. Katiya's floor wasn't the cleanest, it was spattered with spaghetti sauce and paint, there were even a couple of suspect hairs, but Ken didn't care. He liked to sit down low, on Katiya's level.

"Do you think it's because you have divorced parents?" she pressed him.

This line of questioning made Kenny feel strange. "How the hell should I know," said Kenny. Then, because Kenny was Kenny, he considered what she said. "They just got divorced last year," he said. "I've been lost a whole lot longer than that."

"That sucks," said Katiya. She really felt for him. She used her hand to flip back her hair; she shook it out. "I'm glad I'm not lost," said Katiya, and instantly regretted it.

There was a silence. Now that she'd established intimacy, Katiya said: "Do you want to go to bed with me?"

Ken stared at her. Then he shifted gears into cool-and-groovy. "I thought sex would mess with your Karma?" he said.

"Yeah, well," said Katiya.

"Sure," said Ken.

Neither of them moved to get up and enter the other room. It was quiet then, in that big damp studio apartment. Ken imagined that the remnants of dinner were congealing on their plates. In the dark blue light of night Katiya's hair shone yellow.

"Do you hear that?" said Ken. It was a white noise, a metallic hum that just wouldn't give up.

"It's the refrigerator," said Katiya.

"Oh," said Ken. "It's messing with my boner."

They were in bed. They'd been going at it pretty well for around twenty minutes. Then Ken asked Katiya about birth control and Katiya told him that she was on the Pill. That's when Ken lost his erection. Why? he wondered. Was it because it proved that she'd had sex before? Was it because it made everything feel so deliberate? Was it because talking about it took responsibility and he couldn't claim even to himself to be caught up in the moment?

Katiya took matters into her own hands. Ken tried to imagine Sylvie going down on him. But it was no use. He lay on his back, his head resting on Katiya's one pillow. Katiya rolled over, put her head on his chest and kissed his neck.

"I'm sorry," Ken said.

"Are you kidding," said Katiya. "I'm just glad to be lying here with you."

Ken mumbled a few things that Katiya couldn't make out.

"Hmmm?" she said, and he repeated himself, mumbling as indecipherably as before.

It doesn't matter, Katiya thought, we have all the time in the world, I can ask him about what he said tomorrow. She'd loved him so long now from afar. She could wait. There were endless hours ahead for them to talk. Katiya was sure that Ken was going to be her new boyfriend.

Ken looked at the digital clock. It was 1:30 in the morning. "Look," he said, "it isn't you, it's me."

"Remember we're in this together," said Katiya.

"I got to get out of here," said Ken. And he sat up and swung his legs over the side of the bed. "Scott's counting on me helping him out tomorrow morning."

Scott was the housemate that Ken was getting sick of. Scott was spending the summer painting houses. Ken had never helped Scott out before.

"Cool," said Katiya, although it was obviously not cool.

Ken jumped into Scott's jeans. He danced around to get the hips right. He pulled on his white guayabera shirt. He flipped his hands through his hair and looked at Katiya lying with the sheet wrapped around her waist. Her breasts slid to each side of her chest and Ken had an urge to take them in his hands and push them back up again. Her hair was fanned out like an angel's.

"Baby, give me a kiss," Ken whispered.

Katiya sat up and wrapped her arms around him. She kissed him long and full on the lips.

"This isn't just a one-night thing?" she asked him.

"No," said Ken, "of course not. What kind of boy do you think I am?" He grinned his crazy-grin.

Her heart twisted.

"I'll call you tomorrow, okay?" he said to her.

Katiya nodded okay back to him.

"Don't get up," Ken said. He pushed a golden lock behind her ear, he brushed her cheek with one finger. He kissed her on the nose. "You are so beautiful," he said, and sighed. And then, "I'll let myself out."

Katiya watched from her bed as Ken went back into her kitchen. After he turned on the light she saw him slipping into his shoes, no socks. The socks he left beneath her kitchen table. Ken blew her a kiss from the doorway, flipped that light off, and headed up the stairs.

Alone in her bed, Katiya wondered if she'd ever see Ken again.

It was later than he thought when Kenny got into the old blue Buick his father bought used for him last winter. The sky was so light, the moon so bright, it could have been any time in the world—it could have been no time. There wasn't any traffic at all in that sleepy town and Ken drove fast because he liked to.

When he got to the rotary he decided to take the long route home, by the lake. There was a little A-frame out that way and when he reached the crest of the hill a few yards up the road from it, he could often see this woman lying in her loft bed, at the top of the house. She had a different guy up there with her every other weekend. One was strong and burly, one was lanky, slight and familiar-looking—Ken was sure he had seen him up at the college. It was a ritual now, whenever Ken was out late on a weekend night to drive slowly by the A-frame, and get a glimpse of the action. The woman seemed pretty, although most of the time he passed her in a blur; and even though he never met her, nor even had any desire to, Ken felt as though he knew and liked her. It was hard to be divided between two people—Ken knew what this was like. Wasn't that the crux of his situation, his mother and his father, Sylvie and other women, Cara and the whole world? Ken had sympathy for the A-frame woman. So he took the lake road, this time as fast as he could, the front windows rolled down in that old jalopy, and stuck his elbow out. He steered with one hand. The night air tasted good.

Back at Katiya's Ken had been angry, he felt exposed,

how did she dare to pretend that they were so intimate? Now, out beneath the stars, relishing the speed of his speeding car, he breathed in the cool dampness of August, the musk of the lake water, and his anger drained out. All that mattered was that he drive away from her as fast as was humanly possible. His skin smelled like failed sex, fishy and bitter. He rolled down a back window with an electronic device. The rear window on the left was broken, cracked and held together by duct tape.

What *was* his life's work, Ken wondered. What did he want?

He thought hard. He wanted to be swimming, right now, right away. He wanted to ride a horse. He wished he were an artist like Katiya, a scholar like Sylvie, a musician like Jake, so that he too could quit school and go play rock and roll. He wanted to be a politician, an important scientist, a movie star, a zoologist. He wanted to spend the rest of his life in bed. He wanted to sleep with hundreds of women, to taste them, to compare the composition of their insides, to understand what was different about each one of them. He wanted to fuck their brains out. He wanted to be monogamous. He wanted to get married yesterday, stay married forever. He wanted children. He didn't want children. He wanted to be rich, he didn't want to be tied down by material possessions. He wanted to be a Buddhist, and an atheist, and what he was by birth, which was a Jew. He wanted to be a Native American. He wanted to be a girl.

Ken wanted all this stuff and he wanted none of it. He wanted to squeeze life raw between his hands.

"Nothing is enough," he said aloud to himself, in that rattling speeding car. "Nothing is enough for me."

I need everything, Ken thought. And instinctively his foot flattened down the gas pedal. He wanted to thrust himself forward, out of the here and now, barrel into his future. Ken wanted to rush headlong into life.

The road twisted and turned, the car banked from side to side. The hill crested, but the little upstairs room in the A-frame was dark, that lady must have turned out the light. Did she know he watched out for her? Ken craned his neck to see if he could make sense of any shadows. The car sailed over the hill.

Ahead was a tree. It was giant and dark and spidery, waving thick arms in the low burn of his headlights. It was all there in front of him, relief; everything that he ever wanted, everything that he needed. The tree was the center of his world; it was nothing. The tree was Ken's bull's-eye.

"I need everything," Ken said, again, and again, the tree playing matador, the Buick a thrusting blue bull. "I need it all," said Ken, aloud in the racing car when there was no one around to hear him.

"I feel good!" he cried as he was hit head on by the exhilaration of speed and danger and air and dark and light, by being alone out in the night, by knowing that his future was coming as eagerly toward him as he was rushing out to greet it.

"I feel good," said Ken out loud to no one, not even one of his many gods, as his foot switched preferences from gas to brake pedal and he pumped that brake in concert with his pumping heart; he pumped with all his might.

The wheels locked, the car was burning rubber, the tree watched as Ken tried his best to switch direction, to defy its attraction as if it possessed a magnetic charge. A moment ago he'd wanted to enter it, but just as suddenly, Ken was changing his mind. He felt good, he'd said so aloud which made it more true for him, and he was so high now that the barriers were melting between his spirit and his body, and he had nothing but survival on his mind. He was exalted to his essence. Wasn't that what he was after his whole life?

But the tree was getting closer, and the present had his future by the throat. "I will be a better son, a better brother," Ken tried to barter; but the gods weren't listening to his lies. The car was careering closer, and the tree blocked out the light. In a second it would all be over—nothing could save his ass this time. There wasn't anything he could do but shut his eyes and take the ride. Because the kid was out of luck. And he was out of time.

Helen Schulman was born and raised in Manhattan. She is presently teaching at New York University and in the Graduate Writing Division of Columbia University. Her first book, *Not a Free Show,* was published in 1988.

DATE

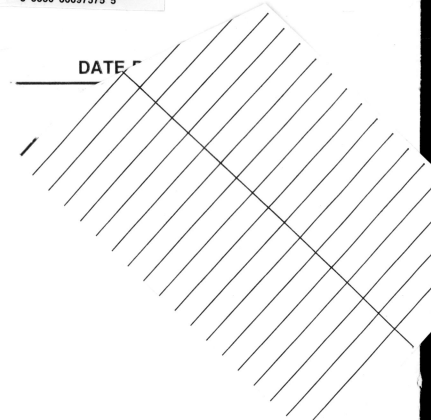

PRINTED IN U.S.A.